TRUTH
CATCHER

TRUTH
CATCHER

ANNA SALTER

PEGASUS BOOKS
NEW YORK

TRUTH CATCHER

Pegasus Books LLC
45 Wall Street, Suite 1021
New York, NY 10005

Library of Congress Cataloging-in-Publication Data is available.

ISBN: 1-933648-25-2

9 8 7 6 5 4 3 2 1

Interior design by Maria Fernandez

Printed in the United States of America
Distributed by Consortium

For Lee and Lynn Copen

Here's to missing you, kiddos

My mother named me Breeze. She was waiting for me one hot Arizona August, swollen and overdue, when a steady breeze came up out of nowhere and blew all day and night. She said the breeze brought me with it and, when it went, left me behind.

Today I was a long way from Arizona. I have been a long way from Arizona and my mother since I was two years old. Today I was sitting in a Washington State prison where I was waiting to interview a sex offender, something my sweet hippie momma never envisioned for me. I am a forensic psychologist and one of the things I do is evaluate sex offenders for possible civil commitment, which was what had brought me to Judas Island Correctional Center in Posedan, Washington.

Oddly enough, Judas Island Correctional Center was on the mainland, just south of Seattle—no island in sight. The interview room was a small windowless square furnished with standard prison decor: bolted-down metal furniture and vinyl floors. I heard footsteps and looked up as Daryl Collins entered the room.

He was forty and balding with thin wisps of hair carefully combed down over his forehead. The mouth was thin and wide; the eyes were deep set and hazel with a hard cast he couldn't entirely hide. He was a big man with hunched shoulders, and unlike many inmates, he didn't look like he had been weight-lifting or working out. Nonetheless, his face was unlined and looked younger than it was. Prison doesn't seem to age inmates; time just seems to stop for them when they go inside. The officer with Collins halted just inside the door, leaned against the wall, and folded his arms. Collins, manacled at his waist and ankles, walked across the room toward me.

"Please sit down, Mr. Collins. I'm Dr. Copen," I said. "I understand you're willing to talk with me."

"Certainly, I'll talk with you," Collins said, settling into the chair. "I got nothing to hide. Not anymore. I gave all that up a long time ago." The moment he spoke, I had a better sense of Collins, and not one that had anything to do with his words. I am a synesthete and my neurons are a little bit cross-wired, if you want to put it that way. When I hear voices or music or even some animal cries, I don't just hear the sounds, I see colors and designs. I especially like seagulls because their voices are a kind of soft-curved red. I don't even have to close my eyes to see the colors—they are right in front of me, with shapes and textures I don't even have words for. And the colors sometimes go with something else that's hard to describe, all kinds of sensations in my palms.

It's not like there's something wrong with me. Science says synesthesia's normal—although pretty rare—rare as in one person in twenty-five thousand. My neurons are just, well, crossed. It's not a big deal for me—it's all I've ever known, but I don't advertise it. People don't do well with different.

To my ears Collins's voice sounded soft, easygoing, and diffident, although it didn't look any of those. It was a brassy color with an olive tone. It had angles although I didn't have a name for the shape they made and I couldn't identify the sensation in my palms, either, only that it wasn't pleasant.

"Thank you for agreeing to meet with me," I said, launching into my spiel. "I am a psychologist retained by the State of Washington to do an evaluation of you. My job is to determine whether you meet criteria the legislature has set for a sexual predator. If you do, you could be civilly committed at the end of your term of incarceration and not released until you have reduced your likelihood of reoffending sexually. If you do not meet the criteria for a sexual predator, you will be released when your term of incarceration is up."

I ran through all of it, even though I knew he had likely studied the law more than I had. Sixteen states now had laws that said each sex offender was to be evaluated at the end of his prison sentence. If he was found to be a "sexual predator," he could be civilly committed instead of released when his time was up. In that case, he'd be transferred to another secure facility for treatment. He'd have to stay until the treatment program decided he had lowered his risk to reoffend—which meant he could stay forever. The "forever" bit was the part that upset offenders. Most had attorneys before I even began my evaluation.

"I am not for or against you. I am an outside, independent evaluator. You may agree or not agree to this interview. If you do agree, you can refuse to answer any questions you choose. You may also ask me questions about the process. If you do not agree, a report will be filed anyway, based on file review.

In that case, I will note your refusal in my report but will not interpret it. People refuse the interview for a variety of reasons and I understand that refusing is not indicative of being either more or less likely to reoffend."

Collins sat back and watched me as I spoke. He had an earnest look on his face and his hands lay relaxed in his lap. I took a breath and went on. "This interview is not confidential. Anything you say can be used in my report, which will go to the court. My notes will be available to both attorneys. Here's a release form that says all this, which you will have to sign for me to continue. Do you have any questions?"

"Well," he said, "I only have one. I was wondering if we could meet without the guard, privately. He could stand right outside the door, of course. The things is, I'd be talking about my childhood, about things that happened to me. Maybe it's going to the court, but it doesn't have to be known at the prison."

I looked at him in disbelief, then glanced up at the officer who was still leaning against the wall, his arms folded across his chest. He was looking steadily at me, no doubt waiting to see how I would react. A staff member had paid dearly for agreeing to be in a room alone with Collins. Why would Collins even ask?

"I read the records," I said.

"That was a long time ago."

"I repeat. I read the records."

"Look, I was out of control then, crazy. It was before I found the Lord. I'm a different person now. You can ask anyone. I haven't had any kind of conduct report in the last five years. I just feel I could talk much more honestly without someone listening in."

I reached in my briefcase and searched for a few minutes,

then pulled out some pages and put them in front of me. "Mr. Collins," I said, "let's review this to make sure we're both on the same page here. Ten years ago your therapist terminated you from group. She felt you were not taking treatment seriously, and that you were threatening and controlling other group members. You asked for a termination session. There should have been an officer in the room—after all, you had threatened her—but somehow you talked her into not having one. You barricaded the door and raped her repeatedly for hours. You told the officers that if they used gas or battered it down, you'd kill her. You raped her until you were tired of it and then opened the door. That you would even request being alone in the room with me or any staff member surprises me very much. The prison would never agree even if I did."

He didn't respond for a moment and perplexed, still not sure why he'd bother to ask, I simply stared at him. Then suddenly I got it. If I agreed, it would drive a wedge between me and the authorities. I'd have to argue he wasn't as dangerous as they thought, which would likely have some sort of impact on the report. Cognitive dissonance would keep me from telling the prison he wasn't dangerous and telling the court he was. It was clever, I'd give him that.

"People can change," Collins said finally. "I know I've changed. I was on speed then. I was in the depths of my depravity. I hadn't found Jesus."

"No."

He just looked at me, but I added nothing. I knew from experience that anything else I said would give him reasons he could argue with. Saying no worked much better. It's a good, solid word. I don't know why more people don't use it.

"I really don't know if I can do this interview under these

circumstances," he said. "You're asking me to talk about very private things with someone else listening in."

"That's up to you, Mr. Collins," I said easily. "If we do this interview, we'll abide by prison rules. Whether we do it or not is your choice." I knew to never try to persuade sex offenders to do or not do anything. It was a handle they could use to manipulate you. It was up to Collins if he wanted to do this interview. I didn't have a stake in it either way.

He sighed, picked up the pen and signed the consent form I had placed in front of him.

"All right," he said. "I have one more question. Have you found the Lord? Do you believe in Jesus Christ, our Savior? I have a right to know who I'm talking to, Dr. Copen. Because I don't think anyone could understand what has happened to me if they hadn't found Jesus. Have you been dyed in the blood of the lamb? Because if you have, you know the change that can happen to a man. You know the love that can hold you like a baby in His arms."

I opened my mouth to speak when, suddenly, Collins came out of his seat and leaned far across the table toward me, his face inches from mine. "Do you know, Breeze," he said softly, "do you know the love that can hold you like a babe in His arms?" The voice seemed to slip under my clothes like fingers and his eyes had turned as dark and shiny as marbles. An odor came off him that smelled like overripe fruit laced with testosterone. He'd placed his forearms on the table next to me and I could see the brown hairs on his arms standing up like bristles. The guard stood up immediately and said, "Sit your butt back down, Daryl."

Collins smiled a satisfied smile and sat back. I knew at that second I had seen Daryl Collins, and there was nothing he'd do for the rest of the day that would tell me more. He was never going to be a first-class con man, although he probably didn't know that. The best con men make you feel instantly like friends. Testifying against them makes you feel guilty, as though you've let a friend down. For Collins, the hunger to see fear flair up in any eyes across from him had been too strong. At the end of the day he was a simple thug. He'd always go back to the violence, even if he didn't need to, even if it hurt him as it had this time. He just had too much fun doing it.

I slowly leaned back also, my face as expressionless as I could manage. I folded my arms and studied him. I said nothing at all. Anything I said would give him a kick. Protesting it would tell him it bothered me, which is all he wanted in the first place.

And what was there to protest, anyway? If I wrote down every word he'd just said, there was nothing in them to suggest any kind of threat. Still the sense of threat had made the hair on my neck rise. More than anything I hated his using my first name. Of course, it would have been easy for him to get it. Just ask his attorney who the evaluator was on his case. Knowing how he got it didn't help. The intimacy he'd wanted to project had been there: a hairy, oily kind of intimacy that made me feel like I'd been violated.

I waited for a few moments and then spoke. "Mr. Collins," I said, my eyes flat, "can you tell me about the sexual offense for which you are currently imprisoned?"

Collins looked down and away for a moment before he spoke. When he looked up again, he was back to the reformed penitent. "It's all there," he said, waving his hand dismissingly at the records in front of me. "Do we really have to talk about it? I was a different person then. I hadn't found Christ. Why dwell on the past? Still, if I hadn't gone through all those things, I wouldn't be the person I am today." He shrugged.

"It's all part of the Lord's plan. Even so, I just wish I could find some way to make it up to her. I pray for her every day, but it feels like I ought to be doing more."

He was handling the role pretty well. Even without the lurch though, I wouldn't have bought it. I had an advantage he didn't know about. Synesthetes are all different, and my particular brand of synesthesia involved seeing changes in the texture of the voice when people lie. The moment he started talking about his religious conversion, his voice had changed from smooth and brassy to scratchy and rough. There must be some kind of change in the tone when people lie, because that's all the synesthesia responds to. If so, the auditory changes are too subtle for me to hear. They translate, however, into something very easy for me to see.

"OK," I said, "what about the previous criminal offenses you had, for instance the one you were originally incarcerated for? I believe you robbed a Seven-Eleven. You would have been out by now, if you hadn't raped the therapist."

"I've already said there's no point in dwelling on the past." The edge was creeping back in his voice. When I didn't speak, he went on, "All right. I've never denied I was a wild kid. I just didn't seem to have any sense back then." He sighed, as though weary of having to say it one more time. "That night I was going to a party and I got almost there when I realized I left the beer and my wallet home. Instead of going back to get it, like a fool I just walked in a Seven-Eleven and took a couple of six packs."

"Well," I said, "how was it you remembered your gun but forgot your wallet if you weren't planning on a robbery? Do you usually take your gun to parties?"

"In my old neighborhood back in Dallas, we did. It was a dangerous neighborhood and you didn't last long if you weren't carrying a gun. That's just the way it was back then. I guess I'd gotten into the habit. I'm the first one to say it was foolish, the whole thing."

"Mr. Collins, you didn't just take a couple of six packs. You robbed the cash register."

"That was an accident. I wasn't planning on robbing the cash register. The clerk thought I was, and he opened up the drawer and started throwing money at me. Like a fool, I took that, too. I wish he hadn't panicked like that. I wasn't going to hurt anybody."

I looked at the records in front of me and almost smiled at his brazenness. "The clerk testified you pistol-whipped him and demanded the money," I said quietly. "I've seen the photos of the clerk's injuries. They're impressive."

"Oh, the pistol-whipping, that was my fault. I'm ashamed of that especially. He threw the money at me, and I started to leave with it and the beer, when all of a sudden he got some kind of foolish notion in his head that he should try to stop me. It's stupider than shit to tackle a man with a gun. He did though, and I hit him up the side of the head, just to make him back off. Like I said, I wasn't trying to hurt anybody."

The surveillance camera said otherwise, but I moved on. "Mr. Collins, you have a long criminal history. I believe you have four arrests for assault, five for drug dealing, two DUIs, four for Breaking and Entering, and one conviction for assaulting a community-center worker when you were an adolescent. It's hard to explain all that away as youthful impulse or accident."

"Most of those are just arrests . . ." He stopped. That line of defense didn't fit with the role he was taking. "I've already told you. I was young and stupid in those days," he said. "Praise the Lord, God can redeem anyone," he went on," even a sinner like me." That was his story and he was sticking to it.

—◄०►—

Four hours later I was tired. I had asked all my questions, given all my tests. The tiredness didn't come from the time; it came from the lies. Something about malevolence just takes a bite out of your soul. And maybe being tired had something to do with what happened next. Off to the side, just at the corner of my eye on the edge of my peripheral vision, I saw the specter of a small girl. She stood just there, looking at me rather than Collins. If I cut my eyes over toward her, I saw nothing. It was only when I looked straight at him that I saw her at the corner of my eye. I literally rubbed my eyes, but she was still there. It rattled me, and I tried to keep the confusion off my face and concentrate on Collins. What the hell was this? Was I losing it?

I blinked and rubbed my eyes again. It didn't do any good. Synesthetes are known to have more paranormal experiences than other people, only nothing like this had ever happened to me. It was probably just something to do with the synesthesia, I told myself. Given I already saw things other people didn't see, why couldn't my head make up something else? Still, I had a gut feeling the little girl had something to do with the man in front of me, even though there was nothing at all about any little girl in his records.

What I did next surprised me, and later I couldn't explain it. I was tired, and I was confused by the image, but that's no excuse. I knew, even as I did it, that I shouldn't.

"What about the little girl?" I asked. "The little preschool girl."

He had been slouching forward staring at his hands, but now his head jerked up and he stared straight at me.

"What little girl?" he said, so quietly I could barely hear him.

I wanted to say, the one I keep seeing in the corner of my eye, the one who keeps looking right at me.

"Blue dress with yellow daisies," I said. "I think you know the one I'm talking about." I was truly winging it now but that's what she was wearing and I was betting Collins would recognize it. I don't know how I knew that, but I did.

He opened his mouth to speak, still staring at me, then shut it. Finally he pointed at the records on the desk in front of me. "There's nothing in those records about any kid," he said, which, of course, wasn't anything close to a denial.

"Really," I said. "If it wasn't in the records, how would I know about it? All I do is read records."

"I don't know what you think you know. You can't prove anything about any kid," he persisted. My sinking heart settled somewhere near my feet. He had already flunked the statement analysis test. He had not once denied there was a kid or that he had harmed her. Instead, he was focusing on what I knew and how I knew it. Innocent people don't act like that. They deny things outright; they don't evade the question.

I started to speak again when Collins rose from his seat. "I've got to get back," he said. "Count's coming up." He turned to the officer who was now sitting in a chair behind him. "I'm done here." The officer put down the magazine he was reading and got up. Collins moved to the door without another word. He started shuffling down the hall, each step brought up short by the chains on his ankles. Only once did he look back at me and I couldn't read the expression on his face at all. Beside him the guard seemed to be strolling casually, but I noticed he always kept one hand on Collins's arm. Even when he had been reading, I always felt his attention had been more than half on Collins. I watched them go, then turned and went back into the room.

Still thinking about Collins I packed up my things. He'd get by some, I thought, but even without the tip-off of the lurch across the table, he didn't have what it took to make the big time. People just wouldn't *like* him—even if they believed him—and being liked was a con man's stock-in-trade. Still, the memory of his sudden leaning forward and the look in his eyes was sticking to my skin like stale sweat. Maybe he was bush league as a con man, but he was first class when it came to reaching across a table in a maximum security prison and, in front of God and everybody, sliding fear across the table like a high card. And for no reason at all except the sheer hell of it.

I looked around one last time. The little girl wasn't there. Then again, I didn't think she would be.

chapter 2

Warden wants to see you," the officer at the desk said as I stepped out of the room.

"What?" I said. "Why?" In the five years I had been going in and out of prisons doing sexually violent predator evaluations, no warden had ever asked to see me. Prosecutors asked to see me. Defense attorneys. Relatives. Victims. Even media sometimes. Never a warden. Whether or not one of their large collection of inmates was convicted of being a sexual predator didn't usually concern them. If he wasn't found to be a predator, he was released. If he was, he was transferred to another facility. Either way, he was gone.

The guard at the desk just looked at me. "I'm sorry," I said. "I'm just surprised. Do you know why?"

"Sure," he said with a grin. "He always tells me."

I shook my head at the stupidity of my question, got directions, and headed for his office.

—◇—

"Dr. Copen," the warden said, rising from his desk and shaking my hand. "Joseph Stevens. Please sit down." He was solidly built with a crew cut and he obviously still worked out. He had one of those necks as wide as his head—a weight-lifting neck—but the years were cutting lines in his face and he looked like he was getting up toward retirement time. His greeting and his manner were stiffly formal—he had a military air about him—and that kind of greeting never, as far as I knew, meant anything good. Nonetheless, he had a steely dark blue voice that shaded into softer tones, and I liked the voice and him right away.

I smiled in greeting, then sat quietly without saying anything, just waiting. I had followed all the protocols, gotten permission to enter the prison, had the offender sign the release form. I had no cell phone or keys with me, and I hadn't brought in so much as a plastic knife to cut an apple. I hadn't even worn an underwire bra because I knew it would trigger the X-ray machines. So what did he want with me?

He looked as though he was waiting for me to speak, and when I didn't, he cleared his throat and said, "I'll come to the point. I'd like to know what your report on Daryl Collins is going to say."

I was so surprised I blinked. Why did he care? Collins would be gone from the prison whether or not he was civilly committed. Then it hit me: He must have known her, the staff member that Collins attacked. He could have been here ten years ago. Sure, he knew her.

"I don't know for sure. I haven't scored the actuarial instruments yet, the ones we now use to assess risk." I paused. He was looking down at the desk as though thinking how to phrase what he wanted to say.

"But I won't evade your question," I went on. "I don't think he's going to meet the criteria for civil commitment. He's vicious, to be sure—that's clear from the records. And manipulative. He's surely going to go on committing crimes. The law, however, requires that he have a diagnosis that leads to sexual offending and that he be more likely than not to commit another *sexual* crime. He's just not a specialist in sexual crimes, and that's what the law requires."

"He committed a sexual crime," the warden said evenly.

"Oh, I know he did," I replied, "—the one against the staff member while he was in here—and frankly, he's probably committed more than one. On the other hand it's the only one on his record. Whatever else he may have done, he hasn't been charged or convicted for."

"I have a report I'd like you to read," he said. "He's bragging to a snitch about 'fishing for bitches.'"

"Which is?"

"'Fishing for bitches' is his term for a practice he and his brother had of luring twelve-year-old girls to his house where he would take them in the basement and the two brothers would rape them. He had the walls covered with mattresses to hide the screams."

"He didn't get caught for it, did he?" I said.

"Does that really matter?" he asked. "You can't be serious."

"I don't write these laws," I said calmly. "He's got nothing on his record so there's no way to *prove* he committed any previous sexual crimes, unless the jury wants to believe your snitch, and I'm guessing his résumé is as bad as Collins's. There's no real way to get around the law on this: it has to be proven that he's likely to commit another sexual offense."

I saw the look on Warden Stevens's face and went on, wanting him to understand this wasn't something I could just make happen. "Look, I don't want to see a dangerous guy on the streets anymore than you do. I just doubt there's much I can do about it. The way we do these evaluations now, we don't just interview these guys and then give an opinion. Too many psychologists got conned. I'm sure you've seen guys like this con people all the time. So now we use objective instruments to measure how high risk they are. They work like the actuarial tables that the insurance companies use. The offender gets points for different factors and then we look at the recidivism rates for the people who have that number of points.

"I won't bore you with the details. The bottom line that Collins has no previous sexual charges or convictions means he's not likely to score high on these tests. Previous sex offenses are huge factors on the actuarials. On one of the tests, half the points come from that alone. And for all their flaws, these instruments do work a whole lot better at predicting risk than clinical judgment does. They've replaced clinical judgment in the court system for exactly that reason."

"You and I both know he's going to do it again," he said bitterly, "and that doesn't make any goddamn difference at all. One more time," he muttered, "the law is going to set someone free who everybody knows is going to go out and hurt someone."

"I won't argue with you," I said, although he seemed to be talking to himself more than me. "The loophole in the law is that risk of violence isn't enough, it has to be sexual violence. I'm pretty sure he'd score high on the instruments that measure a high risk for future violence, but that's not going to matter."

"You're just going to throw out the snitch's report?"

"It won't factor into the actuarial instruments," I said. "They require a charge or conviction. The snitch could testify anyway, but is he the kind of person a jury would believe? In my experience it's always the psychopaths who snitch because they have no loyalty to anyone. Which means the defense will shred him on his own record. Am I wrong?"

Warden Stevens sighed and leaned back, "Do you know what happened to her, the woman he raped?"

"I read the report, yes."

"No, I mean afterwards."

I hesitated before I answered. I didn't and would as soon not know. I had seen enough victims to know that having an experience like that was pretty much like eating cut glass. Things inside that woman would keep getting cut up long after the door had opened. Still I could hardly say I didn't want to know.

"No, sir," I said. "I don't."

"She came back fairly soon after it happened—too soon, some thought. I guess it was. She moved to a new office, of course, but that didn't help. She wouldn't close the door and finally, she had it taken off. She quit talking to anybody. She broke up with her fiancé. She wasn't . . . she wasn't the same person. There was something . . . I don't know . . . something missing in her face." He glanced up apologetically as though he expected me to criticize his vagueness. "Have you ever seen that," he asked, "when something just seems missing?" I didn't speak and he just shook his head.

"Eventually she left. Not just here. The town, the state. Someone said she'd been hospitalized. I don't know if it's true. She's out there somewhere. I wish I believed she was better."

"Warden, stop me if this is inappropriate—why wasn't there an officer in the room? He had made threats against her and he had a history of attacking staff. I'm guessing there was supposed to be."

"Another screw-up. He talked her out of it. Said he'd had a change of heart. That he didn't mean the threats. Said therapy was personal. He wanted to terminate without anyone listening in. Her fiancé was head of the security shift that day. Collins talked her into it and she talked him into it. Nobody told me anything about it until it was too late." He paused and the anger on his face seemed to sharpen the creases; I guess not being asked still rankled. "I wanted to fire someone over it—badly to tell you the truth—but there wasn't anyone to fire except her and her boyfriend and . . ." He shrugged. We both knew they had gotten a lot worse than being fired.

"You're going to do what you have to do," he added. "But whether you think you can prove it or not, this man is dangerous and you know it."

"Sir," I said, "I promise you I'll look at this as carefully as I can. I have to tell you though, if he doesn't fit the law, he doesn't. You and I both know a lot of dangerous people get released from prison every day. And it's not going to matter if I say he fits, if he doesn't. I'm not the judge or the jury. If I try to make somebody fit the criteria for a sexually violent predator who doesn't, the defense will hand me my head, and he'll still get set free. I can't make a case that isn't there."

"Juries are capricious," he said. "They're like the NFL. On any given Sunday, anything can happen."

I couldn't argue with that.

"Do what you can," he said. "He's going to hurt somebody if they let him out." I couldn't argue with that, either.

As I got up to leave, I had a thought and turned around. "Warden, can I ask you something?"

"Sure."

"Do you get staff who are working with him—chaplains,

counselors, volunteers—do any of those people ever request to meet with him alone, despite his record?"

"All the time," he said, smiling wryly. "All the time."

Outside the sky had turned the color of sludge and the air felt wet and heavy. Rain doesn't always seem to fall in the Northwest; sometimes it just seems to materialize in the air. The sky and the prison were both shades from the same grey palette and hard to tell apart in the worsening light. I tried to imagine any set of circumstances where you couldn't tell a prison from my much beloved Carolina sky but failed. The bright Southern sky over the Outer Banks where I lived would make this prison look squalid and ugly—as alien as an inner city alley on a mountainside. Even when it stormed back home, the storms tore up the world with a fierce energy. This endless dampness, this gray woolen air that was the hallmark of the Northwest, had nothing in common with the carbonated spring rains in Carolina or the vivid razor rains of a bad winter. I took one last look and started the long walk to the parking lot and my car.

I couldn't get a flight out until the next morning, so I braved the endless Seattle traffic and headed for an airport motel. There was a sea of red dots ahead and white dots behind, the cars themselves emerging only briefly from the fog and then disappearing again, like gray metal ghosts flitting by in the darkness.

It wasn't just the wet, gray air or the claustrophobic traffic that was affecting me. The tiredness from the interview hadn't let go. I never felt good after interviewing a truly vicious human being, and sometimes it lasted quite a while. I wondered how other people felt about it, people who didn't see voices turn scratchy or have weird sensations of heat in their palms when they listened to lies, but I think it probably affected everybody one way or another.

It was the price I paid for not doing therapy with victims anymore. I had nearly drowned in the well of misery that showed up on the hour every hour in a therapist's office. I reached the point where I couldn't listen to one more broken and battered child, not one more dissociative, depressed adult. I worried all the time about my self-mutilating, suicidal clients. I just felt too bad for people to survive as a therapist. Other people's feelings seemed almost as vivid as my own to me and as hard to let go of. Maybe it went along with the synesthesia. Who knew?

Whatever the reasons, dealing with conning and manipulation was easier for me than dealing with trauma and suffering. I couldn't fix conning, and I knew enough not to try. I had no real empathy for psychopaths and rapists and pedophiles, and that saved me. Most days I just watched, took notes, and wrote up my little reports—reports that separated out the ones the law could keep off the streets from the ones it couldn't. Sometimes, just sometimes, those reports were enough to keep another child from being molested or another woman from being raped, and I figured that wasn't such a bad way to make a living.

Even so, every once in a while some tale of malevolence got to me. The tale of the naive counselor was bad enough, but what really stuck in my head was the "fishing for bitches" story. I could practically hear the twelve-year-olds screaming in the mattress-padded rooms.

I made it to the motel. After sitting around listlessly for a few minutes, I walked over to the window and pulled back the curtains to look for some kind of view. A parking lot greeted me. The sodium lamp gave a sickly yellow cast to the wet asphalt, and the cars looked like dead bugs floating on a greasy black sea. I closed my eyes and thought of my home on Blackbeard's Isle. The sun would be putting on a show now, sliding into the sea and painting long canary streaks across the waves as it went, sponging huge rose and purple blotches across the pale blue sky.

There were living things in this world. The island where I lived was full of them, but none of them were here. There were even made things in this world that had souls: sailboats and some small planes and every hang glider ever made. Motels weren't on the list. I had never met a motel that was anything but a dead spot on the planet. No living thing stayed long enough to impart any spirit to the place. We were all drifting through, and our spirits touched nothing. The chairs, tables, and beds were shells, pictures of themselves with none of the feel of things that had actually been part of the life of a living being. There was no energy here to sustain the spirit, and my batteries were running low. What would happen, I thought, if someday on the road my batteries died completely and I couldn't get back home? Now I was losing it.

Morning brought the long flights home. I did not have a clue, not a premonition, not a thought that within twenty-four hours I'd be heading out again like a rocket, all because of a teenager's voice on the phone in the middle of the night.

chapter 3

The clock was creeping up on 3:00 a.m. when the phone rang. I was so grateful to be back home on Blackbeard's Isle that I had fallen into a deep trench of sleep, the same one I always fell into after traveling. I came up slowly, too sleep-befuddled to be coordinated, and knocked the phone off the hook when I tried to answer it. "Yes?" I said finally, when I had scrambled around and recovered it. I was too tired to even think that it was sure to be bad news. What else is a phone call at 3:00 a.m.?

"Are you my mother's friend?" the voice said, a bright orange starburst exploding in my mind's eye at the sound. The voice was teenage and shrill and something else, angry maybe, or just upset.

"Am I what?" I said, trying to focus. I didn't recognize the voice. This must be some mistake. "Who is this?"

"Are you my mother's friend?" the voice said again, this time impatiently and closer to the phone, as though someone might hear. I closed my eyes to focus on the words because the colors were distracting me, much more than they did during the day. Of course it didn't help. The color was in my head, not out there, so it continued to pulse like an electric orange star going supernova.

"Who's your mother, hon?" I asked finally, sitting up.

"Jena," and I heard the tears. "You know Jena. You must. She talks about you. All the time. She used to, anyway."

"Jena?" I said. "Jena Jensen? From Clark?"

"If you're my mother's friend,"—the starburst seemed to darken in anger and then implode—"why. . . aren't. . . you . . . here?" I heard a tremor at the top of it that sounded like the beginning of something—tears, perhaps or even a wail. I started to say something—I don't know what—when I heard a shout in the background and the phone went dead.

Could this be Jena's daughter? Jena, my best friend throughout my whole, entire childhood? I didn't even know she had a daughter. So where was Jena? Jena with the dirty-blond hair speckled like a lion's mane and the large eyes and the big nose and the mother who nodded off at the breakfast table, her eyes dilated to the size of dimes. Jena with the prettiest voice I'd ever seen, a sort of swirling aqua with tiny yellow sprinkles in it. Jena with the busy surgeon father who was never there and, when he was, just walked past the nodding mother and the silent Jena. I was grown before I realized those drugs had to come from somewhere and it was unlikely her mother was buying them off the street. I had lost touch with Jena years ago. Now memories of her came back in the kind of vivid clarity that, for me, is usually only found in colors.

The thing I remembered most about Jena wasn't the nodding mother or the stale cereal in the cupboard: it was her dreams. Week after week from fifth grade through eighth, Jena told me dreams she had at least once a week about a secret agent who had thrilling, death-defying adventures, unlike anything that happened in Clark, North Carolina, where we both grew up. Before she woke, he'd always receive an envelope telling him where the next assignment was. The next time she dreamed about him, that's exactly where he'd go.

Once I accused Jena of making the stories up, of not having dreams at all, and she had looked more surprised than anything. "Make them up?" she said. "How would I do that?"

It was a stupid thing to say. I, of all people, should have known that you could have something a little unusual about you and not be lying. Jena was the first and only person in my childhood I told about the colors and about my palms. I didn't have a word for it then so I just described what I saw. Jena didn't even blink. I had the feeling that stranger things than that were going on in her head.

When high school graduation came and everyone else was obsessed with jobs or college or getting married or leaving Clark or not leaving Clark, Jena never said a word to me or anyone about her plans. So I was floored when, the day after graduation, she came by my house on her bike and told me she was on her way to California. She had planned it carefully. Her saddlebags held only one change of clothes but an assortment of extra tires, tools, maintenance paraphernalia, and maps. She was joining up with a bike tour for part of the trip and on her own for the rest.

I was wide awake now so I went out on the small balcony off my bedroom and tried to think. All that came to me were memories of Jena. Passing notes in fifth grade. Talking late at night on sleepovers till one of us dropped midsentence. Clamming on a sandbar and then losing all the clams when my twelve-foot sailboat tipped over on the way back.

The phone call had freaked me, and I tried to talk myself down. Maybe this was just an overwrought kid, and whatever she was talking about wasn't nearly as earth-shaking as she thought. Maybe I was tripping out over this for nothing.

I didn't believe it. There is something about genuine fear, distress, whatever you want to call it, that can't be faked. I've heard it a few times in my life, and I've never known an actress to get it right. This voice had the real thing. Whatever could produce that fear was real, too.

I didn't have anyway of tracing the phone call. The island's phone system wasn't sophisticated enough to even have call waiting. How was I even going to find her? I walked back in and saw the small laptop sitting on my desk. There was always the Internet. Like everybody else, we had access to the Internet on Blackbeard's Isle, and the vast neural network that it accessed encircled the planet like a hairnet with very fine mesh indeed. We were all caught up in that net. Pieces of us— phone numbers, addresses, credit card numbers, driver license numbers, criminal records, property exchanges, taxes paid or not, child support—all were stuck to that net somewhere. The search engines that probed through the billions of connections hummed like lasers cutting through paper. Jena was somewhere in that net and these days anyone anywhere could be found with very little trouble and virtually no expense.

I turned on the computer. Opening up the Internet was like entering every mall on the planet all at once. Ads popped up in front of me, urging me to travel to the Caribbean, buy a better toilet cleanser, and increase the size of my penis. I sighed. It was like letting the world beyond Blackbeard's Isle right back into my living room. I shuddered, got up abruptly and hit a button on the stereo. Yo-Yo Ma spilled into the room and immediately golden globes began drifting down in front of me like hot air balloons floating by. What a shame he could never see them.

It only took ten minutes to find Jena. It required no more than calling up Google and typing in "finding people." A dozen sites jumped up where, for really paltry sums, I could find pretty much anybody. I remembered her birthday because it was only two weeks after mine. Armed with that and her full name, the Internet extracted her with tweezerlike efficiency from the hundreds of millions of others. I now knew where she lived. I knew that she was married and when—almost exactly three years ago—plus I knew her husband's name. I knew that she had no civil judgments against her and no criminal record.

Just for the hell of it, I ran her husband also. I didn't have his birthday, but I knew where he lived because he lived with Jena. Armed with his name and address, I found out enough to know Jena had been playing a long shot when she married him.

I stared at the phone for a few minutes and then decided what the hell and picked it up. It was the middle of the night but so was the call to me, and I was betting it came from the same number. Was this an emergency or not? There was only one way to find out. My hands seemed steady enough, but I felt light-headed and out of breath. The phone rang five times before it was picked up.

"Hello," Jena said. I was so relieved I didn't speak for a second. "Hello?" she said again. "Who is this?" The relief vanished as I realized the pretty swirling aqua with yellow sprinkles I had loved had changed. I couldn't see any swirling now and the sprinkles were more elongated and looked harsh. The colors were no longer vivid but ragged and uneven.

"Jena," I said finally, "this is Breeze." I waited for her to reply but she didn't. "It's Breeze," I said again. "Are you OK?"

She still didn't speak. "Talk to me, Jena," I said softly. There was still no reply. It was eerie. I could feel her presence so strongly it was almost like being in the same room although I heard nothing. Then I heard a click and she was gone.

I had no pets, no spouse or children. I didn't have a time clock to punch or a boss to call. I didn't even have a boyfriend to leave a note for. I looked at the address on the Internet one more time, and picked up the phone to call the airlines. Jena was family. No way was I leaving it at that.

The first ferry came at an ungodly early hour, and if there was any consolation to leaving Blackbeard's Isle so soon after coming home, it was the sunrise that blossomed behind the boat as the ferry headed west to the mainland. Sunrises each seem to have their own personality, and this one had a considering, even-tempered air about it, but with a kind of light gaiety about it. The sun seemed to float lightly amid an array of small and subtle colors, like a child playing with pastels might make.

There were other days when the sun seemed to scream across the morning sky trailing blood-red streaks behind it, which was a different sort of day altogether. This day was starting in a kind of light and easy peace, at least as far as nature was concerned.

I took the braid out of my long red hair and let the wind pick it up. Even worrying about Jena didn't entirely erase my pleasure at being on the water. The part I liked best was the betwixt and between, when there was no shoreline anywhere to tether me. I watched Blackbeard's Isle shrink to a faint line, like a lover headed to another fate, then walked forward on the ferry—as I always did—just to make sure nothing lay ahead.

Nothing ever did. There wasn't anything between the last shore and the next but the low drumming of motors churning through the swells, the cawing of the hoarse sea gulls diving for handouts, and the sea itself, stretched like an endless protective bumper between me and the busyness on shore. I loved this ride. No offenders, no papers, no court dates, no reports, not even the endless minutiae of shopping and cleaning and, well, living. Out here, I had no appointments to keep, no phone calls to make.

Pamlico Sound was in fine form today. The wind was starting to rise and waves were already forming whitecaps. Despite the halcyon sunrise, the forecast said a nor'easter might be coming in, and that was never a good time to leave the island. Nothing beat standing on the shore and watching a noreaster tear up the world: disregarding niceties and propriety, whipping flags and weather vanes till they flapped and spun and showing no respect for Mr. Donovan's obsessively tended garden. Everybody talks about a storm's fury, but I've never seen one without a sense of humor.

But today even the pastel sunrise and the hypnotic rhythm of the swells couldn't keep the shore away entirely. The phone call last night kept replaying in my mind like a toothache that always returns. The problem with worries is they take you away from the colors. Even the cawing of the seagulls didn't arch in the sky like they usually did.

The motel where I kept my car was a stone's throw away from the dock. I didn't need anything except a scooter and my old red jeep at Blackbeard's Isle, and that's all I kept there. The morning was crisp and clear, the blue above a bright parasol over a sandy forest filled with small, sweet chirping birds. From the small houses that lined the landing came the scent of magnolias. I greeted Josie, my car, like the old friend she was and headed up the road to Betsy's house.

Betsy was my touchstone, the one person I checked in with, coming and going to Blackbeard's Isle. I even rented a room at her house to keep my work clothes. Call me crazy, but I couldn't seem to let Dr. Copen anywhere near Blackbeard's Isle. When I left the Outer Banks to work—and that was usually the only reason I left—I dressed at Betsy's house, did what I needed to do, and then came home. Everything about my working self from the car to the clothes stayed off the island. Breeze, no degree and no last name, beachcomber, lover of driftwood and oyster shells, lived on Blackbeard's Isle.

The road to Betsy's was an old country two-lane. Snakes and skunks and small critters of one sort or another routinely flitted across it, but today there was nothing except low, dense brush framed by live oaks with old Spanish moss hanging down like witch's hair. This part of the coast was swampland and we had the water moccasins and cottonmouths to prove it. Josie took the ten miles to Betsy's house in a slow, even beat befitting the easygoing sunrise. There was no way to hurry on this road and Josie didn't like to anyway. Rumor had it the contractors were paid by the foot way back when the road was built, so it twisted and turned continuously, and went by everybody's house who lived there at the time.

I parked and walked in Betsy's back door. I'd missed Betsy both coming and going on the last trip, but this time it was early and I was hoping—really hoping—she'd be home. A glance at my watch told me Betsy's soap opera wasn't on yet. Betsy had watched the same soap opera every day since high school and nothing, so far as I knew, ever interfered. She had taken a nursing degree at UNC after graduation, then returned home to marry a boy she'd dated since ninth grade. She started working as a nurse until the hospital insisted on a rotating schedule—which meant she'd miss her soap—so she'd said fuck it. Jimmy had started an auto-body shop and was making good money so she decided to stay at home and wait for the children. They came, a boy and a girl, three years apart, with the grace to inherit Mama's smarts and Daddy's work ethic. They were both at UNC now, the younger one having started in the fall. I'd been worried about my friend ever since.

I called to Betsy and a moment later she appeared in the kitchen while I was looking for a soda in the fridge. I said, "Got a minute?"

"Oh, I think I've got a few," she said dryly. She had a cigarette in one hand and was wearing her bathrobe. Lately she seemed to wear it all day some days. She had a voice the color of smoke with blue tinges shaped in a sort of spiral.

"Want one?" I said, holding up a can of Dr. Pepper.

"Pass me a beer, girl. It's too early in the day for soda."

I handed her the beer without comment and we both sat down at the kitchen table. I looked at her. She'd put on twenty pounds somewhere in the last few years, mostly after the last kid, Mary Alice had left for college. She'd been smoking more, and the lines on her face showed it. And this drinking beer in the morning was new. Betsy had never been much of a drinker.

I was pretty sure things weren't going well with Jimmy. He'd never been a real talker. Now that the kids were gone, it seemed to be bothering her more. Something was bothering her. Maybe just no kids and not enough to do.

I thought about saying something. I always thought about saying something every time I saw her these days, but decided—this time like every time—that today wasn't the day. There was a small hard ball of resentment somewhere in the back of Betsy's eyes. So far that look hadn't fastened on me and I wanted to keep it that way.

"Jena Jensen," I said, putting up my feet on a nearby chair.

"Jena Jensen?" Betsy opened the can in front of her and took a swig. "Now that's a name I haven't heard for a while. I never did know what you saw in that girl. Mousy little thing."

"Oh, I don't think so," I said.

"Oh, come on," she replied. "Always had her homework in on time. Always had her cardigan buttoned to her neck. Worked the drugstore on weekend nights. Never partied that I knew about and I raised enough hell to know. Never dated. What do you mean you don't think so?"

"You remember the time that witch—what was her name—Beecher, said any kid who didn't pass some stupid-ass test couldn't go on the class trip."

"Sure," she said, and neither of us could help smiling at the way it had worked out. We both knew—the whole class knew—it had been aimed at a couple of developmentally delayed kids in the class whom she didn't want to take. No doubt she thought they would have embarrassed her in Washington, or maybe they were just too much trouble.

"Remember when she passed out the papers, they all had passing grades. The kids were cheering. And she was yelling she didn't write those grades."

"Oh, I do, I do," Betsy said.

"I'm pretty sure that was Jena."

"No way."

"I think so. First of all, who else was smart enough? All the kids' papers that might have flunked had been rewritten. They deserved the grades they got. And the real papers never showed up. Besides, all the handwriting had been faked. Pretty good fakes at that. None of our usual juvi delinquent types could have pulled that off, or would have even tried. Besides, she never looked up from her book."

Betsy raised her eyebrows.

"Anybody who didn't expect it would have looked up. Jena just kept reading."

"Unexpected depths," she said. "No wonder they never figured it out. Nobody would have looked her way. Hat's off to you, kid," she said and raised her beer to a ninth grade Jena. "Why do you ask? Where is she now?"

"I don't know," I replied. "I'm worried about her. I'm going off to try and find her." I told her about the phone call and about what happened when I called back. "I was hoping you could tell me something."

"She came back once, years ago," Betsy said thoughtfully, "before you moved back. She didn't stay at her father's house, I remember wondering about that at the time. She had a knapsack and was camping. I asked her if she wanted to stay here, but she said she liked to camp. Said she'd camped all over South America. You think that was true?"

"Sure," I said. "She'd do that. You ever hear anything else about her?"

"Not me. I'll ask around. Best reason to go to church. Only reason, really, to catch up on things." She flicked her ash and took a long drag on her cancer stick. I hated the smell and the smoke. Still it was Betsy's house, and I wasn't willing to lose her over it.

"I doubt anybody knows anything," she went on. I don't think she ever had a friend here except you. You guys were thicker than thieves."

"It was the voice," I said. "I'd have probably skipped right over her, too, if it hadn't been for that. It was amazing-looking. I could have watched that voice all day." Betsy was one of the very few people who, even now, knew I was a synesthete. I hadn't told her until we were in college. It wasn't that

I was ashamed up of it; it was that I didn't like getting treated like a curiosity—or worse, a freak.

"You know, she loved mountains," I said, thinking about what Betsy had said about South America and wondering if Jena had gone there to climb.

Betsy looked quizzically at me. "She had pictures of all the great Himalayas on the walls in her room: K-2, Annapurna, Everest," I said. "She knew more about them than I know about this county. She knew every route up them and who did it when. Hell of a thing for a girl growing up on a coastal plain. I wonder if she ever took up climbing. There are some major mountains in South America. When was this that she came back?"

"Oh, Lord, I don't know. The kids were little, that's all I remember. Probably not more than five years after high school. I remember her asking about you. I said you were doing that graduate school thing you did. Didn't she ever contact you?"

I shook my head.

Betsy shrugged and got up. "Well, I don't know." She walked over to the fridge. "You're coming and going all the time, girl," she said. "Weren't you just here?"

"In and out," I said.

Betsy stopped with her hand on the door. "You know, I really don't understand you people. I'm willing to go anywhere in the world as long as I'm in Hyde County when the sun sets. I don't know what you people are looking for out there."

"Today's different," I said. "I'm going to find Jena. But you know why I go out there—to make a living. We just don't have enough rapists and child molesters and murderers on Blackbeard's Isle to keep me busy. Not anymore. Not since the pirates left."

"Liar, liar," she said. "If you had to stay here full time, you'd end up, well, like me."

There was a pause and then I said softly, "What are you going to do, Betsy? You need to do something."

"Have another beer," she said, opening the door.

chapter 4

Jena adjusted the gooseneck lamp so there was a perfect circle of light centered exactly on her desk and spilling on the floor. It was possible, she supposed, to get a smaller light that would just fall on the desk. That would be much more precise, but really she did not want to be blind-sided by people stopping at her desk, and this way she could see the shoes. Shoes that just went by on the way to the bathroom didn't come into the circle, but those that stopped at her desk did.

Her boss's shoes, for instance. She could even read a little of what Dave wanted to say in the way they shifted. If he just stood beside her desk, balanced on both feet, it was about work, and the fastest way to get rid of him was to look up long enough to hear him out. She didn't really have to look up more than once, and sometimes she could just say yes and he'd say what he needed and leave.

Sometimes, however, he started shifting from one foot to the other, and that meant he was starting in on her again: on the change in her, how worried he was, did she need help, how he wanted her to talk again to the police lieutenant he knew. All idiot suggestions for another woman from another planet. Then she would just drift inward, just slip backward into some very quiet place where she hardly heard him at all, like she did last night when Breeze called, but she didn't want to think about that.

Dave was shifting today so she braced herself, but he just handed her some papers and left. How confusing. He really shouldn't do that. She needed to get another job, somewhere they hadn't known her "before." Just thinking about the energy that would take exhausted her.

She settled in with the numbers in front of her. She knew it was a clerk's job, this business of keeping track of purchase orders and shipping and other minor administrative tasks. Which was why she'd asked for it. The business of managing the office had gotten too complex. There were too many decisions to make. One day she had realized it was too hard to come to work and make all those decisions and, worse, have to talk to people. The looks on their faces were intolerable, almost as bad as looking in a mirror, which she had not done, thank God, in a year now—maybe more. She didn't entirely remember when she had stopped looking in mirrors.

Numbers were different. A kind of quiet certitude came over her when she added figures up. It all had to come out exactly right at the end of the day or she couldn't leave. Once she had stayed two hours late, and she'd paid for it at home. At least the numbers had finally come out right, or she'd have been there all night.

Lately she had taken to arranging the purchase orders and the other paperwork so they lined up right at the edge of the desk, exactly even with the side of the desk and the bottom.

Not a millimeter over. That helped too. Except some mornings when she came in, they had been moved slightly, which was freaky. She tried to think it was the cleaning lady and not Jerry going through her things, like he did at home. It could be him. You never knew with him. Once she found a list he had made of everything she had, including how many tampons. He watched everything, kept track of everything.

Sometimes she tried to imagine life without him, but the prospect of it just seemed blank. It was easy to pretend things would be fine, when really, there would be a huge void if he left. She hadn't felt like a person for a long time, not like anything really, and he was real, if nothing else. And what about the drugs? How would she get them without him? So he couldn't leave. Then she'd be left with just Lily who needed things all the time. Rides to her friends' houses. Report cards signed. Shopping. Teacher conferences. How was she supposed to do those things on the bad days? There were a lot of bad days.

Sometimes she tried to remember life before Lily. Life before having to make sure there was food in the house and clean clothes and someone home every day of the year. Life when she could just grab her backpack and go climbing. Remembering wasn't all that good an idea. It brought back Lily's father and the mountain morning when the rain turned all the lichen on the rocks into glass, and he took a step before he was fully hooked in . . .

She closed her eyes and looked hard at the numbers. It was dumb to think about leaving anyway. Leaving was out of the question because Jerry was more scary as a shadow outside her door than he was actually being in the house. Or was that true? It was true he'd be more dangerous, but more scary? That presupposed she could still feel fear, and she didn't think she

could. Or maybe she was always afraid so there was no difference. Either way you looked at it, whatever it was she felt these
days was always the same. Maybe Dave or someone else would
label it fear. It didn't matter very much what words they
wrapped around it. One thing was certain: she'd forgotten
how to feel safe.

She looked down at the paper in front of her and realized
she had lost track of the numbers while she was thinking, and
panic seized her. She could still feel panic, at least. At numbers
that didn't add up, or shoes that weren't lined up exactly even
in the closet, or flatware that wasn't perfectly aligned on the
table. Which was probably crazy. No doubt Breeze would
think so. She didn't want to think about that. Breeze wouldn't
likely even recognize her if she saw her. Thank God she only
called. You can't see someone on the phone.

She couldn't help but think about Breeze sometimes, even
before the call. When her own sense of being a person faded,
and she couldn't find a point of view or a place to stand, she
pretended she was Breeze. She had had one friend in her
childhood, and she was still real when the rest of the world
had faded into myth.

She had had Breeze's number for a long time now, written
in permanent marker on the inside of her watch. It had taken
a long time to find a permanent marker with a fine tip. She
had done it though, and now the number was there night
and day. She never took off that watch. She took showers
with that watch. Whenever the numbers started to fade, she
wrote them again.

Whatever Jerry did to her he had never taken off that watch.
She liked to think she had the number memorized anyway, but
sometimes when he was hurting her, she could hardly remember
her name so she didn't trust she could remember a number.

Strange how large Breeze had grown in her mind. When she left Clark, she'd thought about calling her, but somehow never had. She'd been on the road pretty much all the time: climbing, moving around, and then again, well, she didn't like phones all that much, anyway. The truth was she didn't know why she never made the call. Maybe because she'd left Clark and the South behind and had been reluctant to open the door even an inch.

Breezes calling her—that wasn't part of the plan. If she had talked to her, Breeze would have come. No way could she have fooled Breeze and . . . what then? What would happen then? She wouldn't make suggestions like Dave did or whine like Lily did. She wouldn't let it go and walk away. Likely Jerry would kill them both. And even if he didn't, there wasn't enough of her left to start over.

Still, she couldn't give up that phone number. I could leave, it said. As long as she had it, she had a back door open. There was some small room in her that he hadn't gotten to. He knew it, too, that one room stayed locked. What he didn't know was where the key was: written on the back of her watch.

B y late afternoon, I had made it all the way to Chicago. I felt uneasy about going out to Jena's house at night, so I decided to wait till morning when there was less chance her husband would be home. I didn't have a plan if Jena wasn't there either.

I fell asleep early in a motel on the outskirts of Chicago, but sleep brought no respite. All night Jena and I climbed K-2, a tougher climb than Everest, and one that climbers say is different. Everest merely has its moods, but K-2 has a malevolent feel about it—or so climbers say—as though its very nature was malicious. It particularly likes killing women climbers, and does so in appalling numbers. It kills a higher percentage of women who try to climb it than any other mountain.

Jena and I were in the "death zone," the area above 26,000 feet where the body can't acclimate and the tissues start slowly shutting down, the air too thin to sustain life for long. All the time you are in the death zone you are slowly dying. Stay too long and eventually you die—simple as that.

All night Jena was leading on a knife edge covered with ice and snow that was breaking away with each and every step. There was no bottled oxygen and I couldn't think. I kept calling Jena to turn back, but the wind was swallowing my words.

I slept fitfully and woke frequently. Each time I fell asleep, I slid relentlessly into the death zone with Jena. Finally I gave up and just got up. The dream made me uneasy, so I pulled on a pair of jeans and went outside to clear my head. It was raining slightly, a rain as light and feathery as fingertips. I held my face up but hardly felt the soft drops.

Strange I could dream so vividly about a place I had never even been remotely near. That's what I remembered most about talking with Jena. She talked endlessly about the mountains. She told stories about all the great expeditions, and she had made them come alive. I made those last few exhausted steps to the top of Everest with Hillary, had been with Bonnington on the first ascent of the south face of Annapurna, and was on K-2 with Schoening when five men on his rope fell and he held them up alone. Jena would lean forward when she spoke, hands flying, an unfocused light in her eyes.

When morning came, I climbed into my rental car and started taking on the Chicago labyrinth. I finally found Jena's house but stared at it, perplexed. I could have seen Jena in a city loft or a remote cabin or almost anything quirky. The bland, suburban home in front of me didn't fit.

I got slowly out of the car and walked up the front driveway. Now that I was there, I sort of wished I wasn't. I felt like I was approaching a hornet's nest, and a part of me wanted to leave it alone. The house was quiet and nothing looked unusual. Nonetheless, my palms were sweating and an amber haze lay over everything. Sometimes my own emotions got in the way of what I was seeing, and today was one of those days. I was nervous and that always cast a tint.

I knocked on the door and waited, thinking all of this was probably for nothing. Most likely they both worked. Silence greeted the knock, so I raised my hand to knock again, when the door opened so suddenly I took a step back. The man standing there was blond and wore a powder blue shirt that matched his eyes. He wasn't all that tall, only about five feet nine. He looked quick and strong, like a gymnast, but without the large shoulder muscles. At that size I was eye to eye with him. He was drop-dead good-looking, so much so that I wondered for a second if I had seen him on TV or something.

He didn't say anything, just stared at me, and it took me a moment to speak because something about him, the golden-boy good looks or maybe the flat and appraising eyes put me off balance. He gave me the kind of once-over that was universal in the good old days of Playboy bunnies and jokes about dumb blondes, a frankly sexual look without any of the warmth or playfulness that would have made it even vaguely amusing. He took in the red hair pulled back from my face, the five-nine runner's frame, and the gray-green eyes without a word.

"Hi," I said. "I'm Breeze Copen. I'm looking for Jena Jensen, an old friend of mine." The moment I said my name I knew the next sentence was superfluous. Nothing changed on the surface, but I could feel the charge in the air. There was no question that this was the right house. Somehow I knew that the moment I saw him.

"I'm sorry I didn't call. I was passing through and my plane was delayed. I thought I'd take a chance and run out."

"How did you find Jena?" He said it bluntly, without apology. The voice was copper-colored with a sort of swarthy darkness mixed in. The texture was weird, sort of puffy, almost like seersucker only puffier. The voice looked almost bloated and made me think of floaters, dead bodies that had been in the water too long. Darkness usually meant anger, but I couldn't hear any. To my ears the voice sounded neutral, even casual. It didn't look that way.

I raised my eyebrows and tried to look puzzled. "I saw an ad," I said, "on the Internet for looking up old high school friends. It had a free coupon and I thought of Jena. I haven't talked to her in years. They gave me her address and, since I was passing through, I thought I'd surprise her." I was always amazed by how well I lied.

He smiled belatedly, and the smile was warmth personified. It was as though once he decided there was nothing behind the visit to worry about, his whole persona changed.

"Forgive me," he said. "I'm Jerry Roland, her husband. I'm a writer, and when I'm working, I find it hard to switch gears. It takes me a moment to get my head out of the story. I'm sorry. Jena's out of town on business."

"Oh, no," I said. "Just my luck. What kind of business does she do?"

"Consulting," he said. "She works with different businesses in the area."

"Really, what's her field?"

"Organizational development." He said it easily, although the voice's texture had grown rougher, but I didn't need that to know he was lying. He made no move to invite me in.

"Could I have her cell number?" I asked. "I have to go today, and I'd like to give her a call sometime."

"She doesn't have one," he said. "She did, but it drove her crazy. She finally quit carrying it. Said she couldn't get anything done. Well, you know Jena. She's not the most techno-logically minded person. Look, I don't mean to discourage you, but Jena has pretty much put Clark behind her. She never felt she fit in there. I don't know . . . " He let it trail off.

"Ah," I said. "I see."

"She said she'd call in when she got to the motel," he offered. "I can tell her you stopped by. She'll get back to you if. . . well, you know."

"Of course," I said. "I understand."

"Can I can give you my number?" I asked, knowing it was meaningless. It was the kind of thing I'd say if I believed him, and I wanted him to think I did.

"Just a moment," he said and closed the door in my face. He returned with a pad and paper and dutifully wrote my cell phone down—as if he'd keep it more than a nanosecond after I left. He smiled that smile again and all I could think of was that song they play on the golden oldies, Rod Steward singing, "If I listened long enough to you, I'd find a way to believe that it's all true."

haven't found a way to believe it, I thought as I drove away, or maybe I didn't listen long enough. Ten to one, Jena was at work somewhere in Chicago. The question was, where? Southerners are stubborn; it's either a pitfall or a virtue, depending on what we're up to. Today I thought it a virtue.

To find Jena, I had to find a way to get back on the Internet, and it took a little doing. More than a little, actually. I spent an hour trying to find a pay phone that had a real honest-to-God phone book in it. I gave up and started asking gas station attendants and clerks in stores where I could find an Internet café. I still had no luck and was about to check into a motel just for its business center, when I drove by a computer store. The guy working behind the counter knew of an Internet café, and an hour and a half after I started looking, I was sitting at a café drinking good Ethiopian coffee and looking up Jena again.

It had been easy last time to find her home address. I had simply gone through a "finding people" company and searched through the info they compiled. Unfortunately, nobody seemed to compile work addresses. Finally, in desperation, I just typed in her name and "Chicago," and was astonished when she popped up right away in a list of staff on a Web site for a company named Horizons. Jena was their office manager—if it was the right person—and the company had listed their phone number and address.

I got out a map and started driving around Chicago again. Would he have called her? I didn't think so. I was betting he wouldn't even tell her I came. I got confused and made wrong turns and cursed city traffic—wishing all the time I was back in the tiny village of Blackbeard's Isle. Eventually I pulled up to a white stucco one-story, a pleasant enough building set off in a tidy business park.

The receptionist behind the desk was in her fifties with a square jaw and a Joan Crawford coif with her hair pulled back over her ears. She was talking with a man with dark, curly hair who was leaning over her shoulder and going over some papers. I waited for them to finish and tried to settle on an approach. At least I hoped to find out if Jena was in town and confirm she worked there, even if I couldn't see her for some reason. The man spoke for a moment longer, then straightened up and turned to go.

"Can I help you?" the receptionist said, and her voice looked like a lime-colored balloon, the kind of bright color you associate with children's books. The voice didn't go with the hard lines of her face and gave me hope she wouldn't be a pain in the butt to deal with.

"I'm looking for Jena Jensen," I said. "I understand she works here." Immediately the man stopped and turned around. He looked at me sharply, which alarmed me almost as much as the middle-of-the-night phone call. Why would even mentioning Jena's name get such a reaction? At least I knew I was at the right place.

The receptionist glanced at him and said, "And who should I say is here?"

"Tell her an old friend," I said. "From Clark."

"I'll take her back," the man said, opening the door behind the receptionist desk and holding it for me. I followed him into a large room with cubicles set up in the middle and offices lining the edges. Despite its bland layout, it was an attractive room with rust carpeting, cream-colored walls, and clean, compact fluorescent lighting without the harsh fluorescent tones of yesteryear. He turned right and walked past the cubicles to an office on the far side. At the door he stepped aside again and ushered me into a large corner office dominated by a huge metal desk sitting in the center of it. Clearly, this was his office, and I wondered why I was there. He walked in behind me and closed the door.

"I'm Dave McQuaid," he said, holding out his hand. "I'm Jena's boss." His voice was a crumbly soft yellow, and he had kind, hound-dog eyes. He had looked taller when he was leaning over the desk but standing, he had a long torso and short, stocky legs. He had probably been built like a fire hydrant once, before a decade or so had turned his shape into a "business body," the kind created by too much work, too little exercise, and an American fat-loading diet. He was carrying maybe fifteen pounds more than he should have, and he was soft at the edges. Still, he looked comfortable to be with, the kind of guy women liked to snuggle up with.

"Breeze Copen," I said and got a brief, dry handshake in exchange. We both sat down. I waited. We both knew I was wondering why I was in his office and not Jena's.

"I just wanted to talk to you for a moment. How well do you know Jena?"

"Very well twenty years ago. We were best friends growing up."

"And now?"

"I haven't seen her in twenty years."

"What brings you here all of a sudden?" He wasn't looking at me when he spoke but down at a pen he was fiddling with on the desk. His voice had those mottled white spots that always went with worried. It was unsettling, though, to see this man nervous. It didn't fit. He looked solid and easy-going and not at all like a natural worrier.

I didn't speak until he finally looked up. "Why don't you tell me what's going on?" I asked. "Why are you asking all these questions?"

He sighed, dropped the pen and sat back. "You don't know anything?" he asked.

"I got a call," I said. "A friend was worried about her and wouldn't say why. I came to see why."

"But you didn't go to the house," he said. "You came here."

"Well, I did go to the house," I said. "A man who smiled too much said she was out of town."

"Ah," he said, "and you didn't believe it."

"I didn't like his eyes," I said. Which wasn't the whole story. I absolutely hated the texture of his voice. That probably wasn't the thing to say.

"How'd you find us?"

"Internet," I said. "You can find anybody."

He sat back and looked straight at me. "OK, I don't know you from Adam, but what the hell. I'll tell you what I know, because who knows? Maybe you can do something. We sure as hell haven't done squat.

"Two years ago, Jena applied for a job here. My office manager had taken a temporary maternity leave and then decided to stay home with the baby. We'd been trying to get by without one, thinking she was coming back, and things had just sort of been slowly falling apart. I don't know if you want to hear all this, but I don't know how to tell you without starting at the beginning."

"It's fine," I said. "What do you do here?"

"We place ads for businesses," he said. "We don't make up the ads ourselves. We're a marketing company. We research where the ads should go, which consumers read what, that sort of thing, and then we place the ads in the most strategic places. Sort of getting the most bang for the advertising buck," he said. "It's not rocket science but it's a competitive market, and we have to be pretty efficient at what we do to survive. Almost everybody is in sales and on the road a lot, so the office management position is important here. It's sort of the glue that holds things together.

"She had a funny résumé, lots of different jobs and then times with no jobs at all, and I almost didn't even interview her. When I couldn't find what I was looking for, I interviewed her on a lark.

"She had something," he sighed. "I guess you'd call it pizzazz. If you saw her then and now, you wouldn't believe it. Hell, I don't believe it and I've been here the whole time. She was thoughtful and funny, and she said some of the gaps had to do with mountain climbing. Said she'd work for a while, save up money and then go climbing in different places. South America, mostly, I think.

"Then after she had a child, she stayed home with her as much as she could. She'd save up so she could stop working and go back to work when she needed to. She said she had recently moved here, and now that her daughter was older she wanted to work full time. I asked her why she moved and she said she'd gotten remarried and her husband had a job here, at the university. Said she was settling down.

"Well, I doubted that part, the settling-down bit. In my experience people with résumés like that keep moving. But so what? So she wouldn't stay forever. I thought maybe she'd help us get things together, and next time around maybe we'd find someone for the long term. In any case I was desperate. That's not all of it. To be honest, I liked her—when I met her, that is."

"You don't like her now?"

"I don't even know her now," he said, bitterly. "I don't know . . ." He shook his head. "In any case, it seemed to work, at first anyway. She was good at her job and she was good with staff. They liked her, too. She could get things done without offending people and she was really funny. I can't say she ever had a close friend here, but that's fine in an office manager. Plus she was creative. She even made suggestions for changing ads and they worked. I was actually thinking of making some ads ourselves, hiring some people and getting her involved with that end, when it just seemed to go to hell in a handbasket."

He was staring in the distance now, his eyes moving back and forth as he remembered. When he didn't go on, I interrupted gently. "So what happened?"

He looked over at me, pulling himself back to the present. "I didn't notice anything at first, but maybe I should have. I'm pretty busy and probably I'm not the most observant guy in the world. My wife dyed her hair one day, and I didn't even notice. She still gives me shit about it. Anyway, one of the sales reps came in one day and asked me what was going on with Jena. I asked her what she was talking about. She said hadn't I noticed Jena wore long sleeves all the time, no matter what the weather.

I thought she was crazy. The place was air-conditioned. Why shouldn't Jena wear long sleeves if she wanted to, but she said go out and look at her hands. I asked her what I was looking for and she said, 'Just go look.'

"So I did, and her hands were just black and blue. Somebody must have held them down and pounded on them. God knows what she was hiding under those sleeves, but you can't hide hands. I asked her about it. She said it was nothing, said she fell. I am no doctor, but I do not see how you could get those injuries from falling. They were so swollen she could hardly move them. I think some of the bones were broken. Anyway, it got worse after that.

"More bruises, more long shirts and then one day she turned her head and I noticed a line around her neck. There was just no way it could have happened unless someone put something around her neck and pulled. I went batshit. My wife works in a rape crisis center, and I had already been talking to her about this. I called her, and she came down to the office. We both tried to talk to Jena about it which did no good at all. So I called the police. I have a friend who's a detective, and he tried to talk to her. She wouldn't even speak to him. The end result was zip, except that I think we almost lost her. I think she came close to quitting that day. I think she would have if she hadn't had to tell him she quit.

"So we backed off, mostly. Sometimes I can't help it, I try to talk to her still—I don't know what else to do—but she acts like she's deaf. She doesn't even answer me anymore, just keeps her head down and acts like I haven't said a word.

"The worst thing, if you think anything is worse than finding out somebody is being strangled, the worst thing is what she's become. She has just turned into some kind of zombie. She doesn't speak to anybody unless she is forced into it. Her pupils are dilated half the time, and I know she's on drugs. I should fire her for that and for the fact the whole office is upset about this all the time, but I don't have the heart. What would happen to her if she didn't have someplace to come to every day? Besides, I'd be on drugs, too, if I had to live her life.

"Of course, she got to the point she couldn't do the job. I don't know what I would have done about that. I didn't have to deal with it because she asked for a demotion herself. She said she wanted to just do purchase orders and supplies and other administrivia, so I set that up. Begged me to tell her husband we were downsizing if he asked, not to admit she requested it. It brought in less money, of course, and I gather he's not working now. She didn't have to ask me twice. I'd tell him she'd grown two heads if it would keep him from beating on her.

"You won't believe what you'll see. She sits in the corner of the room now, like some sort of . . . something—I don't know how to describe it. It can't go on like this forever. He's going to kill her, or she's going to kill herself, or she's going to overdose on drugs, and we'll never know whether she did it herself or he fed them to her. I'm going to feel like I should have done something, but I'll be damned if I know what. My wife says it's going to kill me. I tell you I can't even sleep at night thinking about it."

He paused and ran his hand through his hair. I had sat frozen listening to him. I was having trouble processing all this. This was Jena of the wild secret agent adventures and the Himalayan stories? Jena was somewhere in this building with lines around her neck, beaten black and blue? Of all the people I knew, this was not the person this could have happened to. Someone had made some mistake.

"Jena Jensen?" I asked. "This just doesn't . . ."

He just looked at me and my voice trailed off. "I know," he said after a moment. "I don't blame you. I wouldn't have believed it, either, knowing what she was like before. I'm sorry for dumping all of this on you. I'm just pissed off about it all the time."

"Jesus," I said softly. "I just . . . never . . ." My voice drifted off again. I couldn't wrap my head around it. It all sounded so bizarre. These kinds of things happened to someone else, a client, someone on the news, a nameless victim of one of the offenders I interview—not to someone I knew personally.

"What do you know about her husband?" I asked, mostly to buy time while I tried to process this.

"Very little," he said. "The mystery man. He came to an office party early on. He was pleasant enough. I didn't see anything. He's very good looking and I remember some of the women commenting on what a 'catch' he was. Sure. Like catching cancer. We haven't seen him since then, thank God, because I don't think anybody on the staff could be civil to him, and who knows what he'd do to her if we weren't. He has called a few times checking up on her, different excuses to make sure she's here. I don't know what that's all about. She doesn't have the energy to walk around the block. She doesn't leave her desk for lunch, doesn't take breaks. Just sits there."

We both sat silently for a minute and then I said, "Well, I'm grateful to you for cluing me in. I think I would have lost it if I had seen her without some kind of preparation. I'll go talk to her," I said, and then more to myself than him, "about what? I can't just plow into her about the abuse." I fell silent, trying to figure out what to do.

"Well, you can't do any worse than we have," he said, "no matter what you do. Listen, feel free to bring her back here. I'm going to be in a meeting for a while." When I didn't speak, he added gently, "I don't know that there is an answer. It's like watching somebody in a car without brakes who's just picking up speed. Maybe it can't be stopped. That's what my wife thinks, too. Sometimes I think this whole thing was a done deal a long time ago, when she first got involved with this guy." I sighed and got up. Nothing was coming to me. I guess I'd find out what I was going to say when I got there.

We walked through the large main room past rows of people working in cubicles. No one seemed to take much notice of us—I guess visitors were common. All the way I had some crazy hope it wouldn't be Jena, but as we rounded the last cubicle there she was, sitting in the last cubicle in the corner in the very back of the room.

I stopped, at a loss for a second. It was Jena, although I doubt I would have recognized her on the street. The woman sitting at her desk and staring at the floor was rail thin, wearing a long shapeless dress with long sleeves. Her hair had not been washed recently, and it hung dispiritedly at her collar. That seemed to hit me most of all. As a child her hair had been tawny and full, and I had always thought it looked like a lion's mane. Now it was flat and unwashed and one side looked longer than the other, as though she cut it herself without paying too much attention.

She wasn't wearing makeup. Nothing about her spoke of care or attention or even minimal worrying about what other people thought. She'd gone too far to even put up a facade. Dave started to speak but I shook my head and waved him off. I walked over to Jena's desk, then paused, not sure what to do next.

I was standing right next to her, but Jena didn't look up. I knelt down beside her and finally, she did look up, her eyes flaring with alarm. The face had the outlines of Jena's though it didn't seem like her. The eyes were larger than I remembered—

or maybe the face was just thinner—and instead of pupils they seemed to have endless dark centers, dry wells without luster or light, that showed no promise and found no refuge. The darkness in them was not the kind born of mischief and glitter but seemed dull and turned inward, the kind found only in faces of those who have lived with truly brutal people.

She didn't have to speak for my palms to feel something soft and—I don't know—faint, brush up against them. I couldn't feel enough life force left in this woman to keep a candle burning. Even so, recognition was swimming in her eyes and, oddly, a look of fear. She glanced around, as though fearful someone would see me.

"Hi," I said softly. "Long time no see, girl. Are you OK?" And then I surprised myself by reaching out to touch her arm.

She jerked back automatically with panic in her eyes, and I realized she was beyond any kind of conventional comforting. For sure, she could not be touched.

"OK," I said, pulling my hand back. "We need to talk. Dave has offered us an office or we can go for a walk."

She shook her head without speaking and looked down again.

"Why not?"

"I can't," she said very quietly. Her voice was hoarse and small, and I could barely see it.

"Jena, I talked to Dave, and he told me a little bit about what's been going on. I promise you I won't hammer you to do things you can't do right now, so please don't think this will be a replay of him or the police. But I am not leaving this office until I talk to you. If Jerry calls, Dave will put him through just like he would if you were at the cubicle. If I have to, I will follow you home and knock on your door if you won't come with me."

It was brutal and unfair but I didn't know what else to do.

She sighed and put her pen down very carefully. She moved it twice before she seemed satisfied that it was in the right place right on the edge of the desk, and then she stood up rigidly and looked at me and waited. Dave hadn't been kidding about the zombie part. For the second time I was at a loss. Was this a real person standing in front of me or not? I turned and walked back to Dave's office, and she followed me obediently.

When we arrived, I pulled out the big desk chair for her, but she just looked at it and shied away. She pulled out the only other chair in the room, a small chair for clients, and sat down very carefully. She smoothed her skirt evenly and sat quietly. I couldn't sit in the big chair and loom over her, so I sat on the floor in front of her. I was careful not to touch her.

I tried to figure out where to start when Jena spoke. "I didn't want you to see me like this," she said, her voice faint and hoarse.

"I know," I said.

"I knew you'd come," she said. I wondered that she didn't ask me how I'd found her, or how I knew to come. Did she know her daughter had called me? Somehow I didn't think so.

"I was thinking about Clark on the way over," I said.

She didn't say anything, just waited.

"Do you remember sitting on your roof on summer nights? Remember when your dad was gone and your mom was too, in a way, and we'd sneak out your window and climb up to the peak, holding onto the edge. That scared the bejesus out of me. I always wondered that it didn't seem to bother you at all. I went anyway because I didn't want to admit how scared I was and besides I wanted to hear the stories. Do you remember? You used to tell me about K-2 and Annapurna and all the great expeditions?"

I didn't know why I was talking about this except that was the Jena I knew, and maybe if she remembered who she had been, we could find someplace to meet. For sure, I didn't know who she was now and wondered if she did. A flicker of something crossed her face. She could easily be brain-damaged by now, but everything wasn't gone. She'd recognized me, and cared about how she looked to me, and she had long-term memory, anyway.

"I remember," she said very softly.

"I loved it," I said, "when you talked about the Himalayas. It was almost like you knew them, even then. The way you told the stories, the mountains were the real stars, not the climbers. They felt more real to me than some of the people I knew because they were so real to you. Did you ever make it over there?"

"Not to climb," she said wistfully. "I climbed in South America—a lot—but I never had the money for a Himalayan expedition. I did go on a trek there once." I had to strain to hear her, but at least she was talking.

"How high did you get in South America?" I asked.

"Sixteen thousand feet," she said, "and technical." A fleeting look of pride crossed her face which astounded me. Something ran through me that felt a lot like hope.

"What was it like?" I asked. "The climbing?" She paused, and at first I thought she wasn't going to answer.

"The world goes away," she said. "After a few hundred feet. Even in this country you can't see the cars or the houses or anything. Even in Yosemite, which is nothing but a tourist trap on the ground. Even a few hundred feet up, it looks like it must have before any of it—before the McDonalds and gift shops and all the other crap. And once you're on top you can see forever. The sky. It's bigger than the earth and you're living in it. I don't know. All you think about is weather. It just runs through you. I still dream about it."

So did I, although I didn't say it. I don't know if anybody else would have understood what she meant, but I did. That was the thing. That had always been the thing.

"What was your favorite?"

"Patagonia," she said. And she said it with such wistfulness it might as well have been Shangri-la or the Promised Land. "It's not a mountain; it's a region. The mountains aren't that high, but it is remote beyond belief and really, really beautiful. The storms are alive and more powerful than anything you see on this earth. It really is the last best place on earth."

"Jena," I said. "Let's get out of here. Just for one afternoon. Dave will cover for you and call me on my cell phone. Just a few hours to talk. That's all."

She hesitated, and then she said. "If I go, will you promise not to go to my house, ever?"

"OK," I said, knowing I was lying. I could easily imagine circumstances where I'd have to break that promise.

"It's really important. You can't go to my house," she said again. "You don't understand."

"What?"

"If you show up at my house, I'm dead."

Fear rose up right through my core, and I tried to swallow it back down. I didn't know if I should tell her now I'd already been there or not. I decided I'd wait and tell her later. She had to know before she went home.

chapter 7

J ena followed me out of the building with Dave swearing
he'd stall Jerry and contact us in the unlikely event that
he called. He'd gone out to talk to the receptionist in
person, and he watched us get in the elevators with a hope-
fulness that made me feel guilty. I knew he was hoping for
something that wasn't likely to happen.

Jena was nervous as soon as we left the building and constantly scanning everything around us, looking for him. I
liked to think she'd become paranoid with all the beatings.
Then again, I didn't know how many times he had surprised
her when she didn't expect him. We found a small restaurant
where she could see everybody in the place and she sat down
with her back to the wall facing the door. She seemed to relax
a little then. I wouldn't say she felt safe, just that she looked
less anxious than she had on the street.

She ate almost nothing but had two glasses of wine. I didn't
know if that was a good idea. I didn't have any wine. She'd
gotten me to the point I half expected him to charge through

the door, and I thought he'd be hard enough to deal with sober. The wine loosened up something in her brain, and she talked more freely than before. At least it meant she could.

The talk was mostly about Clark and our families. Her mom had died in her sleep. Jena suspected an overdose, but there was no autopsy. Her dad had retired. He was older than her mom, in his forties when they had her. He had Alzheimer's. He was in an assisted-living place now—even Clark had one. I knew the talk needed to move from Clark to now, but didn't know how to do it without losing her.

"How long did you climb?" I asked.

"Years," she said wistfully. "Until I had my daughter. I couldn't climb after that. I couldn't leave her. Her father was a climber, too. He died on a climb, not long after she was born."

"I'm sorry," I said.

"He was a really good man," she said. "And he climbed with the grace of a cat. I wish he hadn't died."

It sounded so childlike—"I wish he hadn't died."

"And you remarried?"

She looked past me at the door, as though just mentioning him might make him appear. "A few years ago. Actually, I met him a long time ago, then lost touch. He was a hotshot climber at Yosemite. Artificial climbing on big walls and all that, but he'd wanted to do the big stuff. Besides, he didn't think anybody took Yosemite weather seriously. It can be blisteringly hot on the walls in the summer. When people think of weather, though, they think of cold. They don't take artificial climbing seriously, either, for that matter. He'd wanted to prove he was a real climber and he joined an expedition I was on." She looked away, remembering. After a moment she said, "It didn't go well."

"Why not?"

"Climbing's like that," she said. "It's hard and dangerous, and everybody's under a lot of pressure so they get cranky. People click or they don't. A lot of times they don't. He didn't click with the group leaders. He always wanted to lead all the hard stuff. I just thought he was trying to prove he could. They didn't see it that way. They thought he was a showoff. And people complained he didn't carry his share of the weight when we were slogging all the equipment up to base camp. I thought they were too tough on him. I felt bad for him . . ."

I didn't speak and after a moment she went on. "I didn't see him again for years, and then I ran into him after John died. He was giving a talk on a climb up Cerro Torre. It was a place I'd always wanted to go. I went up to talk to him afterward."

"Will you tell me about it?" I asked. "About what's been going on?"

"No," she said, looking down at her glass.

"Your daughter called me."

"She did? Lily?" She seemed startled, as though it had only occurred to her now to wonder how I found her. "She hates me. I don't blame her."

"I don't know what's going on, but I know she doesn't hate you. She was furious at me for not being here to help you."

She just looked at me for a moment, then said, "I'm worse than my mother."

"Maybe right now," I said, "but not forever."

"You don't know what forever is. This is forever."

"It could end today."

She didn't speak. Then she said, "He'd find me. You're the first person he'd think of. I've talked about you. He'd start by finding you, and that would lead him to me."

"Well, he might find me, but he wouldn't necessarily find you."

She looked at me questioningly.

"He wouldn't find Betsy. He doesn't even know about her. I'm sure you could stay with her if you were worried about his finding me."

"I don't really know Betsy. She was your friend, not mine. I only saw her in a couple of classes."

"That's the point. Which means he doesn't. And believe me, Betsy needs a cause right now. She's got a shotgun and an attitude and she lives at the end of nowhere."

"I can't," she said. "You don't understand."

And I didn't, until I remembered what Dave had said about the drugs.

"You take drugs," I said bluntly. "And he gets them for you." She didn't say anything.

"How do you think this is going to end?" I asked. "Do you think you can do it forever? How long can you do it? Six months? Do you have a year left in you? I'm sorry. I promised I wouldn't harangue you. You won't need the drugs if you get rid of him. If you don't, even the drugs won't help forever." I felt the urgency rise in me like a sour taste in my mouth. I didn't want to harass Jena, but it was rolling out of me anyway.

"What did Lily say?" she said suddenly, not listening to me at all. "Where did she get your number?"

"I don't know. I thought maybe you gave it to her. Why does it matter?"

She didn't speak for a minute and then she pulled off her watch and handed it to me. I looked at it, puzzled. Still she didn't speak. I turned it over and saw my number written on the back. For a moment everything stopped, and I closed my eyes and felt a kind of dizziness. Lily was right. I should have been there. Jena had always been somewhere on the back burners of my mind—one of those people you're going to get back to someday—but I never had.

"Lily knows about this?"

"No, she can't." I heard panic in her voice.

"Why not?"

"Because if anybody knows . . ."

"He could find out?" I finished for her.

She nodded.

"She wouldn't tell him though, would she?"

She looked at me with a look that said I didn't understand anything.

"How does he treat her? Does he . . .? "

"No, he does something that's almost as hard. It's like shunning."

"Like what?"

"Like what the Amish used to do. He pretends she doesn't exist. He doesn't speak to her. He doesn't set a place for her at the table. He buys food for two. I have to shop for her. Most of the time I fix her dinner, and she eats in her room. She thinks he hates her. She doesn't even stay home that much anymore; she stays with her friends."

"So why would she tell him? She wouldn't."

Jena just shook her head and I realized this wasn't working.

"She could have gotten it on her own," I offered. "I didn't have any trouble finding you. Does she take computer classes at school?"

"Yes," she said. "Yes, that must be it." I didn't know if that was it or not. Maybe Lily found me through the computer or maybe she knew about the number on the back of her mother's watch, but it seemed more important to calm Jena down than to figure out something we couldn't figure out anyway.

"Jena, we can leave this restaurant, pick up Lily and head for the airport. This can end today."

She paused for a long time, and just stared at her wineglass. After a while I thought she just wasn't going to answer. Then she said, "We could take Lily?"

"Of course. We wouldn't leave your daughter. Did he adopt her?"

"No."

"So what's the problem? He doesn't have any legal say over her, and her father is dead. You're the one with custody, right?"

She nodded slightly. "Then what?"

"What do you mean?" I asked.

"After we get on a plane."

"Then we go to Betsy's and hide the two of you until this blows over. Look, I work with guys like this. If he's who I think he is, he'll just find someone else."

"You don't know him."

Which is OK by me, I thought, but didn't say it. "He's not as bad as you think," Jena added. "Some of it's my fault. A lot of it."

"Fine, so maybe you're bad for him—I don't know. It can't be good for him, turning him into some kind of monster. Even if you're doing it to him, it has to stop."

"He needs me."

"Jena . . . "

"You don't cut the rope on someone. You just don't."

"What about Lily?" I asked. "It's not OK to cut the rope on him, but it is on Lily. What's it like for her to live with someone who treats her like she doesn't exist?"

She didn't answer. "Look," I went on. "I evaluate people like him all the time for my job. He can be funny and charming—right—anytime he wants to. When he's smiling that dazzling smile of his and those blue eyes bore into you, he looks like he'd take stray cats home. He's got another side though, doesn't he, and you never know when you're going to see it. You remind him he said he'd take you to a movie, or paint a room or take out the trash or any of the normal things in life, and all of a sudden he's slamming your face into a wall. Once he starts, he just keeps slamming it, and he won't stop no matter what you do."

Jena was looking at me sharply now. "How do you know he has blue eyes?" she said quietly, staring at me. " What did you do? Did you go there?"

I couldn't deny it. "I went there this morning, looking for you."

"Oh, my god. You lied to me."

"No."

"You did so lie to me."

"No, I didn't. You didn't ask. I said I wouldn't go to your house in the future. You never asked. I was going to tell you."

She just closed her eyes and leaned her head back against the cushion. OK, it was kind of a lie. I could have told her sooner, and I would have eventually.

"I'm sorry. I didn't have anyway of knowing he'd be home. I just thought he'd be at work, that if anybody was at home, it would be you."

She didn't answer. "Look, at least get Lily out of this. Do it for her if you can't do it for yourself."

At that she looked up and pausing, seemed to consider it. "All right," she said. Her voice was flat and uninspired, more resigned than anything. If this was freedom, the advantages weren't apparent to her yet. What would happen when she woke up from this numbness? Would it be like frostbite, where everything is numb until you thaw it. Then the pain grows until you can't think? Would she start howling and never stop?

"Do you mean it?" I said. "Can we pick up Lily and go?"

"I mean it," she said, but her voice didn't match her affect. Her face was hollow and expressionless, like this was just one more ordeal to be gotten through. I tried not to read too much into it. It was way too much to ask for her to have any kind of normal emotional reaction right now. She was going on rote, doing what she was told.

"OK," I said, "where's Lily?"

"In school," she said.

"Which gets out?"

She told me. I looked at my watch. We had twenty minutes to get there before Lily headed home.

I called Dave on the way to pick up Lily. He promised to have two tickets waiting at the airline counter, three if he couldn't get them on the flight I was already on. I offered him my credit card but he said we'd settle up later, and I had a feeling I'd never get the bill. He sounded overjoyed, much too confident for my taste—I was still waiting for Jena to change her mind. Still, she had a settled air about her now, as though the decision had been made.

We drove to the school and arrived just before the bell rang. We waited for Lily to come out, and when she did, I saw a tall, dark teenager with Jena's mouth and eyes and a stranger's frame. Lily was taller than her mother and had bigger bones. She had a swimmer's shoulders but a pudgy middle, which said she wasn't swimming or probably doing anything all that active. She had green frosts in her short, dark hair and round metal bracelets up and down one arm. The look she gave her mother was complicated: hostile and worried and contemptuous all at the same time. Anything but glad to see her. When I introduced myself, her eyes widened and she glanced at her mother to see if she knew. I didn't want to get into it, then so I just hustled everybody into the car and started off.

"Where are we going?" Lily said.

I waited but Jena said nothing. With Lily in the car, it was as though she had used up her last available quota of energy and had faded back into the woman I first saw at her desk. She stared out the window as though Lily wasn't there.

"We're leaving," I said. "We're going to the airport."

"Leaving?" Lily said. "For how long?" The voice sounded panicky.

"I don't know," I said carefully. "You both have to get away from Jerry right now. He's bad for both of you. I don't know when you can come back." Except never, I thought.

"What about my clothes?" she said. "What about my friends?"

"We'll buy you new clothes," I said.

"What about my friends," she said. "I can't leave my friends. Who will I talk to?"

Her comment caught me off guard. Did she have a clue what was at stake here? A flash of anger swept through me like an afternoon thunderstorm. Could this be the kid who was so worried about her mother she had called me in the middle of the night, crying on the phone? I tried to shake off the anger. Could it be I was a little tense about this thing to be angry at a confused teenager? After all, what else did she have except her friends?

"We'll figure it out. You can always use e-mail and instant messenger. Not to mention phones. The only thing is, Lily, you won't be able to tell anyone where you are. Not for a while. You understand that?"

She sat back. "It's OK," she said. "My friends would never tell."

I felt the anger rise again. Great, I've known this kid for five minutes and I was having homicidal impulses. Good thing I'd never had children. Whatever. We were in the car and headed for the airport and we'd take it one step at a time.

He couldn't have known. I knew that, but still I was nervous the whole time. Parking seemed to take forever, and the line to the counter was short, but slow. I couldn't help constantly looking around. Jena, surprisingly, never seemed to look up. She kept her eyes on the floor as though fending off all the sights and sounds, all the noise and confusion. She was so different from when we went to the restaurant that it surprised me. Why wasn't she worried? But he couldn't know where we were, and maybe she knew that.

Or could he? If so, how? A tracer on her car wouldn't help him. We'd left hers at work. A tracer in her purse would. If he had that, though, why would he check up on her by calling like Dave said he did? Had he followed me? Oh, that would work. I had no experience with tails at all and hadn't even thought to look for one. But I didn't think he'd have let us get this far if he had.

No matter how I reasoned it out, I still kept scanning everything around, looking for him. They say the hardest wait in the water is when the lifeboats are on the way. That's when people fear the sharks. The plane and freedom were tantalizingly close, and it was our one shot. I kept checking Lily. It wasn't beyond her to slip off, and that would be the end of it. Having gotten over the initial shock, however, she seemed in good spirits, as though she were going on vacation. She and her mother didn't speak, and I couldn't have said whether they were connected or not. I was clearly more nervous about Lily than Jena was. Jena seemed to pay her no attention at all, and when Lily went to buy a magazine, I was the one who casually got up and went with her.

When Lily and I got back, they were starting to call the plane, but Jena wasn't there. I had a moment of fear, then saw the note on her seat that said "bathroom."

I stood while Lily kept looking at her magazine, and we both waited while they called the first-class cabin. All the time I was staring down the corridor, looking for Jena. They started calling economy. Something started to turn in my stomach. I don't know when I understood, but by the time they called our seats I knew. It was just too fucking late to do anything about it. I had been watching the wrong person. All I could do now was get Lily on the plane.

"Lily, let's go," I said. I had her ticket. I had all of them, including Jena's, although I was pretty sure she wouldn't need it.

"Where's my mother?" she said frowning, and closing her magazine.

"She'll join us," I said. "Let's just get on the plane."

Lily stood up and turned to look down the corridor. When she turned back around, she looked at me accusingly. "Where is she? She's gone, isn't she? She left me."

"Lily," I said, "she will never come if you don't get on that plane. If you do get on that plane, I think she will come eventually. But no, she isn't coming today. If you don't get on that plane, neither one of you is ever likely to get away from him. And when she's dead, he'll start on you."

She just looked at me and then back down the hall. "I hate her," she said. "I don't care what happens to her. She deserves whatever he does to her." Then to my relief, she picked up her magazine and walked toward the plane.

I called Dave while the plane was still on the ground and told him what happened, and what I would need from Jena if he could get it. He promised if she came back to work, he'd get it. Neither one of us could guess if Jerry would let her come back to work. I could see the darkness settle at the bottom of his voice.

As for me, helplessness settled down over me like a weight. I'd failed to talk her into leaving him, and I couldn't make her. The ties to Jerry were stronger than her need to survive. With Lily gone she'd lost the last reason she had to buck the tide and stand up to him. She was like someone who was falling in front of a moving car and couldn't break her fall. But with whatever energy she had, she'd pushed Lily out of the way. Give her credit for that.

Jerry would know where Lily was, of course. I doubted he'd beat it out of Jena, although he'd probably try. It wouldn't matter. I'd showed up the same day that Lily had disappeared, and the blue eyes I'd seen on Jena's doorstep had been quick.

Somehow I didn't think it mattered that he knew. As long as Jena was there, he'd probably leave Lily alone. For one thing, Jena was going downhill rapidly and he'd be unlikely to want a witness around when it came to the end. For another thing, he'd never beaten Lily, just ignored her, so he might be just as happy with her gone.

I settled back in the seat and looked over at the dark head staring fixedly on Britney Spears. I closed my eyes and felt the sharp, angry energy next to me vibrate like an electric bass. A long way away I could feel something else, a sort of forlorn keening way out on the edge of things—but whether it was Jena or Lily or the girl with yellow daisies on her dress, I couldn't say.

chapter 8

ily hardly spoke on the plane and gravitated to the TV the moment we walked into the motel room in Raleigh. She watched it nonstop and didn't want to leave the room even to eat. I ordered pizza delivered to the room, all the time feeling like Lily wasn't really there. I tried to tell myself she was just upset about leaving her mom. She would liven up when she saw the beauty of the coast.

I found out otherwise. The kid was not a nature buff. As we drove through rural North Carolina the next morning with the windows down, I watched the red clay of the Piedmont turn into the loose sandy soil of the coast. Low shrubs and tall, skinny pines lined the road, and as the coast approached, we saw more and more of the wind bent live oaks I love the most. I had bought my house more than anything because of a tree I called Grandma, a huge live oak in the front yard. The flora made no impression on Lily. She hardly ever took her nose out of her magazine, and then it was only to ask if we were going to stop at any malls.

Never mind, I thought. Wait till she sees the sea. The land on the coast was merely backdrop for the sea, and you can't be human and not have the sea reach down into every molecule of DNA and stir things up. We came from the sea. We were mostly water still. Our very breathing in and out echoed the pattern of waves thrown up on the sand as though we couldn't leave without taking the rhythm with us. I had no doubts that Lily, for all her adolescent cool, would respond to the sea.

If she did, she hid it well. I took her through Beaufort with its historic houses from the 1700s and pointed out their second story widow walks, where wives had once kept vigil, watching for their husbands' ships. I drove down Main Street and we watched the wild horses on Carrot Island, little more than a stone's throw from the town dock. Beaufort was in fine form—pulsing dots of light lay on "the cut," the small body of water that flowed between Beaufort and its satellite island. A plethora of sailboats of all sizes and shapes sat anchored in the channel. I can't say the response from Lily was over-whelming, although she did look out the window, which I suppose was something.

We headed home, down east to the Cedar ferry that would take us to Blackbeard's Isle. Along the way I took a detour to go past parts of the Inland Waterway. Giant oaks stretched over it with Spanish moss dripping all the way to the ground. Had we stayed a while, we might well have seen some of the water snakes that made the Waterway their home. Who knew? Alligators roamed in the back coves still. I offered to stop and explore. Lily said if I did, she'd wait in the car.

By then she had looked at her magazine until she must have memorized every word, and I was losing patience with her constant fiddling with the radio. We fought over the volume endlessly. Country was king on Southern radio, which seemed to astound Lily. In her world, country music was just a rumor—except for Faith Hill. It seemed she was an exception, although I didn't know why.

I was disappointed that Betsy wasn't home when we arrived at her house. I needed to talk to someone over fourteen. There was nothing to be done about it so I changed to my cutoffs and we headed for the ferry. Lily didn't seem the slightest bit curious about Betsy's house or my clothes-changing ritual. She had asked for my cell phone to call her friends. I didn't know what she'd say, and I wanted to talk about it first. Lily told me it was none of my business, so I kept the phone. I could feel some kind of power struggle starting up between us, but I couldn't seem to stop it.

She stayed inside on the ferry trip over. Since the ferry windows were filmed with salt from sea spray and you could hardly see out, this meant she saw nothing of Pamlico Sound. I stood on the back of the ferry and watched the gulls dive for handouts, wondering what I had gotten myself into.

I put her on the back of the scooter when we got to Blackbeard's Isle and we headed home. It looked like the scooter was something of a plus to Lily, although she wanted to drive, which I pointed out wasn't, strictly speaking, legal.

My home is an old and weathered cape, which I am slowly remodeling. It has cedar shingles and white clapboard and it fits the island. What if the floors tilt some and the kitchen could be the original? To me, it has character and it's homey, plus Grandma sits out front, the live oak as wide as an easy chair. Lily didn't even glance at the tree, and I couldn't stifle the hurt when she looked at my home like it was a flophouse. She rolled her eyes. "This is it?"

"What do you mean?"

"It's decrepit."

"Not really. It was built in the twenties and it still has some original work inside."

"The twenties." She rolled her eyes. "How do you live here?"

My head ached, and I was starting to feel sorry for myself. I had stopped in Chicago to see what was wrong with a friend and had ended up with an alien in my home: a wiseass, junk-eating, surly-mouthed teenage mall bunny who didn't have the God-given sense to appreciate the sea. I didn't like this kid, and I didn't like myself because of it. She was Jena's daughter, after all, and she'd watched her mother being slowly beaten to death. She'd seen more violence in her young life than I had in all of mine. But when do you have a right to get angry? How obnoxious can a kid be before it's OK to wish they lived on another planet?

I said nothing else but went inside and Lily followed me. When I turned around, she had a cigarette in her hand and was fumbling in her purse for a light.

"Whoa, Lily."

"What?"

"You're what, fourteen?

"Almost," she said, shrugging. "So what?"

"So you can't smoke. It isn't even legal to buy them."

"You're not my mother."

"Think of me as your camp counselor," I said. "We still have rules."

"It's none of your fucking business what I do."

"Come on, hon. It's my house."

"And you're going to stop me—you and whose army?"

I sat down slowly on the closest chair and shut my eyes. "Why do you want to smoke?" I asked. I said it just to get her talking,

She paused. "What's it to you? I like it, that's all."

Stopping and looking was what I should have done much earlier, but I had been preoccupied. I knew the voice was a pulsing orange from the phone call, and I hadn't really looked closely at it since I'd been with Lily. The orange was now lighter and almost transparent. I saw worry lines in it. More than anything, I saw the kind of transparency that went with fear.

"You're scared," I said.

"What?"

"You're scared—for your mom? Scared of what he'll do to you if he finds you? Scared of leaving your friends? I don't know what, but you're scared."

"You don't know anything."

"I know you're scared. I can *see* it."

"You can what?"

"Figure of speech. I can tell you're scared. I underst—"

"I am not scared," she yelled. "You drag me down here because my mother is a total wimp. It's not my fault she's a goddamn doormat, that she lets that asshole beat the shit out of her. Well, I didn't ask to be here in this stupid–ass house. And I'll smoke if I want to."

I was calmer now. Her voice was light and mottled, which went with crying or close to it. I opened my eyes. "I'm sorry but you can't smoke here. I can't deal with the smell or the yellow stains on the walls. Not in my presence, either. If you get caught trying to buy cigarettes, you'll have to deal with the consequences yourself—I won't bail you out. I know I can't stop you when you're out of my sight, and I won't follow you around. I do have some rules when you're here though. No smoking in the house or anywhere around me. Let me show you to your room and I'll see what I can come up with for dinner.

She rolled her eyes but put the cigarette away. I took her to her room and wasn't surprised when she said it was too small.

Then she headed for the living room, and stopped short when she didn't see what she was looking for.

"Where's the TV?"

"I don't have one."

"In the whole house? I mean you have one in your room, right?"

"I don't have one."

"You don't have a TV?"

"That's what I said."

"How do you expect me to live here without a TV?"

"Excuse me," I said and went in my room and shut the door.

Fortunately, Betsy was home. "Betsy, what do you know about thirteen-year-olds?"

"Well, darlin', I had two."

"No, I mean the kind that are totally obnoxious and that you desperately want to kill and then feel like an idiot because that's entirely the wrong reaction."

"Honey, there isn't any other kind. Where did you run into one?"

"In my living room about thirty seconds ago." I gave her the condensed version of Jena and the airport and the trip home.

"Oh, Jena," Betsy said sadly. "God bless that child. Lord, she has surely lost her way. All right. I'll come over tomorrow. I've got to run some errands in the morning, but I can probably make the noon ferry. In the meantime quit harassing that poor girl and just let her be. And for God's sake, let her call her friends or she'll run away before I can get over to rescue her."

"I don't think you've got the picture here, Betsy. I'm the one that needs rescuing."

"Uh-huh," Betsy said. "Don't pick me up. I'm bringing my own transportation."

"You don't need the car," I said. "And I don't mind running down."

"I'm not bringing the car," she said and hung up.

I'm willing to admit I don't know anything about mothering. Maybe it's because I never had any. My mother, Elsie, is still alive, for all the good that's ever done me. She's a hippie—a few are still left—living somewhere in the desert outside Phoenix.

Dad had been a hippie too, or maybe just a hippie wannabe. Back in the sixties, disillusioned with Vietnam and race relations and whatever else caused thousands of young people to leave the straight world, they had both dropped out of school. But Dad was visiting the hippie world while my mother emigrated.

It took me a long time to get my dad to talk about all this. Finally, when I was twelve, I lost it one night and screamed at him that my mother didn't love me and what was wrong with me, so he told me about her.

He said my mother was the gentlest person he'd ever known and the most trusting. He said she bought hook, line, and sinker into the hippie world and even when she was pregnant, he couldn't get her to stop taking drugs. She said they were natural because they came from plants. I was grown before I thought to wonder if my synesthesia was genetic or the product of my mother's drug use.

He said when I was born, she couldn't make the switch to the kind of responsibility a child brought. He tried for a couple of years, but things just got worse. She took no real responsibility for me and got too stoned to feed and change me. He got more and more nervous about leaving me alone with her even for short periods.

Then one day he came home and I was crying, standing in the kitchen with a diaper completely soaked with urine and weighted-down with feces. I had cat food smeared on my face because it was the only thing I could find to eat. Cat shit was oozing between my toes. When he changed my diaper, my bottom was already raw, and I was crying with a stom-achache—probably from eating cat food.

He packed his things and mine, got in the battered old car they owned together, wrote her a note, and drove away. She never came out of the room where she was meditating. He drove all the way to Clark because he knew he could get help from his parents to raise me while he worked. The only thing he felt bad about, he said, was taking the car. She was out in the country and needed some way to get around. When he got to Clark, the first thing he did was borrow money from his parents—enough for her to buy another old clunker—and sent it to her, along with our address and phone number.

It was five years before we heard from her, and then it was a note about how my spirit had chosen North Carolina over Arizona, and telling me she understood. We were children of the universe, she said, and our spirits should be free to choose their home. A spirit named Rada was looking out for me. She had seen him when she meditated, and he had said I was doing fine.

I never told anybody about my mother except Jena. It was another bond between us. Everybody else in Clark had normal mothers. They worked or they stayed home. They yelled at the kids and most swatted them. Some were nicer than others, but they all went to the PTA and signed report cards. Except for us. Sometimes I thought Jena's mother was what mine would have been if she had moved to Clark. Of course that was all wrong. Jena's mom was a Southern housewife who could pass as normal in Clark if she needed to. The one picture I had of Elsie showed a woman with a long red braid down her back and a homespun, shapeless shift with sandals. She would have stood out in Clark like a Christmas tree at a Chanukah party.

Over the years I occasionally heard from her. Usually it was a message from the spirits that she had been told to pass along. She mellowed some, it seemed, or just endured, but she appeared to be getting along in the world. She was weaving, and once sent me a scarf she had made that was truly beautiful. I touched it, and my palms grew warm and ached. My head told me there was nothing between us, but I could never get rid of that scarf. I had it still, the sad total of what Elsie had to give me.

Nonetheless, after all the offenders I had interviewed, it was hard to be angry at someone who had no malice in her. Elsie did no harm, simply trusted the world way too much. At night, sometimes, I wondered what her voice looked like and wondered too when I'd get the courage to go to Arizona and find out. I wore my hair in a long braid down my back, just like my mother did, although I had told myself countless times it had nothing to do with her.

One thing's for sure. My experience with Elsie had not given me any clues for how to deal with Lily. Kind as he was, my father was not a mother. Nor did he provide one. He never remarried—he never even got a divorce and he never had a live-in girlfriend. My grandmother was reputed to be a motherly type, but she died shortly after we got back. I got my information on periods from a teacher I trusted, and when Kotex started showing up in the bathroom, my father never mentioned it. He did what he could and just ignored the rest, trusting, I guess, that I would figure it out. I never had a sibling so I knew as much about children as I did about armadillos. I had been one, but not one like Lily. I had been a tomboy and lived outdoors, and Lily offended nearly every sensibility I had.

But what could I do about it? Lily was living with me—that much was certain. She was living with me because Jena had entrusted her to me. There were things you did in this world and things you didn't. You'd have to be a slimeball of the first order to send a kid to foster care, or worse, back home to a mother who was your childhood best friend and was now getting beaten to death. Jena didn't need to ask and I didn't need to answer. It was understood between us. Lily was mine, until Jena came back for her, if she ever did.

chapter 9

Early morning was the best time to work, while the house was quiet and Lily was asleep. I sat down at my desk while the sky was still an early morning rose, and pulled out all Collins's records. My office used to be a dining room. The one structural way I changed the cottage was to have a picture window installed there, so I could see the sea in the distance while I worked. The view might be distracting, but it made me want to sit down at the desk, anyway.

I started looking through the papers. In front of me lay the minutiae of a wasted, hurtful life. The only question about a man like Collins wasn't what he'd do for this world, but what he'd do to it. In Collins's case, he was prepared to do a lot of different things—not just commit sexually assaults, which is the only thing that counted under the sexual predator law. Collins was an equal opportunity offender, the kind who might scam you out of your life savings, mug you in an alley, or, if the mood struck him, rape you. He hadn't even gone to prison for sexual assault. That had happened after he was already in for armed robbery. It was hard to predict what he'd do next. He probably didn't know himself.

I didn't doubt the story about "fishing for bitches," but he hadn't gotten caught for it and I couldn't prove it. Without that, he had no prior sexual charges or convictions at all. This meant that on the RRASOR, the simplest of the instruments for assessing risk, he didn't look that bad. The RRASOR had only four items, and half the points came from previous sex charges and convictions. In regards to the other three items, he picked up a point for having victims he wasn't related to, but that was it. He had no points for young age—he was over twenty-five. He got no points for male victims—his only known sexual victim was female. Men with male victims reoffend more—God knows why. Out of the six possible points, he had one. Men with a 1 on the RRASOR had, on average, an 11 percent reoffense rate in ten years.

That wasn't the end of it, however. I had other instruments to consider. I turned to Static99, current front-runner in the world of risk assessment of sex offenders. Static99 included RRASOR items and had a few more besides. The addition of the new items didn't change his overall risk level. His score was a 4 and 6 was the cutoff for high risk. At a 4, the group he was in had a 36 percent reconviction rate for a new sexual offense over fifteen years, which wouldn't meet the legal criteria for more likely than not. Hence he did not meet the legal criteria for a sexual predator.

There were two more instruments to look at. His risk on the Minnesota instrument, the MnSOST-R, wasn't any different: he didn't score as high risk on that, either. Finally I scored him on psychopathy. He scored well over 30, which meant he was a psychopath, one of those strange folks without a conscience. But then, that had been pretty clear from the interview and his history. None of this said he wasn't dangerous. It just said it couldn't be proven that he'd commit another *sexual* offense.

I looked at the findings one more time and then got up and took my coffee upstairs to a small balcony off my bedroom. I dragged a small rocker outside, sat down and closed my eyes to think. It had rained the night before and each lift of the morning breeze sent water on the wet leaves showering down. A small branch bobbed up and down on the rail and, tapping it with each bob, kept forest time. Trees don't wear watches: they bob and rustle and shake and bend and shimmy sometimes. They mark time by ever changing rhythms instead of splintering it into equal fragments, each one the same, the way people do. I do my working down below in my office, but my thinking up here, where no glass comes between me, the muted silver-olive of the cedars and the rustling of the trees dancing the Texas two step with the eager breeze.

Maybe the scores were right, I thought. In truth, Collins was a psychopath and a thug. He was a violent criminal. He didn't specialize in sex offenses. Frankly, he was more likely to get caught for a bank robbery than he was for the rape, which was all these tests measured—who got caught for what. The truth was, he didn't fit the law. Dangerous or not, he'd have to be released. Probably he would be, anyway. Nonetheless, the warden was right: he'd surely hurt someone if he got out. I thought about it for a while and then decided there was still one remaining option.

If I could use the Internet for find Jena, why couldn't I use it to find the therapist he'd raped in prison? I went back inside and started in on the computer. It sounded like a good idea, but I tried and I couldn't find anything about her currently. I had her name, of course, Sarah Reasons, and I found records of her up to ten years ago. She existed in cyberspace up until the assault, then nothing.

I called the warden, and he put me in touch with a couple of her friends and I found out why. She had changed her name—the cut glass had kept grinding—and she had gone east, about as far from Collins as she could get and still be in this country. All that didn't come out right away, of course. It took the warden's calling her friends and vouching for me and then her friends's calling her and getting her permission to tell me. She had sworn them all to secrecy, and they had all honored it.

At the end of the morning I still didn't know her new name, but her friends had given her my number, and Warden Stevens was hopeful she'd call me. I was less sure.

I was still waiting for a call by midafternoon when I heard a racket so loud it felt like a jet had landed in the front yard. I couldn't think for a second, but the sound was revving up and down, and I was pretty sure that jets didn't rev their motors. Thank God, mechanical sounds don't produce colors or designs, or God knows what I would have been looking at. I ran outside and found Betsy in the front yard where, in blue jeans, a tank top, and a leather jacket, she was sitting on top of a large silver and blue Harley. Lily had slept through most of the day, and I didn't even know she was up until she ran out behind me.

"Oh my god, Betsy. Where'd you get the Harley?" I yelled over the noise.

"I bought it. Lord, these mothers are expensive, but worth every penny." She patted the chassis fondly and revved the motor again.

I was dumbfounded. "You bought a Harley?" I yelled over the motor. "Why?"

"I wanted to." She revved it one last time, then turned it off. Silence fell, and in the silence I could hear my ears ringing.

She turned to Lily. "You must be Lily. I'm Betsy. I'm a friend of Breeze's, and I grew up with your mom. Go get dressed, and I'll take you for a ride."

"Betsy, I'm not sure this is . . ."

"Hush now, I brought an extra helmet." Lily was already running back inside to get dressed.

"Never mind," I said, sighing. It would have taken two members of the Carolina Panthers to keep Lily off the cycle at this point. "Have you had anything to eat?"

"Not since breakfast," Betsy said. "I'll take anything you got. You doing OK?"

"No."

"You'll get used to it," Betsy said. "It grows on you."

Like barnacles, I thought, but didn't say it. We talked for a minute in low tones about life with teenagers, and then Lily came running out of the house wearing low jeans and a short top that left a gap where her belly button showed. It must have been what she'd had on under her long-sleeved shirt the day before. Even Betsy balked at this and told her to put something on over it for protection. Lily ran back to get her shirt, and I noticed she didn't seem to have a problem with doing what Betsy said. When she came out the second time, I asked her what she wanted to eat when she got back. As far as I knew, she hadn't eaten since last night.

She shook her head. "I don't eat during the day," she said.

I opened my mouth to say something, but Betsy shook her head slightly and frowned at me. She started the motor and this time I got my hands to my ears in time. I watched the Harley kick up dust as Betsy wheeled it around. I headed back to the house, the picture of Lily on the back of the bike stuck in my mind. It was the first time I'd seen her smile.

When Betsy came back, she brought back a different kid, or so it seemed. Lily's eyes were bright and she was talking, actually speaking words. Her cheeks were red, and her spiked hair lay flattened against her head. The muscles of her face seemed more relaxed, and little kid excitement shone in her eyes. She was talking all about the cycle and gesturing broadly as she described what she'd seen and bought on Blackbeard's Isle. I realized I'd never seen her really use her hands to talk before and wondered why that was so. It was as though she'd been all scrunched over.

Betsy had taken her on a tour of the island with an emphasis on places to shop. They'd hit the only one open, the variety store, which sold groceries and clothes and drugstore items all in one. The clothes they bought would get her through the next few days. Nonetheless she told me that Betsy said I should take her off the island right away to do a real shop so could we go that afternoon? I had a feeling that I'd hear that phrase again: Betsy said this; Betsy said that. Lily even ate a late lunch with us and, for all her claims she didn't eat in the day, managed two sandwiches. After that, she took a stack of magazines she'd bought and disappeared in her room.

"You enrolling her in school?" Betsy asked.

"As soon as the permissions from Jena come," I said. "I've already asked Jena's boss to get them for me. I need Lily's birth certificate and some kind of transfer of guardianship. Dave said he'd work it out—assuming she comes back to work. Who knows if Jerry'll let her? I don't even want to think what she's paid for this."

Betsy just shook her head. "How can a soul get so lost in this world?"

I didn't comment as I didn't know. "What'd you do to Lily?" I asked. "You brought back a quasi-human being." I started to clear the dishes. It was spring and the windows were open and somehow I was getting the idea maybe I could survive this.

"I don't mean to give you a short answer, girl," she said, "but it's all in the knowing how." I laughed. It was what my grandfather had said when I asked how he carved the sails on his model ships so they looked like they were made of cloth.

We left the dishes and went outside to sit under Grandma so Betsy could smoke. "Betsy, I have to keep telling myself she's Jena's daughter."

"I know," Betsy said. "But what you see now ain't all there is."

"And you know this how?"

"She called you," Betsy said. "Why would she do that if she was the tough, wisecracking kid you think she is?"

I didn't say anything. It was true I couldn't reconcile the mall bunny who hated her mother with the voice on the phone.

"Girl, all you're seeing is the smoke and mirrors that teenagers put out there. You haven't even met Lily. It's like some kind of age template. They all have the hair and the CD players and the smart-ass talk. It's years before you see the person peeking out."

"And there's always somebody home?"

"Not always. More than a few of them are nothing but shells. I don't think so this time, though."

"Why?"

"I repeat. She called you. That took something." She sighed. "Think of it from her point of view. Her lifeline right now is a woman whom she believes could have helped her mother but didn't," she said bluntly. "When this friend finally shows up, she abandons her mother again and makes her abandon her besides."

"I didn't . . ." I said, my voice rising.

"Don't start," Betsy said. "It isn't logical. As for her mother, how can she make any sense of her? Some part of Lily has got to know she's dying as surely as if she had cancer. Hell, she does have a cancer. So here Lily is with no mother and no way to take care of herself. Don't think for a second she hasn't considered what's going to happen if you throw her out. Get real."

"But she isn't even vaguely civil," I protested.

"That's not how it works."

I digested what Betsy had to say, and we sat while Betsy smoked and I thought about it. Then I sat up with a start. Lily and Jena had driven out of my mind what I really wanted to talk to Betsy about.

"Betsy," I said, and looked around to be sure Lily was out of earshot. I didn't know how to say this, and I most certainly didn't want Lily to hear it.

"What," she said absentmindedly. When I didn't speak, she asked again. "What?"

"You don't tell Jimmy everything, right?"

"Humph," Betsy snorted. "Not by a long shot."

"I need to know you won't decide I'm crazy, and that you definitely won't tell Jimmy who would think I'm crazy."

"You're not crazy," Betsy said, "and Jimmy isn't all that interested in my friends anyway. Or my life," she added.

"You haven't even heard what it is," I protested.

"You're not crazy," Betsy said.

"Maybe not crazy," I said. "Maybe just hysterical."

"Will you cut it out already?" Betsy said. "I can't stand that psycho-babble. Just spit it out."

"I saw something that wasn't real."

"No shit," Betsy said.

"I don't mean that," I replied. "Something else."

"Like what?"

I didn't reply for a minute while I tried to think how to say it.

"Just spit it out," she said. "What do you think I'm going to do, shoot you because you see a squiggle or two?"

"It's not exactly a squiggle. I interviewed this offender, up in Washington State. Late in the interview, I started seeing like a specter in the room, a little girl right at the corner of my eye in my peripheral vision. She just kept staring at me. Nobody else saw her, of course. She was so vivid to me I could see the details on the dress she was wearing. "

I paused but Betsy didn't comment.

"OK, I know this is my imagination and I'm not trying to say it isn't. The feeling I had was that she was one of his victims."

"What kind of victim?" Betsy said.

"A dead one, I think," I answered.

"I was afraid you were going to say that," Betsy said, taking a drag on her cigarette.

"Well, I don't know, Betsy. There's no way to find out for sure. The records don't say anything about a kid. Of course," I added, "my head could be making the whole thing up. I see shapes and colors when people talk and they're not real. Maybe it's some kind of cross-connected neuron thing, just like the synesthesia."

"Uh-huh," Betsy said, not sounding convinced.

"The only good thing," I said, "is at least she didn't talk to me."

"That's good?" Betsy said.

"Schizophrenia," I said. "The hallucinations are almost always auditory. They lied in the movie of A Beautiful Mind. He had auditory hallucinations. They made it visual so it would work in a movie."

"Oh, come on," Betsy said. "You're not schizophrenic."

"Easy for you to say," I said. "You're not sitting there with a preschool kid staring at you in the middle of a prison interview. I couldn't stand wondering—so I asked him."

"Say again?"

"Well, I didn't say I was seeing a little girl, if that's what you mean. I asked him to tell me about the preschooler."

"And?"

I didn't meet her eyes. "He reacted like he'd been shot," I said. "Maybe it's a coincidence, but he didn't like the question. And his voice changed. It was a brassy color with an olive sheen. Then it got lighter and more scratchy-looking."

"You didn't tell him his voice got light and scratchy, did you?" Betsy said.

"Oh, come on, Betsy."

"So where did he think you got the info? You said you didn't see anything in the records about it?"

"Not a thing."

"So?"

I paused. "I don't know. He could think anything. He could think there's something in the records he doesn't know about. He could think the police told me about a suspicion they had. He could think I talked to some associate of his."

"Is he getting out?" Betsy said.

"Probably. He's a good bet to."

"Girl," she said. "I love you dearly, but you can be dumber than a post sometimes." She kept smoking and didn't say more.

I thought about what Betsy wasn't saying. She had a point. The truth was offenders didn't really fear anything except a murder rap. It was the only thing that could slam the door forever. Routinely, they'd say, "I can do ten" or even "I can do twenty." But no one said "I can do life." Not to mention that in Washington State, murder was a capital offense, so he'd be lucky to get life if he really had a preschool victim. He probably was very interested in where I got the info.

All of a sudden his lurch across the table came back to me.

It had been the eyes that had bothered me, much more than the silken malice in the voice. Once I'd had a friend with a pit bull who had never given me any trouble at all, and I had never feared him. Then one day when I was reaching down to pet him, he had lunged for my throat. In the split second before he leaped I had seen his eyes change. They had gone from normal dog eyes to something only the zebra sees before the kill. I had known when I saw the eyes he was going to attack. It had just happened too fast for me to move or even speak. Luckily my friend had called him off in time.

Betsy and I sat quietly. She kept smoking, her eyes a long way away and troubled. I just kept looking at Grandma and remembering. I don't know what I wanted from Betsy. Whatever it was, I didn't get it. All I got was a bad feeling that I'd done something wrong. And then an old quote came to me from the Civil War, "Mistakes are much worse than sins because sins can be repented of and, hopefully, forgiven. But mistakes laugh at repentance and continue to amass their consequences."

chapter 10

W hat do you want?" the voice said, and for a
moment I wasn't sure who it was. It was late on
the second day of my searching for Sarah Reasons
and I had almost given up hope that she'd call back.

The voice was a dark mossy green with something else in it
that I didn't quite have words for. It was patchy or something,
full of places where the green frayed out. I couldn't tell what
was in those places. It wasn't really black; it was just like a big
nothing. I couldn't say the sound of her voice had much
warmth in it either. Thinking and talking about Collins was
probably a little lower on her list than dental surgery without
anesthesia.

"I'm sorry. This is . . ."

"Sarah . . . well, Reasons, although I don't go by that now.
Anyway, I was told you were trying to reach me."

"Yes, I was. I'm doing an evaluation of Daryl Collins . . ."

"He's not getting out."

I paused. "He's served his time," I said carefully. "He will get out unless he gets caught by the sexual predator law. As I told your friends, that's why I'm doing an evaluation—to see if he fits the criteria for civil commitment."

"No sane person would let that man out."

"It's not likely anybody's going to have a choice," I said. "It's not clear he fits the only law that could keep him in."

The phone was silent, but whether she was trying to keep from exploding or hanging up I didn't know.

"I was wondering," I said, "if you know anything about him that isn't in the records. Anything he said or did that I should know about. Anything that would help me in this report."

"Everything is in the records," she said. "Every last sordid, sick, disgusting detail."

"That may be," I said, "but the records don't reflect what it was like, not really. I want to paint as vivid a picture of it as I can in this report." I paused and decided to tell her the truth. "Because I don't have much else," I said. "Severity isn't sup- posed to count although sometimes it does. Sometimes it makes the difference."

"No," she said. "I'm not going to go there. You can't make me."

"No, no, no," I said. "I'm not trying to make you do any- thing. I'm just . . . OK, I need to know, are you going to be able to testify? If this goes forward, the DA will want you to and . . ."

"Testify?" she said, and the pitch of her voice rose like she had inhaled helium. "Are you crazy? Sit in a courtroom with him? Why would I do that?"

"To keep him in prison," I said simply.

"Like he's ever really been in prison," she said bitterly. "Maybe to you, but not to me."

"What do . . ."

"Do you want to know what it's like?" she said. "Do you really want to know? In the last few minutes before I go to sleep, he's there, and when I wake, in the first few minutes, he's there also. That's the way it's been all these years. It's no different than it was on that first morning. He's never gone away for me. It's a joke that he's in prison. He's never been in prison to me. When I die, in the last few minutes, he'll be there too."

I didn't have anything to say to that.

"I wake up in the morning," she said, "and I have this hollow place in my chest. And I literally think I'll fall apart if I get up. I have to imagine in my mind running bandages around my chest to hold it together before I can get out of bed. I carry that image with me all day long—the bandages holding me together."

"I know this is . . ."

"You don't know anything," she said biting off the words. "My therapist asked me to imagine a safe place," she said. "An image I can use to calm down when I get upset. You know the only thing I could think of? A boat out in the middle of the ocean. A small boat out in the huge, huge ocean, small enough that not even a plane could ever find it. And the water calm for hundreds of miles in all directions so I could see anyone coming. And a lot of high-powered rifles on board, just in case."

I took a deep breath and closed my eyes as I tried to figure out how to deal with this. This was why I hated dealing with victims. Something in me crawled into that small space she lived in, too. The pain in her voice seemed to leach into my palms and run up my arms until my own chest felt hollow. I closed my eyes, and when I pictured her in my mind, all I saw were small bits and fragments of shattered glass.

"The day that man attacked me," she went on, "life quit being a gift and became a sentence."

I opened my eyes and steadied myself for what I needed to

say. I wasn't her therapist. I wasn't her friend. All I could do was tell her the truth. "That's horrible," I said. "It's horrible to be afraid like that. The only consolation is your fear right now is in your head, and at least you can tell yourself that. That he isn't really there, that he's safely in prison twenty-five hundred miles away. If he gets out, all that will change. Every time you hear a squirrel outside your window you're going to think it's him. And you're not going to be able to tell yourself anything to calm down, because the truth is, it could be." It wasn't nice and it wasn't pretty but it was true.

She didn't say anything for a moment, and then she said, "What do you want? I can't testify. What do you want other than that?"

"For starters, did he ever mention any little girls, about pre-school age?"

"I don't think he had any kids, at least not any he knew about."

"Might not have been his, probably wasn't. Was he sexually interested in kids?"

"Not particularly but that wouldn't have mattered to him. He once said if a female was old enough to spread her legs, she was old enough to have sex."

"Christ," I said, wincing.

"What can I say? He's an SOB. It was one of the things that got him kicked out of my treatment group. He wouldn't back down on that statement. Why are you asking about a little girl?"

"I saw something about one in the records," I lied. "Now I can't find it."

"Like what?"

"Like a dead little girl."

"I didn't see anything in the records like that, unless it came in the past ten years after I left."

"We get all kinds of records," I added. "DA records, police records, victim statement. It wouldn't necessarily be in the prison records."

"Well, I don't know anything about it, but I wouldn't put it past him. Anything else?"

"Yes, his autobiography isn't in the records. Most treatment programs require one. Did he write one?"

She paused. "Yes, I think he did. I'm pretty sure of it. I remember it had much in it. I'm pretty sure he denied everything, except the armed robbery he got caught for. And he blamed that on drugs."

"Do you remember where he lived?"

"Where he lived?"

"I'm trying to get a list of every single place he lived as an adult and even a late teen."

"Dallas–Forth Worth. Somewhere around there. That's all I remember. He hadn't been in Seattle long before the robbery. I don't know if he lived anywhere else. Is that it?"

"Well, I'd like to be able to call and run things by you, like the girl. And I want you to call me if you think of anything. I guess that's all I want," I finished lamely.

"All right," she said shortly. "I can do that. Look, is he really getting out?"

"Probably," I said honestly. "I'm working on it but it doesn't look good."

"He'll come after me, you know, if he gets out."

"What makes you say that?"

"Because he has already. He stays in touch," she said bitterly.

"I don't understand. You're in hiding. I could hardly find you. What do you mean he stays in touch?"

"He sends cards, every year, on the anniversary of the rape. He sends them to my mother but addressed to me."

"Your mother? How does he know where your mother lives?"

"Beats me. Well, that isn't true. I have a couple of ideas. He could have had someone on the outside track her down, or more likely he got it from an inmate clerk. I had her down as my emergency contact person, so it was in my records. Inmates work in the records office. That would be my best guess. The cards don't come from the prison. They don't have any fingerprints on them. I've already tried to prove it's him and I can't."

"But you know they come from him? What do they say?"

"They don't say anything. Just 'Happy Anniversary' or 'I'm thinking of you,' or 'Remembering our special time together.' Just printed cards. Why do you think I'm still in hiding? I've never felt safe, even with him in prison. He could always send someone after me. Obviously he has help, or I wouldn't be getting the cards. Now I think he'll wait and come himself. He told me he would if I testified against him, and I did anyway. I know inmates make a lot of empty threats, but Collins is different. When he threatens somebody, he means it."

The stakes had just gone up. I had thought the trauma had made her paranoid and that's why she was hiding. If he was sending cards, however, she was probably right, he'd be looking for her if he got out.

"If you testified against him before," I said, "why not now?"

"I can't," she said. "I was in shock then and I just did what they told me to. Now, the thought of facing him again—it would take me right back there, right back to that room. Believe it or not, I'm better. I can't go back."

"I'll do what I can," I said. "Call me if you think of anything more, or if you hear from him in any way."

"Look," she said, "you gotta think of something to keep him in. I don't want to sound melodramatic, but if you don't,

I'm dead. So do something," and without another word, she hung up.

God bless her, I thought. It wasn't over for her. "The past is never over," Faulkner said, "it isn't even past." Certainly it wasn't for trauma victims. For her, the other shoe was still hanging, waiting to drop. Even if he never came, she'd be waiting for him forever. It was a particularly vicious kind of revenge. All she had done was trust him enough to be in a room alone with him.

I didn't think I'd ever be tempted to trust him, but I reminded myself not to underestimate how smart he was, either. He had a way of tailoring revenge to the person that wasn't pretty.

I thought about it some more, then decided that, bad as he was, I couldn't make Daryl Collins's scores on the tests come out any other way than the way they did, so I picked up the phone and called Robert.

Robert Giles was the assistant DA in King County, Washington, who would be prosecuting Collins, if it came to that. He always screened his calls, so I wasn't surprised when the answering machine picked up. I identified myself and, as usual, in the middle of the recorded voice telling me he wasn't there, he was.

"Ah," he said. "Island girl. You and Tom Hanks. Talking to a volleyball yet? I never understood how anyone could live without the wonders of modern civilization, Starbucks, I mean. Need a care package?"

"Ah, city boy," I said, "send me a tape of traffic at rush hour. Remind me what I'm missing." Robert truly was a city boy. He would go into the most violent project in Seattle, rather than face any kind of tree that didn't have mulch around it. The true pirates were in the cities now, although not in Robert's mind. "You know, they're thinking of turning traffic addiction into a diagnosis," I added. "Help could be on the way."

Robert laughed. "Let me know when the self-help tape comes out. What's up?" I wasn't all that surprised with the shift in gears. Robert always managed to appear genial, but you found yourself talking about work within a minute of reaching him.

"What's up is an inmate named Daryl Collins, who is coming up for release in a couple of months and who—I'm told—would be your case if he were civilly committed. Last and only sexual conviction was for luring a staff member into a room alone, barricading the door, and raping her for hours. Index before that was an armed robbery. He's your basic criminal. Long history of weapons charges, drug dealing, B and E's, assault. Warden says he's bragged about raping twelve-year-olds. Called it 'fishing for bitches' but he never got caught for it."

"Charming," Robert said.

"Well, I talked to him and he certainly tries—when he's not finding a way to practice his intimidation skills. Currently he's found God. I hate to sound skeptical, but you know what they say: there are more religious conversions in the back of police cars than in church. There's a problem, however."

"He doesn't score high on the actuarials," Robert said.

"Unfortunately, in his case. I'm all for people scoring low on the actuarials—the more low-risk offenders we have the better—but this is one of those violent types, and I always hate to see those guys hit the streets. He's a psychopath and a thug. He's just not a specialist in sex crimes. It's part of his general fuck-you approach to the world."

"Ummm," Robert said.

"I've run the numbers and looked at everything I can think

of. I've even talked to the victim—who has changed her name and gone into hiding, by the way. I can promise you she isn't testifying. It's been ten years and she's still working hard to get through the day. He's helping keep it fresh for her. He sends her cards on the anniversary of the rape, just to remind her."

"How thoughtful."

"That's one way of putting it. This is just a courtesy call letting you know he's a dangerous thug, and the victim thinks he'll come after her if we let him go, but I don't think we have a choice."

"Don't be so hasty," Robert said.

I was so taken back I couldn't think of anything to say. Robert had never before interfered in any call I ever made. He knew I was pretty careful in what I did, so he'd never tried to second-guess me on my own turf.

I said slowly, "Robert, I'm not being hasty. I'm frustrated. I'm serious, Robert. I don't have anything. The victim's changed her name and is in hiding. If you bug her about testifying, she's likely to just disappear again. It hurt my heart just to talk to her. I don't understand where you're coming from. It's not like you to second-guess me or to argue with the actuarials."

"To be honest? I'm thinking about Tommy running for governor this fall." Tommy was attorney general of the state of Washington, a charismatic, workaholic who didn't hesitate to interfere anywhere, anytime with anybody's job. Stories of Tommy were legendary: his staff didn't take vacations, no matter what the law said; women who got pregnant found they didn't have a job to come back to. Tommy started his workday at 4:00 a.m. and thought nothing of calling meetings at that hour. Weekends? What were they? Nobody ever protested—much less sued—because they wouldn't be able to get a legal job anywhere in the state of Washington if they did. Tommy had a long memory and a longer reach.

Robert was a bachelor and a workaholic himself, although not up to Tommy's level. Nobody was up to Tommy's level. I don't think anybody could survive in the attorney general's office if they weren't close, however.

"And this means?"

"The word's already gone out. No waves. He doesn't want any sex offenders released who might go out and do something that would make Justice look bad. Think Willy Horton. You wouldn't believe whom we're prosecuting these days. Put your hand on someone's butt, and we'll come after you."

"I'll try to remember that," I said. "Robert, you couldn't win this one. This is defense attorney heaven. All those actuarials we've been preaching about will be on the other side."

"So what," he said. "Better to try and lose. Then we can blame someone else if he reoffends."

"I don't work for Tommy," I said, which was true and not true. I didn't work for him directly, but no doubt if he put his mind to it, he could reach far enough down the food chain to force someone to fire me. I was an outside expert, on contract, with no civil service protection. He wouldn't even need a reason. "I'm sorry, but this is crazy. I want this guy to stay in prison because I think he's dangerous. Even so, I can't see going through a charade that won't go anywhere so it will play better in the newspapers."

"That's what I love about you, Red," Robert said. He was the only person in my life who called me Red, and somehow I liked it coming from him. "Slow down. You're ahead of yourself. Don't you have anything—anything at all—we can go after?"

"Well," I hesitated and then described the little girl I'd "seen in the records."

"What exactly did it say?"

"I can't remember exactly," I lied. "Something about his being under suspicion in the death of a little girl. It troubles me. I keep wondering if there's more that we don't know about."

"When was this?"

"I'm not sure. It was obviously before he went to prison and he'd only been in Washington State for a couple of months before he got arrested for the robbery. So probably Dallas–Fort Worth. That's where he was before Seattle."

"I know somebody in the Dallas–Fort Worth attorney general's office. I'll give them a call. See who knows him and see if we can find anything out about a murder of a little girl. No matter how big the city, a murder of a small child is something people remember. Just don't file the report yet. Give me some time. Like you say, who knows what there is that we don't know about? And see if you can find that reference in the records."

But there wasn't any reference in the records. I felt vaguely guilty about lying to him. What if the little girl didn't exist outside my overactive imagination? Some well-meaning people would be chasing their tails looking for it. Plus if Robert thought he was a child murderer, the pressure would be even worse to keep him in, which probably couldn't be done, so I'd just increased the pressure on me for nothing.

Still, I couldn't say, well, I do think he's a child murderer, but I won't give you time to track it down. "Call me if they come up with anything," I said. "I actually have to go to Dallas next week to testify in a Salvation Army case. I could talk to the AG's people and look at anything they've got then."

"Anything interesting?" he asked.

"I'm just doing my expert witness thing. Nothing interesting about it. It's just the usual Salvation Army minister running a youth group and molesting most of the boys in it. I'm testifying for the kids, of course."

"It's a sick world, Red," Robert said. "I'll see what I can come up with. Come see me sometime. I've got a great Bob Dylan retrospective and I've found a fine new white wine you'd love. There's solace in front of my fireplace, you know. You just don't take advantage of it nearly as much as you should."

I hung up and let out a sigh. There was solace in his bed, that's for sure. I remembered Robert's fingers trailing gently down my spine, and smiled. Still, I never felt like I belonged there. Robert made love as efficiently as he did everything else. He built the lovemaking as carefully as he presented a case in court. But the lovemaking seemed detached and manufactured, and Robert seemed remote somehow. I didn't doubt that he had a good heart—he worked harder on child abuse cases than anyone I knew. I just doubted I was in it, or anyone else I'd ever seen him with. He was just one of those men you could sleep with for twenty years and never feel you'd touched him.

In the meantime I had Daryl Collins to deal with. No matter what Robert said about calling DAs and following up leads, I felt like Collins was already out the door, and we were just reaching after him, fingertips brushing his coat as he slipped past.

chapter 11

L ily and I were waiting. Waiting for Jena to come. Waiting for the phone call saying she was dead. Waiting for the documents I needed to register Lily in school—a birth certificate, school records, written permission from Jena. Lily's life was on pause, and she was waiting for it to take one direction or another. As for me, in dreams I saw the back of Jena's head high up in the mountains. I kept calling, but she never turned. Whenever I thought of her, a wave of helplessness seemed to soak through me and my palms hurt.

Even so, waiting was more a part of my fabric than Lily's. Lily acted trapped, no doubt by the waiting, but also by the island and maybe too by the inevitability of her mother's slow demise. Trapped by not enough kids, no malls, no movies or cable, and maybe not enough hope that she was ever going home again. She was stir-crazy and soon driving me to the brink, but I quickly realized that leaving Lily at loose ends was not an option. I had work to do, and it wasn't getting done, which didn't matter to Lily at all.

I drove her to the other end of the island, and we took the short trip by ferry to the rest of the Outer Banks. We stood in the checkout line with clothes and cosmetics and a CD player with headphones and enough disks for her to hibernate. I watched the hungry light in her eyes as she stood in the line touching the items we were buying. She wanted to open the CD before we bought it. She kept fingering the clothes. Every line in her body spoke to fear that someone would take all this away before we could get through the checkout. For the first time ever I wanted to put my arms around her and sing a song about buying her a mockingbird. It was sad, really. She had a mother whose idea of paradise was the most remote place on the planet, and Lily found salvation in all things commercial. No doubt they were a more reliable source of comfort than people had ever been.

Nothing except shopping seemed to light up Lily's life. She thought the beach was boring and refused to go. She didn't like kayaking: too much work and what was the point. She didn't want to fish or sail or swim. She had no interest in walks, and over time her presence eroded the one thing I needed to thrive—solitude. I still woke to the sound of birds just beyond the small balcony, still had the early morning rocker and the taste of salt from the sea whose distant lapping was the bass line of my life. But once Lily woke up, the colors of the trees and the sky seemed to fade. I no longer stopped to run sand from the yard through my fingers.

Lily didn't notice. In fact, she mostly didn't seem to notice anybody else in the house. She stomped around and sang hideous songs off key. She whined and complained and demanded to know what we were doing that day. She played the radio way too loud. She ran my phone bill into the strat-osphere talking to her friends and then complained because she didn't have her own phone. She hated even a moment of quiet. She looked like someone in withdrawal—which she probably was. The sensory world had been a deluge of TV and music and commercials and radio back in Chicago. Now it was the sound of a cricket outside the window. Lily couldn't adjust. She was as wired as a kid on speed going cold turkey.

I couldn't do much for Lily. I couldn't make her life start up again or make her sensory detox go any faster. The overload she was used to would have to leak out of her slowly like poison leaching out of a system.

I couldn't even get my own feelings straight. I had moments like the one in the store when I saw her clearly and felt in my bones her lack of malice and her confusion. Then I had moments in the house when I thought her presence was a judgment by God for some unknown sin. I needed to save my own soul, at least for a day, so I sent Lily on the ferry to meet Betsy and stay overnight. Betsy had promised her another ride on the Harley plus shopping and TV. I didn't care if they spent the day watching commercials together just so I got a single day of peace.

The breeze was freshening when she walked onto the ferry, and waves were slapping against the side of the boat. The smell of diesel oil hung heavy in the air. Pelicans on the pilings sat stoically and watched the proceedings. Lily had brought some bread to feed the seagulls, which had surprised me. She hadn't even seemed to glance at them on our first trip over. I wouldn't have known she knew they followed the boat.

I watched the ferry pull out. She had seemed happy on the way over, but as the ferry pulled away she walked to the stern and stared straight at me, gripping the rail with both hands. Her face had lost its luster and took on a starkness I'd never seen. She looked older but no more grown up. I thought somehow I was seeing the bones of her life in her face, the sad truth of a violent childhood without the teenage buoyancy that Betsy had warned me was only a cover anyway. I had a sudden thought that she was wondering if I'd be there when she came back. Impulsively, it seemed, she raised her hand in the air as though to wave, then just held it there. I raised mine back. Somehow I knew I could have asked her at that moment why she called me, and she would have told me. But it couldn't happen. Twenty feet had slipped between us now and the gap was widening by the second.

I watched the ferry cross Silver Lake and head through the ditch to Pamlico Sound before I turned to go. Who was she, anyway? The kid with the stark face who raised her hand in farewell seemed entirely different from the obnoxious twit who lived in my house.

I climbed in my battered jeep and drove to the town boat launch to back my small boat trailer into the water. I had a small skiff with a decent sized outboard motor. It was big enough to take me fishing now and then, and more than enough to get back and forth to Portsmouth Island, just across the channel. Right now I needed to be on Portsmouth so badly my palms itched. It was the equivalent of my tree house as a kid. Crossing the inlet, waves battered the hull, and I realized I was going too fast but didn't care. I'd take the pounding just to get there sooner.

There is magic land in this world. I had run into it a few times and it was unmistakable. I saw it once in Colorado as I rode a horse over meadows that cascaded down past weathered wooden fences with fingers of light trailing down them all the way. I had seen it on some rock climbs in Wyoming, places where the stone dipped and swooped and curved, and felt warm and alive when you touched it. I had no doubts Jena had found it in Patagonia. Here and there, along the way, I'd run across places with a certain grace in the way things were put together, as though a better designer had taken a turn. They produced a strange sense of awe in me that floated like a bubble in my chest. And, no doubt about it, Portsmouth Island was magic land. Unlike all the others, it felt like home.

My people had lived there once, way back when Portsmouth had six hundred residents, as many people as lived on Blackbeard's Isle year-round today. Like many others, they'd left after a violent hurricane in the mid 1840s had shoaled the inlet and taken away their livelihood of piloting boats and lightering the boats too heavy to make it through. The Civil War took a further toll and the population had continued to dwindle. The last full-time resident died in 1970. Now it was a ghost town with a few houses, restored by the National Park Service, dotting the fingers of sandy land that tenaciously gripped the pervasive marsh. On the ocean side, shells piled up without being snatched up by greedy human fingers and breakers rolled unheard.

Still, places where humans have lived have a peculiar feel to them, as though their memories lingered on, or they'd left a residue of living that did not depart with them. Walking on Portsmouth never felt quite like walking in parts of Alaska where humans have never been. I felt no sense of being alien on Portsmouth or of intruding on a different world. Portsmouth was an island of people, six hundred of them once, and somehow the memories of dresses drying on clotheslines and whipping in the wind, of wood fires sending plumes of smoke up chimneys, of a postmaster handing out the daily mail, of young and old sitting on the porches in the evening breeze fanning to keep the mosquitoes away—all were still there in ways I could not say. I could feel it, though.

The inlet between Blackbeard's Isle and Portsmouth Island that I raced over had once been the biggest commercial inlet on the North Carolina coast. It had seen more than peaceful commerce, though. Blackbeard's Isle was more than a quaint label for tourists. It had been a pirate stronghold, literally the driveway to Blackbeard's hideout. Blackbeard had anchored past the inlet in the early 1700s in a cove where the coast curved inward like a cup. He'd built a hideout tall enough that he could see over the dunes and spy on ships going up and down the coast. When he found a ship he wanted, he sallied forth to take it and then returned home to party until the next fat fly went by.

Somehow it was always Blackbeard's Isle that drew the pirates and the pirate gatherings and not its quieter sister across the water. I thought Portsmouth Island loved solitude as much as I did, and when she finally saw the last of the full-time human residents go, she'd probably shaken all her bushes in delight.

I tied up at the dock the National Seashore had built for the small group of visitors that frequented the island and walked up quickly toward the group of silent houses. From a distance it looked as though they sat in the marsh itself but fingers of solid land interwoven with vast expanses of marsh sat under them. I turned left and followed the path that would take me past the church, past the rescue station and past the only inhabited building, a small house out back where park service volunteers took turns living on the island to host the visitors.

I walked the mile or so to the beach, feeling as I always did that somehow I was home. Home isn't the place where, when you have to go there, they have to take you in. Frost must have never felt the sense of being home to even write such a line. Home is the place where the tight spring inside you loosens until you can't feel it anymore, the place where your breathing slows and evens out, the place where you stop looking at your watch. Home is the place where you have a right to be, where you don't have to apologize or ask permission. It doesn't matter if you don't own the land; the land owns you. I wondered if people existed who weren't attached to any land in that way, who didn't belong anywhere. Perhaps that's why some people moved so much and never seemed to look back. But maybe everybody has land they belong to somewhere, only not everybody finds it.

The ocean breeze lifted my hair as I walked past the last dune separating inland Portsmouth from the sea. It was steady as a trade wind and had the kind of tang to it nothing except the sea produces. Everywhere I went on the mainland, I found myself sooner or later sniffing the air and wondering what was wrong with it until it came to me. The air feels dead away from the sea; it's like the difference between being in a closed room and being outside. Even inland water lacks something. Lakes can be stagnant and sleepy, filled with algae and swamp gas, but the sea is always a muscular thing.

I stopped long enough to take off my shoes and wiggle my toes in the dry, light sand at the edge of the dunes. Gingerly I threaded my way around the clam and oyster shells, scotch bonnets, and conchs of all sizes as I crossed the beach to the sea. Even with my head down looking for shells, I could tell I was getting closer to the water from the rising roar.

When I finally looked up, the wind had whipped the surf up and the waves looked like porpoises tail-walking across the water until they finally slapped down with a splash. People say sometimes the surf looks playful to them. It never does to me. This was the engine room of the planet, the mother lode, home plate, the place where everything started, and the steady breeze and endless waves were a kind of deep and steady heartbeat. All roads in time lead back to this place. The sea flung us on the shore as surely as it did the shells beneath my feet. Maybe it was bad sense to keep going and we should have turned around and crawled right back in. I'd never seen a porpoise who looked depressed.

I headed down the beach while time stopped and dissolved into the sand scrunching beneath my toes. The breeze slid like a current over my face. I walked by rounded dunes wearing clumps of tall grass like mohawks and over shells—a graveyard of small critters marked only by their tiny drifting headstones. I could feel the batteries deep inside me soaking it all up, recharging for a world of malls and McDonald's that always, to me, felt alien.

Released from the relentless daily log, my mind began to wheel like a bird floating on air currents. My mother floated by, and I wondered if the desert was to her what the sea was to me. She had not done all that well with the outside world, either, and had turned inward instead. Maybe she found her own sea inside the drug-filled colors. Or maybe we all had an ocean inside of us, one I couldn't tap into but she could. Maybe she found that ocean first and took the drugs to stay there.

My head kept wheeling, and I thought about all the different levels we lived in. About the 1,356 creatures in every foot of dirt an inch thick. About the molecules and atoms and quarks that made up everything. Then again, about the bigness of things: about the solar system and the universe beyond. We had to hop back and forth to even think about these different levels because the gift of consciousness had come with a single strange limitation. We could only think of one thing at a time. The ability to take in all these levels at once, to pay attention simultaneously, to be conscious of everything all at once—

that's what God would be—if there was one. God would be a vast consciousness capable of being aware of everything all at once. At least that would be enough God for me. I tried as I always did, to think on all those levels at the same time, and failed, as I always did. Nothing God-like about me.

I don't know if the afternoon passed or I did. Time was nothing but movement after all, that's what the physicists keep trying to tell us. I couldn't really argue with it. Whenever I thought of time, all I saw was a big quilt laid out, and someone with a magnifying glass moving methodically over it from one side to the other. It was all there, the whole thing, and the moving magnifying glass just gave us the illusion that it was changing—the "persistent illusion" of time Einstein used to fret about.

All I know is I must have spent the day walking around the island, mostly on the beach, though I followed some of the trails back into the woods too. My head needed time like this, time when my quirky mind was released from its moorings and could drift at will—driftwood on a wave of diffuse consciousness. But the world rolled relentlessly away from the sun and soon Portsmouth was falling into shadow.

It didn't bother me. The only thing better than being on a beach in the day was being on one at night. My batteries were still charging and I wasn't ready to go home yet.

I was walking by the channel between Blackbeard's Island and Portsmouth when I saw a man on the beach ahead of me. A pale moon was floating slowly upwards as the island drifted into the soft, enveloping dark. Although the moon was nearly full, the night was overcast and I could barely make him out. A sense of unease swept through me. The last tourist boat had left hours ago, and there were no ferries or bridges to Portsmouth, so it was pretty much him and me on the island.

In my line of work you hear too many bad stories to be all that happy about meeting a strange man in an isolated place at night. Still, if he had his own boat, it was probably someone I knew. He was sitting on a rock and staring out at the channel between Portsmouth and Blackbeard's Isle. He was starring intently at the inlet, and even when I got closer, I didn't recognize him for a moment.

"Charlie," I said in relief when I finally caught up with him. Charlie was "touched" as the old people used to say; schizophrenic, according to the books. Whatever you called him, I had known him for years and he was harmless. Sometimes he took his medication and sometimes he didn't. I always thought life was better for him when he didn't. When he did take it, his face seemed to implode and he seemed out of touch emotionally, as though all he could do was concentrate on the chemical flood within.

When he didn't take the meds, well, life wasn't all that bad. He just thought he was somebody he wasn't: Israel Hands, Blackbeard's first mate. As delusions go, it seemed more creative than average. Most schizophrenics picked Christ.

Charlie lived in a small shack on Blackbeard's Isle, and the beach near the shack was the place he hung out most. Still, he had a small skiff, and I had seen him on Portsmouth before.

Charlie did OK. People dropped off groceries with surprising regularity, and—psychotic or not—he was a hell of a fisherman. He might not be well enough to work, but I'd never known him to go hungry. Tonight, though, I didn't see a pole.

He was staring out to sea and at first he didn't seem to even notice me. He was barefoot and wore pants that stopped halfway from his knee to his ankles, and a red shirt. The clothes were old and torn and not all that clean.

I was wondering if he was on or off meds when he glanced at me and said "Aye, that would be the Cap'n out there. N'er saw the likes of him, before or since. I sailed with him from the Caribbean all the way to Boston and back."

"And a good evening to you, Charlie," I said.

He looked back out to sea and went on. "I came from decent folk, you know. I didn't start out to be a pirate. I got taken off the *Mary Jane,* but there was nothing for it after that. Once you're in with the pirates, the British will hang you if they catch you, and the pirates will shoot you if you leave. So I made the best of it.

"It weren't a bad life. Feast or famine. Not that there were any lack of ships to take. But the Cap'n, he'd blow hot and cold. Drunk for a week sometimes, and ships could sail by as pretty as you please. Then tearing up the world going after everything that floated by. Shot me in the knee once, but it were an accident. Trying to shoot another man and too drunk to aim. I asked him why he did it—we were just setting there playing cards—and he said he had to shoot somebody now and then, just to remind the crew who he was."

I liked to listen to Charlie. He was smart, and he knew more about Blackbeard than I did. The things he talked about were always true. I followed his gaze out to sea and thought I saw flashes of light on the water. It must be heat lighting. Maybe that's what had set him off. Probably he thought it was the guns from Blackbeard's final battle. I wondered if places all over the world had people like this. No doubt men wandered Gettysburg and Shiloh convinced they were still in the Civil War.

"I weren't on board when it went down," Charlie said. "They'd taken me up to Bath to see about me knee. Got back in time to see it from shore. I ain't n'er seen the like of it.

Cap'n didn't go down easy, I'll give him that. Won't stay down, either."

We sat for a moment in silence. "Well, Charlie," I said. "It's a nice night. If the weather holds we could have a pretty fair weekend. You doing all right?"

He looked over at me. "I ain't got nothing against a pirate hunter," he said. "Things worked out different, I could a been on one of them boats. But the pirates go after the pirate hunters just like the pirate hunters go after the pirates." He looked back out to sea and paused. "Take you, missy," he said after a moment. "You got a mean one coming up on you. You be careful now. He's got you to leeward, and pirates have always done well this part of the country."

"Charlie," I said, "What are you talking about?"

"Well, you do have your choices, don't you? This one's more like a coral snake than a rattler. I seen them down in the Caribbean. Hide in the sand, don't give you no warning, no bigger than your finger. Give me a rattler any day. Don't like to be disturbed and will let you know you're on his territory. Big as your arm, some of them. The Cap'n, he were a rattler, the like of which nobody's seen. But not the one coming up on you."

"Charlie . . ."

"I can't do much for you, missy. I made my choice a long time ago. Or it was made for me. Nothing I can do for a pirate hunter. If you get a chance, though, bring your snake down to the water. Things are different here. You never know which way the wind will blow, or who the Cap'n will take to."

I stared at him, but couldn't think of anything to say. He didn't seem to expect any reply. Troubled, I got up and headed slowly back. For some reason, I wanted to be home.

stood dumbfounded as Lily screamed at me. Her pupils were tiny pinpricks of anger and her shoulders shook. A small fleck of saliva had burst from her mouth and was stuck to her panting chest.

"You lied to me," she yelled. "You stupid bitch, you lied to me."

"I did not lie to you. I told you the school was small." Lily had had her first day of school—the permissions had finally come—and apparently it had not gone well. While I could understand annoyance or even anger, I was bewildered by this nearly incoherent rage.

"Small? Small is three or four *classes* of kids my age. That would be small. That would be tiny. Do you know how many people are in my high school? Two thousand. Do you know how many kids are in my class in this retarded, asshole place? Four. That isn't small. That isn't tiny. That's stupid. That's not a school; it's a babysitter with a bunch of kids. What am I supposed to do in a class with four people?"

"Well, the worse that can happen is you're fourth in your

class?" I said, my upset at Lily's behavior coming out all wrong.

Lily caught her breath and glared at me. "That is the stupidest thing I have ever heard. Is that supposed to be a joke? You think this is funny? You think it's funny to be treated like a freak? What the fuck do you care? You just want to get rid of me, like my mother. That's why you couldn't wait to put me in that stupid school."

I looked at Lily. Clearly this was about more than the school, but probably getting into her mother right now wouldn't help. I tried to concentrate on the present problem. She was still wearing the multiple bracelets, the gaudy earrings, and the dark, gothic makeup I knew had made her stand out. I was also pretty sure her belly showing hadn't helped either. No matter how many tourists we had, Blackbeard's Isle was still a small school in the rural South. Should I have insisted this morning that she change? Should I talk to her about it now?

I hadn't known what to say this morning, and I still didn't. Lily seemed to resent any instruction or advice, and I hadn't know whether to tell her or let her figure it out for herself. I had asked myself what Betsy would do and figured Betsy would tell me to leave her alone, so I had. Now I had a feeling I'd set her up.

"Lily, honey, I'm sorry it didn't go well . . ."

"You're not sorry," Lily said. "You don't give a shit. You leave me out of everything. You don't give a damn about me. I'm just an inconvenience to you. I'm buried alive here in this stupid, hick place out in the middle of nowhere, and you don't care. You don't even notice me most of the time. You just sit up there in your stupid rocker, and you don't even talk to me. You wish I was never born," she screamed.

"Whoa, Lily," I said softly. "Calm down, hon. I don't wish

you were never born—nobody does. Listen, about school, maybe there are some things we can do . . ."

"I know what I can do," Lily yelled. "I'm never going to that stupid school again."

"Hon, you have to go to school."

"I don't have to do anything. You can't make me. I'll get a job. I'm not going back."

"You're thirteen. You have to go to school."

"Says who?"

"Well, Lily, the law for one thing," I said quietly. This was getting absurd.

"There's a law against beating people too, isn't there?" she answered.

"Yes," I said slowly.

"Well, so much for the law," Lily sneered.

"Lily, I'm not going to argue about this. You're going to school. You have to. Maybe . . ."

"Don't tell me what to do," she shrieked. "You're not my mother. You're not even her friend. You would never have left her with that asshole if you were her friend. No friend would ever do that. You don't know what he does to her. And it's my fault. You don't get it, do you? It's all my fault."

"Lily," I said, alarmed at how loose her thoughts were getting. I stepped forward and put my hands on Lily's shoulders. "It's not your . . ." She jerked away and backed up, trembling. Her pupils had gone so wide I could see the whites all the way around, and she looked like she was hyperventilating. Reaching for her had been the worst thing I could have done; I forgot how much violence she had been exposed to. Quickly I stepped back.

"It's OK," I said. "It's OK. Nobody's going to hurt you. It's all right, Lily. We'll work it out." Lily looked blank and I recognized the look. I'd seen enough flashbacks in victims to know when someone was dissociating and losing touch with where they were.

"You're on the island, Lily," I said. "Blackbeard's Isle. You're not home in Chicago. Jerry isn't here," I added. "Nobody's here except you and me. Let's sit down. Let me fix you something, some hot chocolate, anything. It's all right."

Recognition came back in Lily's eyes, and with it, the fear and the fight went out of them. A kind of sadness swam into them that seemed beyond my plumb line. Clearly this was a traveler who had lived in countries of pain I had only visited.

"I don't want hot chocolate," she said, and then, with quiet dignity she turned and walked slowly to her room.

I stood in the living room for a moment. I didn't want to leave it at that. It wasn't her fault. How could she think so? I walked to her door and raised my hand to knock on it but then stopped. What could I do that would help? Nothing. She had pretty much lost it, and now she needed time to recoup. What she didn't need was a continuation of the argument or an attempt at solace from someone she didn't trust or even like, it seemed. I dropped my hand and walked away.

I went to the kitchen and made a cup of tea, then went upstairs to the balcony and sat on the rocker. I was surprised to see that my hands were shaking. I wasn't used to this. The professional world I lived in had always held devastated victims and angry, sometimes vicious perps. Lawyers had hammered me. Offenders had tried to manipulate me and occasionally had threatened me. Sometimes victims had tried to own me. But home had always been refuge, a harbor where you could moor the boat and sleep to the quiet slapping of the halyards. Now I had lost my refuge to a girl who had never known any. Lily and I were both at sea.

She didn't go to school the next day, and I didn't have the heart to press her. I went to see the principal and explained we were having a few adjustment problems. She seemed unfazed. She'd taught school for twenty years in Durham before retiring to Blackbeard's Isle and had some idea of how big a change it was for Lily. Give her time, she said. It will make all the difference.

I went back home and tried to decide what to do next. In truth I had little choice. I was leaving for Dallas the next morning, and Betsy was coming to stay with Lily. Maybe it was a good thing. Lily seemed to have me and her mother all mixed up together, and she responded much better to Betsy, anyway. Maybe it was cowardice on my part, and certainly bewilderment, but I decided just to go to Dallas. Let Betsy deal with it. It was clearly no time for amateur hour at mothering. Time to bring in a pro.

The plane eased down through the clouds and settled heavily on the tarmac as though flying was effortful and land it's real home. Probably planes were like people: fly where other people tell you when they tell you and the joy goes out of it.

But if I had to go anywhere, I'd as soon it be Texas. I looked out the window at the flat, dry countryside and got that strange feeling of kinship I always had when I was in Texas. It wasn't home, but it was a relative.

I had spent the whole trip obsessing on Lily. I couldn't ever remember being as mad at anyone in my life as Lily had been with me—with me, her mother, her life, and the planet, too, as far as I could tell.

Walking past security I was still obsessing when I looked up to see a sign with my name on it. The stocky woman holding it wore her bright blond hair so short it looked like a buzz cut. She was dressed in a blue blazer and tan slacks. Lily would have liked the hair, if not the duds. She was leaning against the wall, holding the sign casually in front of her and scanning the crowd with a practiced eye. She spotted me the moment I glanced at the sign.

Surprised, I walked up to her. "I'm Breeze Copen," I said.

"Hi," she said, tossing the sign into a nearby receptacle and holding out her hand. "Mandy Johnson." The voice was a thundercloud gray with a soft wiry texture. The arm she extended was solid and muscular, and I realized the stockiness wasn't due to eating doughnuts. She'd lifted a few weights, which usually went along with being a cop, not a prosecutor, unless things were different in Texas.

"Heard through the grapevine you were coming in. I guess the AG's office got a call from Seattle," she said, confirming my guess she wasn't a DA. "Said you'd be in this evening and we might have a mutual case. I thought I'd give you a lift."

"I didn't know anybody was coming to the airport. I appreciate it."

"Had to be out this way anyway, so why not? It'll give us a chance to talk before you get caught up in things." We started walking toward the door. "Any luggage?"

"Just this," I said, indicating the roller bag I was wheeling. As we walked she didn't glance in my direction, and both of us fell silent. I was wondering what she was doing there. Cops had more important things to do than pick up visitors at the airport.

"So you're here for a case, right? A civil suit of some sort?" she said casually, looking ahead.

"Salvation Army," I said. "A child-molesting youth minister.

What a surprise. I'm testifying for the victims," I added. I knew most cop's opinion of psychologists. We were hired guns who made a ton of money putting rapists, pedophiles, and child-killers back on the street. And the truth was, we had plenty who did just that. But if she thought I was a court whore, she'd tell me nothing, not even why she came to pick me up, which was the first mystery.

"Most of the time I testify in civil commitment cases," I said. "I know you don't have the same law down here. We have one where we can retain sexual predators in a secure facility indefinitely for treatment. Sometimes, though, I testify on the side of victims in other types of criminal or civil cases. I don't," I said, "testify for perps. You are with . . ."

"I'm sorry," she said, although she didn't seem to be. "Dallas PD. You hungry?" Which meant, I guess, that I had passed muster. Either that or she wanted to talk away from the office for some reason.

"Very."

"I know a place on the way into town."

I watched Dallas go by as we drove in, and wondered as I always did how people lived all scrunched up in a city. Still I had to admit Dallas was different from most cities. Sure, people were piled up on top of each other like they were in every city, but you didn't get as much of a sense of it in Dallas. There was something sweeping, something grand, about the place—a sense of space even with all the high rises. It was as though the size of the country outside Dallas just rolled on through the city and diluted the sense of crowding. Dallas had long, wide, empty spaces in its soul, and no matter how many high rises they built, that just didn't seem to go away.

Mandy didn't seem to feel the need to talk, which didn't

bother me. I never had a problem with quiet, but her kind of quiet had a sense of unease about it. She seem distracted, like she was thinking about something or trying to make up her mind.

"So," she said, when we were seated at a small Mexican restaurant, "I hear you've been dealing with one of our more memorable scumbags."

"Ah," I said. "You know Daryl Collins. I guess I'm only surprised because it's been so long. He hasn't been here for what? Ten or twelve years?"

"Yeah, but he didn't take his brother Leroy with him. He's a major pain and a constant reminder."

"What's his brother up to?"

"Leroy's a pill. He's actually a whole lot more trouble than Daryl ever was. Daryl was a petty criminal. Your basic thug. Leroy's a whole lot worse. He's got a much bigger drug network than he and Daryl ever had together and a lot more violence on his track record. He once shot a plumber for not knocking on the screen door."

"Say again?"

"He called a plumber, and when the plumber came out, he saw Leroy on the porch and spoke to him. Leroy told him to knock on the screen door. The plumber thought that was pretty silly since Leroy was standing right there. When he didn't do it, Leroy got his .357 and shot him."

"Wow, how much time did he get for that?"

"Not a day. Plumber changed his mind about testifying. They all seem to change their minds about testifying. I guess if you're willing to shoot someone for not knocking on a screen door, its not hard to convince people you'd do a lot worse if they testify."

"And to think I was impressed with Daryl."

"Small-time," she said. "By the way, Leroy doesn't call himself Leroy. We do, just to needle him. He calls himself Trash."

"Trash? Where's that from?"

"I'm not sure. I've heard different versions. One is that he got it because he's a big trash talker, but my partner swears there's a different story. According to him, there was a kid who called him Trash when he was a teenager. The kid got thrown off a roof—so the story goes—and Leroy has called himself Trash ever since. It's supposed to be a don't-mess-with-me kind of thing. Who knows which story is true? You can't figure these guys out.

"Anyway," she added, "what do you know about the four-year-old who was murdered?"

"Nothing," I said. "I get three thousand or so pages of records to look at when I do these evals. I get police reports from every crime he's committed. I get all the records from the prison. I get previous evals and any psych testing. I get victim statements. It's just a mass of material. Somewhere in there was a reference to a little girl who was murdered. I can't even find it now. I wouldn't even have gone any further with it—he certainly wasn't charged for the murder of a small child—but impulsively I asked Daryl about it and he froze. He just froze like the proverbial deer in headlights, and that got me interested." That part was true anyway.

"That's all?" she said, disappointment slurring the thundercloud gray.

"Sorry," I said. "So there is a little girl?"

"There was," she said, "a four-year-old named Sissy Harper, though we never had any hard evidence that Daryl was involved." She paused and leaned forward. Her voice sounded easygoing to my ear, but it didn't look that way to my eye. The tones were grower darker and more cloudy as though she were angry or just anxious about something. Her shoulders were tense and scrunched forward and went with the way her voice looked, not the way it sounded.

"Twelve years or so ago, the gas company got a call from a mailman who smelled gas when he went up on the porch to leave the mail. Yesterday's mail was still there and the day before's, and that bothered him too, since the car was still in the driveway. The gas company sent somebody over, and he took a reading right outside the door where the smell was. The gas guy was so freaked by the level of gas outside the house he called the cops and we broke in."

"We?" I said, not sure if she meant herself literally or just "we the cops."

"My partner Mac and I caught the case. A uniform broke in and called us. We found the stove turned on, the oven door open, and a dead man named Roosevelt Harper on the kitchen floor with a bullet through his chest and another point blank in his face. Then we went through the house and found a second body, Sissy's, in an upstairs closet. She was Roosevelt's daughter. She'd been raped and beaten, and her thighs were covered with dried blood. My guess is she crawled in the closet to hide after the assault. That's just a guess. Maybe he threw her in the closet. Anyway, the doors were locked so she couldn't have gotten out of the house. She died from the gas."

My stomach was beginning to tighten at this, and I wondered if there would be a picture of Sissy in the files.

"So what's Daryl Collins's involvement?"

"Well, he could have been involved. We never had any hard evidence one way or the other. Daryl and Leroy were the dead man's cousins, on his mother's side, and the word on the street was they were all dealing drugs together. It didn't matter.

We didn't have any physical evidence—period. No one saw anybody go in or out of the house that night. It wasn't the kind of neighborhood where it paid to notice the people going in or out." She shrugged.

"That whole family is full of scumbags. A sort of Ma Barker figure heads it, and almost all her kids have served time—Leroy's actually the exception. He did some time as a juvi. As an adult he's found ways to stay out.

"Anyway, we never had anything to go on. The gun never turned up. We never got anything from the street about it, and we shook down everybody."

"DNA?"

"On Sissy? Well, we thought we might have something, but we had a little problem with our lab at the time. Maybe you read about it. Turns out they were manufacturing evidence. The whole thing broke just after we sent in the DNA. We didn't even ask for a report once it hit. Knew we couldn't use it or trust it, and I don't know what happened to the sample. We never got it back. It wouldn't have done any good anyway. The chain of evidence was broken when the lab turned out to be unreliable.

"Could have been anything, really: a drug sale gone bad or maybe a rival dealer took him out. But the kid? That's a kind of very personal revenge unless the perp was wired with crystal meth. Anything was possible. There were way too many possibilities. Until now. Until you showed up with a question about Daryl and a little girl. We were wondering if Daryl had opened his mouth somewhere along the way. I can't see any way you could have run across something about Daryl and a four-year-old in the files up in a Washington State prison otherwise."

I didn't respond to that. She didn't know it, but she had

nothing more than she had before. "Tell me," I said. "What was she wearing? Do you remember?"

"A dirty blue dress with small daisies on it," she said without hesitation.

"You remember?" I asked.

She shrugged and looked away.

I thought about the girl on the edge of my vision when I talked to Collins and the dress she was wearing. Suddenly my stomach finished its flip-flop, and I wasn't hungry anymore. Whatever I was seeing, it wasn't just coming from my head.

"You got stuff I can look at?" I said, finally. "Police reports, etcetera."

"Sure," she said. "I'm not involved in it now so I don't know the details of what they've got planned for you. You'll probably get a message at your hotel tonight with information about where you can look at them. It's likely to be from Pat Humphrey. She's a DA with a particular interest in Leroy. I know you're interested in Daryl, but I can tell the real interest down here is going to be Leroy. Daryl hasn't been our problem for a long time. But if Daryl was involved, so was Leroy. Back then one didn't shit without the other.

"You know," she added, "I don't think Leroy is going to like it if he hears someone is down here from Seattle looking into this murder. It means something is coming out of the prison about this and that means Daryl has opened his mouth."

"I don't think he's had much contact with Daryl," I said. "I can't be sure about letters, but I have all the visiting lists in the records, and he isn't on any of them. Of course, maybe he's calling."

"Maybe," she said. "I doubt it though. He just doesn't seem the type to stay in touch. Be interesting," she said, "if he got bent out of shape with Daryl about this."

"You never can tell," I said. "I've got to testify tomorrow on the Salvation Army thing. I'll be on the stand most of the day, maybe all of it. I can come the day after tomorrow and spend the day on this, or more if I need to.

Mandy Johnson just nodded and stared down at her plate. Something was wrong here, I thought. The energy next to me was all tight and balled and just not right somehow. The voice looked one way, sounded another. I thought I'd be all right if I ran into her in a dark alley, but I was pretty sure there was someone else who wouldn't. Maybe someone from her past, probably a long time ago. That was the problem with people who had issues with the past. Sometimes they ran into people in the present who reminded them, and then watch out. At least she wasn't lying to me: her voice had never changed.

She picked up her wineglass and twirled it in her hand. "Do me a favor," she said.

"What?" I asked.

"When you go in to read the papers, you'll come across the initial police reports on the murders. Tell them you want to speak to the cops who did the initial investigation, see what they remember. Everybody knows not everything makes it into a police report." She looked up quickly and then back down. "They'll probably try to get you to talk to Mac. Don't buy it. I know the case better than he does."

"OK," I said, but I raised my eyebrows, and Mandy went on quickly.

"I'm still interested in this case and I'd like to have an excuse to go back over the files, maybe work some with you on this."

"Sure," I said. On the one hand, it wasn't surprising that there was some sort of politics involved. There were always politics. The police, the AG's office, you name the human institution—there were politics involved. But I didn't know the players here, or the issues, and I hoped I wasn't getting sucked into something.

"You don't need to mention you've met me," she said, which didn't do anything to ease my mind.

chapter 13

t was the afternoon of the second day before I made it into the police station to go over the files. The attorney for the Salvation Army had cross-examined me for a day and a half and had finally reluctantly let me go. He'd been trying to get me to say something that would excuse a minister befriending poor kids in order to have sex with them. I didn't know what he thought I could say that would make it any better. And I certainly wasn't trying to come up with anything.

Now I entered a low modern building and wondered where the old police stations had gone, the ones in the detective novels, the ones with old scarred rooms and scruffy detectives. The building was set on an incline with the main entrance in the front and the entrance to the jail on a split-level in the back. It was freestanding, a new building with a manicured lawn and professionally landscaped bushes under the windows. Without the sign, you'd have thought of insurance or banking.

The room we stepped into was a waiting room and at the

other end of it, a serious metal door that required either the officer on duty to buzz you through or a key code. The officer on duty manned a bulletproof window next to the metal door. He looked at my ID carefully, consulted a list, then picked up the phone and called someone in the back. A few minutes later a petite woman in a stylish rose-colored suit and stiletto heels walked through the door.

"Hi," she said, "I'm Pat Humphrey and I thought it would just be easier to meet you here." She didn't wait but headed for the back, talking over her shoulder as she went. "Unfortunately, we don't have many of their records in the DAs office, anyway. The Collins brothers never seem to make it to trial. I call them the Teflon boys—well, I guess you got Daryl on something in Seattle. We've had no such luck with Leroy."

She led me down a corridor, and I noticed a large working room on my left where detectives in sports jackets and ties were sitting at sleek gray desks and working on computers. I didn't see a bare lightbulb or beat-up desk anywhere. Individual offices followed, and a kitchen lay across from them, clearly a break room for staff. Finally we stopped at a small conference room that held a large table and ten chairs. A mass of files covered the desk.

"I'm not sure technically you're entitled to this," she said. "I know you're a psychologist and only on contract, but we are taking it that you are working for the police on this."

"Not the police," I said, "the AG's office."

"Whatever," she said, waving it away dismissively. "You'll find we try to do the right thing down here and not get too caught up in the fine print."

She pulled out a chair and sat down. "Now," she said, "what do you have on the murder of Sissy Harper."

"The four-year-old?"

She nodded. "Nothing," I said honestly and then told her my feeble little story of the missing reference in the records.

She cocked her head as she listened. She had a petite face that matched her small frame, and brown hair tucked back behind her ears. The eyes were small and bright, and I thought if humans had evolved from birds, we'd all look like Pat Humphrey—at least those of us who descended from small, no-nonsense birds. The voice fitted her. It was a bright lipstick red, hard and glassy, and I couldn't help but smile. Sometimes people's voices fitted the way they looked; sometimes they didn't. This one fit her to a tee.

If she was disappointed in what I said, she didn't show it. She could have played poker with that face, and I had a feeling prisoners looking for a plea bargain wished they'd drawn another DA.

"That's it," she said. It was a statement, not a question. She just sat for a minute looking at something I couldn't see and thinking.

"Do you have a case against Daryl, a civil commitment case?"

"No," I said. "I don't think so. There's pressure to take it forward, but right now we'd lose. Civil commitment in Washington State means that we have to prove he's more likely than not to commit more *sexual crimes*. That particular law doesn't care if he is going to murder anybody.

"The problem is Daryl has only one official rape on his record. He didn't even go to prison for rape. The truth is, he just commits a variety of crimes. Well, you know him. We can't show that he's more likely to rape someone than mug them or sell them drugs. The civil commitment law isn't made for people like Daryl; it's basically made just for pure sex offenders."

I didn't think that was particularly good news, but Pat

Humphrey seemed to like it. "Good," she said. I guess I'm not as good a poker player as she because she read my face and added, "I'm sorry. To be honest, we don't care a whole lot about Daryl Collins. Daryl Collins is a minor nuisance compared to his brother Leroy. We do"—and it was here I caught the first emotion I had heard as the red of her voice seemed to expand and start to swirl—"care about Leroy Collins. Leroy Collins has made fools of us too many times to count. It's not quite fair to say we don't have records on Leroy in the DA's office. We have records of charges—*dropped charges*—over and over again. It's a sad fact you can't make victims testify," she said as though she wished she could. "On the other hand, the only ones who have been willing to have disappeared—not a great advertisement for cooperating with the police." The bright red had turned darker at that last statement, although the voice still sounded even to the ear.

"So I'm not going to fool around. The answer is simple. Tell Daryl Collins you'll cut him a deal—no civil commitment if he hands over Leroy on the murders of their cousin and Sissy Harper. At present we have nothing at all to get Daryl to talk. But civil commitment can mean a life sentence. That's a very credible threat to Daryl."

I just looked at her. "Back up a minute. Do you know that Leroy killed Roosevelt Harper or Sissy?"

"I know he's capable of it, and I know he's killed other people."

"Do you care if he killed them?"

Now she paused, seeming to weigh and measure me for the first time. "No," she said.

"Why are you going for that one? You don't have any evidence at all that Leroy and Daryl were linked to it, and besides, it's over a decade old."

"Because Daryl has been gone since then. He'd hardly have any evidence about more recent murders. And besides, juries hate offenders who murder children."

"You're thinking a jury would buy Daryl Collins's unsubstantiated word?"

"First, he probably did do it. He was his cousin. We know Roosevelt and Leroy sold drugs together. If Leroy didn't do it, he would have gone after whoever did kill him and he didn't. Hell, if we could get a story out of Daryl, we might turn up something to prove Leroy killed him. Second, even if we can't, if we can just get part of Leroy's track record before the jury, I don't think they'll care that it's just Daryl's word. Texas juries tend not be too picky about which crime you're up for, if they know you're a stone-cold killer."

"This isn't the main point, but I can't see how you could get his track record in. Other crimes are going to be considered prejudicial and not relevant, right? I wouldn't think any judge would allow unrelated crimes to even be mentioned in front of a jury."

"Ah," she said, "I see you know your way around a courtroom. We'll make the claim that he dealt drugs with the victim, and our theory is they had a falling out over their business arrangements. So, yes, past criminal activity would be relevant because it would be part of his drug-dealing empire, and there's a few killings along the way I'd argue were part of those dealings."

"And if Daryl killed her and not Leroy, you'd be handing him a free pass on the murder of a four-year-old?"

"You got anything on Daryl and the four-year-old now? Maybe you haven't noticed, but I'd say he's already got a free pass."

I started to speak. Pat held up her hand, "Say—hypothetically speaking, of course—that Leroy didn't actually commit that particular murder—that Daryl did, or someone else. Say even that the jury let him go, the least that would happen is that Daryl and Leroy wouldn't team up again. That would be a service in itself."

"Given Leroy keeps killing witnesses, why wouldn't Leroy try to have Daryl killed if he really thought he'd be testifying against him?"

"Hard to do when Daryl is in prison."

"Not impossible, though," I said.

When she didn't speak, I said, "Are you saying you wouldn't exactly grieve if he did?"

She shrugged. "No," she said, "Put bluntly, I wouldn't. Look, anybody who testifies against Leroy Collins is in harm's way. He's not going to stop being violent, and I'm looking at a future of maybe putting a series of innocent people in his gun sights. If Leroy has to go after anybody, I absolutely assure you I'd rather it be Daryl Collins than anybody I can think of. I wouldn't mind having a witness for once that I didn't wake up in the night worrying about. The last witness against Leroy was a fifty-five-year-old grocer who left a disabled wife. He was a nice man, and he got involved because he thought it was the right thing to do."

"All right," I said, "in a way I can understand that, but I don't think civil commitment can be plea bargained. I know you don't have the same kind of law down here, so you haven't dealt with it. I've testified in these cases for years and I've never heard of it.

"Anyway, you're talking to the wrong person. You're going to want to talk to the AG's office in Seattle. If it isn't legal to do this, I can tell you that the DA on this one, Robert Giles, won't go for it. He's never shot a crooked arrow in his life."

"I'm not talking to the wrong person," she said. "We may not have your kind of civil commitment—ours is a nansy-pansy law about supervising them in the community—but I know this much: if the evaluating psychologist says no case, it doesn't go forward and we have nothing to plea bargain with. If you take it forward, and the DA agrees to file, then it's up to a jury. Now, you say it isn't legal to plea bargain. I say that if there are some arrangements about what gets filed and what doesn't— well, who's to know. Let's just get it started so it's a credible threat to Daryl, and let me deal with Robert from there."

"You know Robert?"

"I know Robert," and I saw a hint of a smile. My guess is she *knew* Robert.

"I don't want to disappoint you," I said, "but I don't shoot a lot of crooked arrows either."

"You're eighty-seven years old and you're dying," she said. "What are you going to feel worse about when you look back—stretching a point and giving me a shot to put Leroy Collins in prison, or the next four-year-old that he kills? Or the next fifty five-year-old grocer? Or the next girlfriend that tries to leave him? You'll find the details in the files. There's a lot more. Enough that I swear to God, if you don't help me on this, I will send you the clippings of every murder he commits for the next decade." She had leaned forward while she was talking, and her pupils were small and hard. Now she sat back and said quietly, "Expect a steady stream of mail."

I sighed. "Let me read the files," I said.

I had just wanted the files on Sissy Harper's murder and on Daryl Collins, but Pat had left the files on Leroy as well. Curious, I started on them first. By midafternoon I hadn't gotten through half of them. I called Betsy and warned her I'd be another day. Leroy was, indeed, a nasty piece of work. He was as callous as Daryl, only smarter and more ambitious. He thought ahead more. If Leroy had raped his therapist in prison, he would likely have faked multiple personality disorder and gotten away with it. Daryl had a very in-your-face kind of style, but Leroy was a whisper over your shoulder when you unlocked your door. "From the house to the car. From the car to the house," he had told one potential witness. "You have no idea how vulnerable you are." She had one of the better outcomes—she withdrew her testimony and lived. Still, I wondered how many years she spent thinking about that phrase every time she got out of her car.

So if nobody ever testified against them, why had Daryl left Dallas? Maybe the heat was on the Sissy Harper case, but he and Leroy had skated every other time. So what was he worried about? Did somebody know something, somebody Daryl couldn't get to? Even if that were true, what would it have to do with Seattle?

Just as I put away the papers, Pat Humphrey came back in. I automatically glanced at my watch. I had read so long I thought the day was long gone but it was only four. "We have Mr. Collins here," she said. "We brought him in to talk about Sissy. I thought you might want to watch the interrogation."

"He came in voluntarily for questioning?" I said, surprised. "He'll talk to you?"

"Oh, yes," she said. "He always talks to us. I think he enjoys playing games with us. And the truth is, why not? It's never hurt him. He never gets rattled or says anything he doesn't mean to."

I followed her through the corridor and down the steps to the floor below in the back of the building, where the rooms for questioning suspects were located. At least interview rooms hadn't changed over the years. This one had a table and two chairs and nothing else in the room at all. There was a one-way mirror along one wall and, I knew, an invisible system was in place to tape conversations. The chair the suspect sat on was slightly lower in the front. Standard police technique involved cutting off the front legs a little so that the suspect couldn't kick back, and was always slightly leaning forward.

I looked through the window. "He's black," I said, surprised.

"So?" she said.

"Daryl is white—he's his brother?"

"Half-brother," she said. "Momma's never cared what race or religion her lovers were. They just had to be mean. Daryl's father is dead. Supposedly he died of an overdose. The word on the street was Momma had something to do with it. I guess he wasn't mean enough. Leroy's father didn't stick around. No idea where he is but judging by Leroy, he met Momma's criteria for mean."

The man sprawling in the chair was small and wiry. Daryl was a big man, so somehow I'd expected Leroy would have been similar. The voices were too low to hear until Pat reached over and turned a knob on the wall. Then they came through so clear it felt like being in the room.

A middle aged detective was talking. He was a burly guy, the kind who made you wonder if he'd played pro ball or at least semi-pro. He was hunched over a notepad, leaning forward, his hand wrapped around the pen like a bear paw holding a twig. "You have the right . . ."

"Yeah, yeah, yeah," Leroy sneered. He had a voice the color of a wet paper bag with a crinkly surface that was shiny in places.

"You want an attorney?" the detective said.

"Harry, Harry," Leroy said. "Your mama didn't raise no fucking geniuses. Every time you bring me in here, you tell me the same thing, and I tell you the same thing. Get an attorney, and you might as well roll up your money and smoke it. Last fucker charged me twenty thousand dollars for a case never went to trial, no thanks to him. No, I don't want an attorney. Until you have something worth paying for, I never want an attorney."

"Well, I have a solution to this problem, Leroy. You could save yourself a lot of money by pleading guilty now and then."

"Save you a lot of time and money if you just let me be. I'll make you a deal. I won't come down to the police station and bother you, and you stay out of the hood and don't be bothering me. Save you playing the fool with all those charges you can't do nothing with." He looked at his Rolex. "You ain't nearly as pretty as my date tonight. You better say whatever it is you got to say."

"OK, let's talk about Roosevelt and Sissy Harper."

"Who?"

"Your cousin Roosevelt and his four-year-old daughter. Forgot your cousin already? Forgot killing the two of them?"

"Man, that was all a long time ago. That what you got me down here for? What is this? Cold case week?"

"There's no statute of limitations on murder," the detective said, "and we never give up on those cases. Besides," he added, "we've got reason to be revisiting it. You never know where help is going to be coming from these days."

Leroy snorted. "You need all the help you can get. What kind of 'help' you think you got?"

"How long since you seen Daryl?"

"Daryl? Daryl's my man. You ain't been talking to Daryl."

"Daryl's in a state where they can put him away for life, Leroy. It's called civil commitment. Do you really think he's willing to do life to save your skinny butt?"

"What's he doing?" I turned to Pat. "What are you doing?"

"Sh . . . " she said. "They'll hear you."

Leroy just sat for a moment. "Dream on, bro," he said. "The product you're smoking has been cut with something. You want the real stuff you need a more reliable source."

"Why would I make it up?" Harry said. "You know, Leroy, once he starts talking, who knows what he would say? In fact, once he talks about anything, he might as well talk about everything. The more the better because at that point he is going to definitely going to want you in jail for one hundred and fifty years. Immunity for him; life for you. Sounds like a deal Daryl could live with. Sounds like a deal we could live with. You, however—you'd be up shit creek."

Leroy didn't reply, unless the reply was in his stillness. Then, he said, "So you're hoping you can get him to talk, but you've been wishing and hoping to get something on me for the last twenty years. I guess your hoping and wishing won't do me no harm."

"If we're hoping, Leroy, if we're wishing and dreaming and scrambling and holding nothing but our dicks, how come someone's here from Washington State right now, looking into this. Someone who talked to Daryl in the prison. How come, Leroy?"

"And you're telling me this out of what? The goodness of your heart?"

The detective leaned back and crossed his arms. "Door's open, Leroy. Nothing's been signed. You want to hand over Daryl? We'll take the best offer we get."

I'd heard enough. I stalked out of the room, and Pat

145

Humphrey followed me. My heart was thudding in my ears. I didn't slow down or say anything until I got to the conference room where I'd left the records.

"You're putting this thing into play already," I said, furious. "You don't even know a plea bargain is possible and you certainly haven't gotten Daryl to agree to it. You haven't even gotten me or Robert to agree to it."

"You don't know about Robert," she said.

"I know about me," I said. "I know I haven't agreed to anything. You decided, didn't you, you'd try to shake up Leroy no matter what. Maybe cause Leroy to get suspicious of Daryl, drive a wedge between them? What are you thinking, that if Leroy bought it and went after Daryl, Daryl would testify in retaliation, plea bargain or no?" Pat just stood, leaning against a wall with her arms crossed. Neither of us spoke as I put away all the papers I'd been looking at. Finally I got control of my anger.

"If you want my help with anything, anything at all, then I want all the information on the case, and that includes talking to the officers who did the initial investigation. There were two, a man and a woman."

"I can't see any reason you need to talk with them. It's been twelve years. Everything's in the records."

"Everything's never in the records, you know that. Do you have some issue with my talking with them?"

"Mac Robinson is still on the force. You can talk to him."

"And the female officer isn't?"

"I didn't say that. Mandy Johnson's still around, but Mac is the one you want to talk to."

"And why is that?"

"He'll have better information."

"And exactly why can't I talk to both of them and make up my own mind?" I asked.

"I'd rather you leave her out of it."

"Because . . .?"

She shrugged as though it was no big deal. I had a strong feeling it was. Mandy Johnson was persona non grata on this case. I wished I knew why. It was clear Pat wasn't going to tell me.

I went back to packing up. No point in going round and round about it. When I looked up, Pat was gone.

Walking down the corridor on my way out, I hardly noticed a man leaning over the water cooler until he stood up, and I realized it was Leroy Collins. The interview must be over, and he too was leaving. He glanced at me briefly, did a double take, and just stared as I walked toward him. As I started to pass, he stepped in front of me.

"Tall, skinny, red hair with a braid down her back. Oh yeah, you're the one."

I stopped short. "Excuse me," I said.

"You're the one who went to see Daryl. He told me about you. So you're the one down here stirring up all this trouble. Daryl was right about you."

"I don't know what Daryl said, Mr. Collins," I replied. "but I am a psychologist retained by the State of Washington to do a civil commitment evaluation of your brother, nothing more."

"Oh, yeah, and what has any of that got to do with Sissy Harper?"

I opened my mouth to give an answer and then shut it when I realized I didn't have one.

"Some people just got to meddle. They just can't rest until they've gotten everybody all stirred up. You know anybody like that?" His voice was low, like a cat purring, and it just seemed to glide toward me. It sounded eerily like Daryl Collins's when he leaned across the table. "Now you've gotten all of these fine folk all hot and bothered over something that's been done and over with a long time ago."

"Mr. Collins," I said, "I'm sure you don't mean to be blocking my way. Please move."

Leroy stepped out of my path and then said softly as I walked down the corridor, the words hissing after me, curling around my neck and sliding over my face. "You messing with Trash now. I be seeing you."

chapter 14

T hat night I swam in easy, rhythmic strokes back and forth across the hotel swimming pool. There were no pools on Blackbeard's Isle, and although spring was breaking, the water was still too cold to swim. I missed swimming badly in the winter. Summer for me meant that I could wade out in the surf, paddle past the breakers and roll into the gentle rhythm of the swells. I would swim lazily parallel to the beach as long as I felt like it and then hike back.

A hotel pool wasn't much compared to that, but still it was enough to calm me. More than anything, gliding through water seemed to restore a sense of order to my soul, a sort of harmony to my overworked senses.

I was making my regular turn at the end of the pool when I heard a noise and looked up to see four-inch stiletto heels standing on the edge of the pool. For a moment I wanted to put my head back in the water and just keep going. It wouldn't have worked. I had only briefly met Pat Humphrey, but I was pretty sure she wasn't going gently into any good night.

It hardly seemed fair to me. The day was over and whatever was done was done. I didn't want to talk about it. I didn't want to analyze it, apologize for it, accept an apology, obsess over it, or even think about it. I just wanted to swim.

I climbed out of the pool, took off my goggles and bathing cap. "How do you stand that?" Pat said. "I hate swimming. I'm cold, I'm blind, and I'm wet." I looked back at the pool longingly.

"Well," I said, reluctantly turning around. "I guess it's a good thing you're not in there." I picked up my towel and walked over to a table and chairs and sat down.

"What's up?" I said.

She sat down across from me and lounged back in the chair. "I shouldn't have sprung that on you," she said. "I don't know why I didn't tell you first. I wasn't thinking."

"OK," I said.

There was silence. "That's all?" she said. "Just 'OK'?"

How many professions could there be, I thought, where someone could be like this and not be killed? Thank God for the legal profession. Give me your abrasive, your hostile, your diplomacy-impaired yearning to be top gun. But did her children even speak to her?

"Pat," I said, "I wasn't happy with what you did and I wasn't happy with myself for blowing up at you. But it's the end of the day and I'm tired. Why are you here? Did you really come here just to say you're sorry, or do you have something else on your mind?"

She looked out at the empty pool. "All right," she said. "Don't get Mandy Johnson involved in anything to do with this case—for her sake. Believe me, you won't be doing her any favors. Here," she said, reaching in her handbag and taking out a slip of paper and handing it to me. "Here's Mac

Robinson's office number. Talk to him. He was her partner. If he wants to tell you anymore about her, that's up to him."

The next morning I left a phone message for Mac Robinson and went back to the office to go over the case files. Mercifully, Pat Humphrey didn't show up, and I spent the morning working through the reams of material. I didn't learn anything new and was beginning to wonder what I was doing. None of this seemed to have anything to do with whether or not Daryl Collins fit the criteria for civil commitment. Lunchtime was approaching, and I was debating whether I should just pack it in and go to the airport early when Robinson called.

"Pat Humphrey gave me your number. I'm from Washington State, and we're looking to see if Daryl Collins fits our criteria for civil commitment statute as a sexual predator. I don't know if you know about civil commitment . . . "

"I'm familiar with it," he said. His voice was salmon colored, maybe a little creamier than salmon, with a very smooth, warm surface.

"He raped a staff member while in prison, so potentially he qualifies."

"So why do you want to talk to me?"

"The Sissy Harper case."

"We never got Daryl for that."

"I know, and I'm thinking right now it's a dead end, but I saw something in the files about it, and I was down here anyway, so I thought I'd check it out. Do you mind talking to me about it?"

He had appointments all afternoon, but said he'd be at the Y playing basketball over lunch, and if I could meet him there, he'd stop early and talk to me.

I walked over. Spring was further along in Dallas than

North Carolina, and all along the way flowers were in full bloom. Already it was getting warm enough that you could feel the heat of the coming summer gathering strength. Dallas had a powerful summer, the heat pulsating off the sidewalk in shock waves and beating up in your face like blows.

The lady at the desk directed me to the gym where the police played at lunchtime. A full-court game was in progress so I sat down to watch. A couple of subs sitting were sitting on the bleachers so I asked them who Mac Robinson was, and they pointed him out.

He was just under six feet and stocky with a body type that reminded me of Mandy. He was shirtless, and although he looked to be in his forties, he had abs that were washboard-hard. He had a knee brace on one knee, testimony to his style of play.

He wasn't the tallest player on the court or the most skilled. His was a playground shot that showed no evidence of coaching, and most of his shots missed. Nonetheless, he was my kind of player because he out-hustled everyone on the court. He played like a bulldog, charging for every rebound, beating everybody down the court, following his man tenaciously. He was dripping with sweat when he came off.

"Copen?" he said, walking up to me.

I held out my hand. "Breeze," I said. "Thanks for talking with me."

He sat down. "Let me catch my breath. I'm too old for this shit."

"I was thinking you looked pretty good. What happened to your knee?"

"ACL last year. Man, what a pain. Took me six months to rehab it. It's still not one hundred percent. Anyway, what can I do for you?"

"Like I said, I'm doing an evaluation of Daryl Collins. He doesn't have that much of a track record as a sex offender, and he comes up short of civil commitment, but nobody really wants to let him out.

"So, my question is, did you have anything at all that tied Daryl Collins to the Sissy Harper murder? It's not just a murder, it's a rape, so it's relevant to civil commitment."

He took a long speculative look at me and I wondered why. He took way too long to answer.

"I called Mandy before I came. She said she'd talked to you," he said.

"A little," I said. "Pat Humphrey doesn't seem to want her on the case."

"She wouldn't," he said. "Did you tell her Mandy talked to you?"

"No, Mandy asked me not to."

"Mandy and I were partners for five years," he said. "We're still friends. I wouldn't want to see her get in any trouble." I wasn't sure how anything he said to me about the case would get her into trouble.

"I don't know what any of this is about," I said. "Clearly, some kind of politics are going on here that I don't know anything about. I don't have any reason to get anybody in trouble, but I wouldn't mind knowing more about what's going on because then it would be easier to know what I could say. Frankly, Pat and I didn't hit it off that well, and I don't know if I'm going to get any kind of truthful answer out of her about anything."

He snorted. "Pat's not often accused of lying," he said.

"I don't mean . . ."

"Don't worry about it," he said. "I just mean she tends to be a little too up front."

"This thing isn't just some kind of personality clash between the two of them, is it?"

"No," he said. "It's got nothing to do with that."

"So . . ."

"All I'll say is we did and we didn't have stuff that tied Daryl to the murder. We didn't have any evidence, but we did have some reason," he said carefully, "to think Daryl had a motivation for wanting Roosevelt dead. A strong motivation."

I thought about that. Nobody had told me any specific reason Daryl might want Roosevelt dead. Just that they were dealing together.

"You mean the drug dealing."

"More than that," he said. "Stronger than that. It doesn't matter. Like I said, we never turned up any physical evidence."

"Does this thing, this reason Leroy had for wanting Roosevelt dead, does this have anything to do with Mandy?" I asked.

He turned and stared at me for a moment. I didn't know why. I was just fishing, trying to make sense of all this.

"You might say that," he said finally.

"So why don't they want Mandy on the case?" I asked.

"She got a little carried away," he replied and turned to stare back at the court. Just by the look on his face, I knew he wouldn't say anything more.

The next morning I was packing and getting ready to go down to the lobby when the phone rang. "Dr. Copen," the clerk said, "your ride is here."

"What ride?" I said. "I didn't order a cab."

"It's not a cab. It's a limousine. Just a minute," he said something away from the phone. "Courtesy of the attorney general's office."

So Pat was sorry. Probably she was making amends because she wanted something. I just hoped she wasn't in the car and riding with me to the airport. I finished packing and went downstairs. A black man with unusually large shoulders and a small waist was waiting. He took my bag and walked out to the car. "Which airline?" he said, taking my bag.

"Northwest," I said, and he held the door while I got in. I felt uneasy suddenly and wondered why as he walked around the car. When he climbed in, I saw a long, curved scar on the back of his neck and it came together. Pat couldn't have sent a limousine. Government auditors would never clear anything like that. And real limousine drivers didn't have the physique he had, and they didn't sport crescent-shaped scars that yelled knife fight on their necks. I started to get out of the car, but the door was locked from the front and I couldn't. I froze for a minute trying to think what to do when the car pulled away.

I could feel the blood rising to my head. I did not have much time. Not at all. He was picking up speed and God knows where I'd end up. I knew, better than most people, that there would be absolutely nothing I could do at the other end. I said to the driver, "I'm sorry. I'm feeling sick. Can you stop the car?"

He glanced back. "Traffic's bad today. Can't stop now, or I won't get you there in time. Just sit back and relax. We'll be at the airport shortly."

I leaned over so my head was behind the seat and put my finger down my throat. I started gagging and throwing up. I turned my head so it went all over the seat. Thank God I'd breakfast. At the sound of my throwing up, the driver hit the brakes and jumped out. He threw open the back door and said, "Shit, look what you've done to my car." I jumped out, bent double, my pocketbook still on my shoulder, my bag left inside. He moved out of the way to let me by, and I ran over to the curb as though I was going to be sick again. He turned back to stare at the vomit on the seat, and I took off running. Fortunately, I travel in jeans and sneakers.

He turned and yelled and started to come after me. The sound of footsteps only followed me for a few feet though, before stopping. We were in the middle of downtown Dallas, and I guess he didn't want to make a scene. I didn't even slow down or look back. I ran a block, cut down a side street, ran into a building big enough to have multiple exits, came out a different one on a different street, wove through more streets, and ran several more blocks,. Finally I stopped and looked back. I didn't see the driver or the car anywhere. My hands were shaking, and now I really was feeling nauseous. I pulled out my cell phone and called Pat Humphrey.

She hadn't sent a limousine.

"Why?" I said. Pat had sent a police car to pick me up, and now I was sitting in her tenth story office still feeling shaky. Pat was behind a massive desk that would have done the CEO of Coca-Cola proud. "Even in Leroy's sick world, I couldn't have offended him enough to wack me out of revenge. And he has to know that if he killed me, it wouldn't stop the civil commitment process. They'd just assign someone else."

Pat was sitting at her desk nervously tapping a pencil. She had worry lines on her forehead, and her face seemed thinner and paler than it had the day before. "I can't understand it," she said. "He's never gone after anybody in the criminal justice system before. What the fuck is he doing? Describe that scar again."

I did. She shook her head, picked up the phone, dialed a

number and then waited. She spoke with a detective named Roger for a few minutes, and then hung up. "Armor," she said.

"What?"

"A guy named Armor has a scar like that. It's just what it looks like, a souvenir from a knife fight. And yeah, he's one of Leroy's boys. I don't know him, but Roger says he's worked for Leroy for the past couple of years."

"I'm still stuck on why," I said.

"Because he feels like it?" Pat said. "Because he's getting crazier? Because we can't lay a finger on him no matter what he does? How the fuck would I know?"

She seemed brittle and upset. I hadn't heard her curse once the day before, and it was a little disconcerting. She took a deep breath. "This has to do with Sissy Harper's murder," she said. "I can feel it in my bones. That's when we got a rise out of Leroy. When you came down here and we started asking questions about Sissy.

"Maybe it's a good thing," she said thoughtfully. "Maybe it means we're on to something. Maybe he knows something is out there, and that's worrying him. Maybe he just wants to know what you know about it."

I rolled my eyes. I couldn't see how Leroy trying to kidnap me and God knows what else could be a good thing, no matter how much it helped Pat. She saw me. "Go home, Breeze," she said. "I'll have an officer take you to the airport and stay with you until the next plane leaves. You should be fine after that. Here you're a liability to us, and it's a risk to you."

"Just think," I said, "what if he murdered me and you got him for that. Wouldn't that be grand?"

"Leave us some physical evidence, would you?" she said dryly. "Good solid evidence. We'd sure appreciate it." She didn't crack a smile.

chapter **15**

The plane lifted off the ground and into a hard blue enamel sky with white cotton stretched thin across it. The clouds looked shredded, against a sky unrelenting and all too sure of itself.

What had Pat done to me when she lied to Leroy?

In a weird way I understood it. Pat knew what the public didn't know, that she couldn't get Leroy playing by the rules. Playing by the rules she'd end up with more dead grocers with disabled wives. So she tried to get creative. The only thing I really faulted Pat for was that she had underestimated Leroy's capacity for violence. Given all that she had seen of him over the years, that was unforgivable.

I spent the long drive from Raleigh to Cedar going over and over the limousine attempt. I wanted to give myself some credit for getting out of it, but really I just felt like an idiot for getting in the car in the first place. And what would I do if something like that happened again? It would be more violent and more sure the next time. Leroy would have learned his lesson and he'd skip the fancy ploys. I told myself it wouldn't happen. I was a victim of convenience because I was in Dallas. If I laid low and stayed out of Leroy's sight, the whole thing should die down, and there wouldn't be a next time.

The house was quiet when I came in, and I was so relieved to be back in my own world, I felt like crying. Betsy was a welcome sight sitting on the living room couch in a tank top and hip-hugger jeans, reading quietly, her red toenails propped up on a pillow.

"Hi," I said, "where's Lily?"

"Miss Lily's in her room listening to music," Betsy said. "She's got her headphones on. Have a good trip?" Betsy looked remarkably unscathed.

"Pretty bizarre," I said. "How was it around here?"

"We did OK," Betsy said.

"Just OK?"

"Well, that's sort of averaging it out. I did fine."

"And Lily?"

"Well, this whole thing is just flushing her down the toilet, that's all."

"I know school is a shock," I said. "It's too small."

"Oh, Breeze, honey," Betsy said. "It's not just the size. She fits in that school pretty much like a vampire would. All these kids have known each other since they were preschoolers. Their families all know each other. Plus she's got green hair and she's pierced and there isn't anybody here who looks like that. It's not just the clothes. I know you think that, but it's everything about her. All four people in her class treat her like she's a freak. And that's not even the big thing."

"Jeez," I said, "what do you mean? What's the big thing?"

"Have you noticed any mail from her mother?"

"Mail? She's expecting mail?"

"Breeze, God bless you. Yes, mail. She's heard zip from her mother."

"Well, her mother's . . . "

"Going to work every day where she could write a post-card and send it to her daughter."

"Doesn't she get it? Her mother's spaced out and beat up. I doubt she can find her car in the parking lot. She probably can't remember what it looks like. She isn't functional. She's probably brain damaged. That's the truth."

"She's her mother," Betsy said firmly, "and Lily misses her."

I thought for a minute. "Betsy . . ." I started. "I don't know how to do this. I am not a mother. I'm never going to be one. You understand this kid a lot better than I do. I feel like I need you in the house to translate when I ask her what she wants for breakfast. Do you think . . . ?"

"Sorry," Betsy snorted. "Wouldn't work."

"Why not?" I persisted. "I could move my stuff out of the room in your house, if that's it. She could go to school on the mainland. You've got a real regional high school. Not to mention you're bored out of your mind . . . "

"Darlin'," she said, "You're the only connection she has with her mother. She isn't leaving, no matter what."

"I'm a hell of a connection," I said. "I've seen her once in twenty years."

"I don't know what was said in that house," Betsy said slowly, "but I think she believes that sooner or later her mother will check in with you—not with her, but with you. And she wants to be there when she does."

I was startled. "With me?" I said. "What about Lily? She's going to check in with Lily a lot sooner than she checks in with me."

"Maybe," she said. "but Lily doesn't think so and we'll just have to see."

"See what?"

"Who knows her better—you or Lily."

The next morning I got a call from Robert Giles. Leroy Collins hadn't wasted any time calling Daryl.

"I hear Texas was interesting," he said.

"If you think throwing up in the backseat of a limousine is interesting," I said.

"It worked," he replied. "What'd you think of Pat?"

"I think they have to muzzle her between cases."

"Pat wants to be a judge," Robert said.

"Death row will double," I said. "What's the phrase, 'takes no prisoners'? How about 'shoots the wounded and their relatives, too'?"

"Now, now," he said, "she's a very able prosecutor. I think some of the only cases she's lost have been Leroy Collins. She's got a remarkable track record."

"For what?" I said. "Asking for the death penalty on traffic warrants?"

"We could go on," Robert said, "but I have something a little more pressing." He paused like he wasn't sure how to say what he wanted to say, or maybe he just didn't want to say it.

"What?" I said, suddenly anxious. "What's happened?"

"Nothing's happened," he said. "Not really. Not yet," he said.

"Robert . . ."

"Leroy called Daryl this morning. Pat had called me and warned me about that little stunt she pulled, and we thought Leroy might try to contact Daryl, so we had Daryl's calls monitored. We were thinking perhaps one of them would say something incriminating. We live in hope."

"What?" I said.

"In any case," Robert said, ignoring me. "Leroy called Daryl, and he was careful. He didn't say anything that you could take to court though it wasn't hard to make sense of. I have a transcript I can send you, but I'll just give you the gist of it now. Leroy asked Daryl if he had decided to play ball up there, maybe talk to some folks at the prison.

"Daryl said he wasn't playing ball with anybody. Leroy said he'd like to believe that, but he'd been rousted, and something was brewing about a cousin of theirs. He wanted to know how the Washington State people knew anything at all about it, if he wasn't playing ball.

"Daryl said the only thing he knew was what he told him already, that a psychologist had come up and asked him about Sissy. He said that was it, everything. He swore it didn't come from him, no way; it was the first he'd heard of it. He said maybe somebody had turned up."

"Somebody had turned up?" I asked.

"That's what he said," Robert replied.

"What's he talking about?"

"I was hoping you might know," Robert said and then went on. "Anyway, Leroy said that was possible though surprising, and he'd have to find out what was going on. He said the whole thing should have been taken care of a long time ago, and if it had been, it wouldn't be a problem now.

"Daryl said it wasn't his fault. He just caught a bullshit charge. Leroy got on his case again about 'not taking care of business,' and then he said he'd met a friend of Daryl's in Dallas but had just missed out on talking to her. He thought he'd have better luck next time.

"Next time?"

"That's what he said."

"Then what?"

"Daryl said that it better be soon because this whole civil commitment thing was coming up. And Leroy told him not to worry."

"That was it?"

"That was it."

"What's he talking about?"

"Pat doesn't know, but it fits with the limousine business. All joking aside, why didn't you call me, Breeze? That was a very close call."

"What could you do about it?" I said, my stomach sinking as my head replayed what Robert had told me. "Oh boy, I've stepped into something, haven't I?"

"Breeze, I think, well, I think, you should maybe take a vacation. I wouldn't go to a relative's. I think you should go someplace you don't usually go. Probably drive. I wouldn't fly. I'd drive and I'd take cash with you and not use your credit cards. At least for a while."

"Robert, I don't mean to sound disrespectful, but this is a thug. How smart can he be?"

"He has attorneys, people working for him who are smart enough," Robert said. "He can hire investigators as well as anybody else can. I wouldn't count on his waiting for you to go back to Dallas, Breeze. He knows that's not likely to happen. He could spend a lot of money on finding you and it might be worth it to him. He thinks you're the key to whatever is going on."

"Robert, I live at the end of the world. You said so yourself. Where would I go?"

"Oh, I'd think Africa, Asia. I wouldn't fool around."

"Hard to drive there."

"Alaska, then."

"You're serious."

"I had a long conversation with Pat this morning. She seemed shaken by what's come of this, and she wanted to make sure I had an appreciation for the destructive powers of Leroy Collins. She said every single witness who has been willing to testify against him has disappeared. Not to mention that he's also killed prostitutes who work for him, a girlfriend who tried to leave him, and, of course, anybody who might be a rival. She's kicking herself for not thinking he might go after you, but he's never tried to hit a cop or a judge or anybody in the justice system."

"What about this idea of hers to plea bargain the civil commitment?"

"Can't be done. It isn't legal; besides, the timing's all wrong. We have to file on Collins by ninety days before his release. Even if he agreed to testify, the trial wouldn't come up for a couple of years. So once we don't file for civil commitment and he's released, what would make him keep his word and testify? Once he's released, we can't go back and file."

"You actually considered this."

"Just as a mental exercise. Like I said, it isn't legal. Which means, of course, you couldn't put it in writing and there we are again   what would make him keep his word and testify if it wasn't in writing?"

I didn't say it again but it was obvious he had considered it.

"So let me sum up where we are," I said. "You have a friend who happens to be a very gung ho prosecutor who gets carried away at times—right or wrong."

"Right."

"And she had an idea to plea bargain civil commitment up in Washington State in exchange for Daryl's testimony on Sissy Harper in Texas, an idea she got when she heard there was something in the files about Daryl and the girl. Right?"

"Right."

"Which sounded like it might work to her because he could

essentially do life on the civil commitment and she thought he'd sell out his mother, not to mention his brother, to avoid that.

"However, everything happens to be wrong with that idea, which no longer matters because she jumped the gun and threatened him with nothing to back it up, just hoping that either you and I would go along with it or, at the very least, she'd precipitate a falling out among thieves. She was stirring the pot, seeing what would happen, right? She was hoping Leroy would take it seriously and make some kind of move on Daryl or at least get on Daryl's case to the point that he would feel threatened and testify in self-defense."

"Probably."

"But he made a move on me instead. Probably to get information about what was going on."

"So it seems."

"So now he and Daryl are still together and looking at me as the one who can tell them what the police have found out about Sissy Harper. And then there's something about somebody turning up—I don't think they meant me—and we don't know at all what that means."

I'd been sprawled on the couch reading when the call came in, and now I glanced up at the ceiling while I tried to think what to do about this. Lily was out and the house was silent, and the moment seemed to stall out like a motor dying. I felt tired and the whole conversation felt futile. The ceiling was an off white with a textured surface and I just seemed to get lost in it. There wasn't anything to be done about this. It was what it was.

"Breeze?" Robert said.

"I'm thinking," I said, but I wasn't. I wasn't doing anything except staring at the ceiling.

"I can't go, Robert," I said finally. "I just can't."

And truly I couldn't. I'd already torn Lily out of her school, taken her away from whatever support she was getting from her friends. She was barely starting over. I couldn't do it to her all over again.

Besides, if Betsy was right, she wouldn't go. She was spending her days waiting to hear from her mother, and if we went on the lam, her mother couldn't find us. And I felt the same way. In the back of my mind, I had some fantastic hope that Jena would decide at some point to leave. I had Lily. If she left, this is where she'd come, but not if we were gone.

"It's complicated. I've got a friend's daughter who is staying here while my friend is going through . . . a bad time. I need to be where she can find us."

"Breeze, whatever is going on," he said, "this is . . ."

"Anyway, it's scarier to be on the run," I said. "On the run I wouldn't have any support. I wouldn't know the police in the places I was at. I wouldn't have neighbors who could keep an eye out. Nothing would be familiar. Here at least I know everybody. I know the home turf better than he does. It would be like giving away home court advantage." I didn't mention that we were moving into tourist season and about twenty thousand people I didn't know were about to show up. Still it was true, I felt safer at home.

Robert let out a breath and then said very slowly and clearly, "This is a mistake, Breeze. You can't just sit at home and wait for Leroy Collins to show up. You may feel safer, but you aren't safer. From everything Pat's said, he's aggressive and proactive. And his methods for getting information out of people are horrific. At least come stay with me. You and the girl."

Something inside me caught at that. I closed my eyes and saw a thick, woven rope connecting me and Robert. I'd never seen it before and didn't know it was there.

"Maybe for a visit when it's over, Robert. What's the point of putting you at risk, too?"

"This isn't a good conversation," Robert said. "I keep thinking I'm going to be remembering this conversation later, thinking there was something else I should have said or done."

"I don't see what. It doesn't have anything to do with you, Robert. I hear you. I just don't think I'd be better off on the road."

In truth, my argument sounded weak, even to me. I don't know why more people won't leave home when they know the Nazis are coming. You could see the sense of it logically. Nonetheless, more than anything else at that moment, I did not want to be living in motels, eating restaurant food and glancing warily at every stranger. Traveling brought its own anxieties, and I couldn't imagine adding to them the paranoia of knowing I was being stalked. Everything in my gut told me to stay, make my stand here, and let whatever was going to happen, happen.

Maybe Robert didn't agree, but he heard the finality in my voice. After a moment's pause he said, "Take care, Red," and hung up.

I went down to the sea that night while Lily was doing her homework, down to the beach closest to Charlie's shack. It was where Charlie hung out most and I wanted to see him though I didn't know why. I found him sitting on a driftwood tree trunk and whittling what looked like a small boat. There were no lights on the water this time and the sky was clear. The sea was still, and I felt at peace standing on the beach in the moonlight. The light was bright enough to see the calluses on Charlie's hands as he worked, and for a moment I just watched him whittle. He didn't speak or look at me.

"Well, Charlie," I said, more to myself than him; "you were right. A snake's coming up on me."

Charlie didn't look up.

"What's going to come of it, I wonder?" I said. Charlie didn't answer. I didn't really expect him to. Talking to Charlie was more like thinking out loud than having a conversation.

I sighed and sat down on the beach.

For a moment he kept whittling, then he spoke. "Weren't no different then and now," he said. He stopped his whittling and looked out to sea. "There'd be the chase and the first shot and then it was all fire and lead and the blood under your feet so thick you'd slip in it. You could hear the Cap'n yelling over it all with smoke all around his face, like Satan himself. He'd tuck fuses under his hat and the ends hanging down with the pigtails of his beard. He'd set the fuses afire, you know, to put the fear of the devil in them. I seen grown men drop their swords just at the sight of the smoke curling round his face and those eyes of his cutting through you. He put the fear in men so bad they couldn't speak or move.

"But nothing scared him. Nobody or nothing. I don't rightly think he knew what fear was, a thing to feel, that is. Oh, he knew what it looked like—he seen it often enough. And he knew the power of it. Said it were worth a hundred men to him, to have the enemy pissing their pants at the sight of him."

"I think I've met someone like him," I said.

He looked back down at his boat and started whittling again. "You ain't met nobody like the Cap'n," he said. "A man can't be beat that don't know fear. Your snake's a mean one, but he knows fear."

"You could have fooled me," I said.

Charlie said nothing at all and we just sat there, while Charlie whittled and I watched the sea.

chapter **16**

The house felt empty with Breeze gone down to the beach. Thank God for the computer. With no TV Lily thought she'd go bonkers living with just Breeze who was usually up on the balcony in a rocker or sitting out under a tree. Doing what? She didn't even have a book most of the time. Breeze didn't talk much more than her mother did, but her quietness was different. Breeze had a light in her eyes that her mother didn't have, and she didn't have a total asshole like Jerry living in her house. Still, she could see how Breeze and her mother could have been friends. There was something about each of them that reminded her of the other.

A gong told her she had a new message, and she closed the one she was reading to see who the new message was from. When she saw the address of the sender, her chest tightened up so much she couldn't seem to catch her breath. Jena24@hot mail.com. Did her mother really have an e-mail address? It had never dawned on her she might. She had never seen her mom on the computer at home. Maybe she had one at work.

ANNA SALTER

She couldn't bring herself to open it. Why was it so hard? It was dumb that she couldn't do it. She opened two e-mails from her friends instead. She read the first one three times before she understood what it said, and as soon as she closed it, she couldn't remember any of it. Some silly shit about a boy at school.

Why couldn't she open the e-mail? What did she think her mother was going to say? It was probably the same old bullshit. Probably she just wanted Breeze's e-mail address. How had she even come up with Lily's? Probably from her friends. She reached for the mouse.

The lines seemed to punch at her. "Hi, I'm wondering how you're doing. I miss you. Are you in school? Are things OK? I love you. Mom. PS Don't tell anyone I'm writing. I want to keep this just between us."

Her breath slipped out and she realized she'd been holding it. She read the words again, "I love you. Mom." And then she reread them. She read the e-mail so many times she felt foolish, even though there was nobody else around to see her doing it.

Finally, she closed down the e-mail and got up. Without thinking, she found she'd gone into her room. She lay down on the bed, then decided she hadn't read the e-mail right and got up and went back to the computer, feeling panicky on the way. She'd better not be making this up. But the e-mail hadn't changed.

She went back to her room with a restless energy running wildly through her. She picked up a magazine, and thought, what a crock. It was all stupid stuff, and she couldn't find anything she wanted to read. Finally she just held it and didn't notice when she put it down. She got up and walked back to the computer. Suddenly she saw herself as someone else might see her and didn't open up the e-mail again, just stared at the screen. The whole thing was stupid. She'd turned into some kind of dork. Already she'd read the thing a dozen times. She was acting like a baby wandering around the house like—duh. Just because her mother wrote a stupid note. She tried to take a deep breath, but her chest felt tight and hurt, like she had the flu. She heard Breeze's car pull into the driveway, and she closed the e-mail and hurried back into her room.

No way was she talking to Breeze tonight. Breeze was clueless but not dumb. She'd know something had happened if she saw her. Besides, she had to think how to answer the e-mail. She felt that surge of panic again. What if her mother expected her to write back right away and she'd blown it? That couldn't be. Her mother wouldn't know she'd gotten it yet.

What was she supposed to say? She started composing e-mails in her mind. "Hi, Mom, I'm fine. School's a drag . . ." but then what? Wait a minute, should she even say she was fine? It wasn't true. This town was awful. She felt like she was marooned on a desert island. And besides, if she said she was fine, maybe her mom would think she should leave her here. Should she say she wanted to go home? Really, she didn't if Jerry was still there. She definitely couldn't tell her mom to get rid of Jerry. She wouldn't do it and asking would make her mother feel guilty.

Her mind drifted back to the time her mom had said they would leave, and they packed all their things. They just sat in the living room as it got later and later, closer to the time he'd be back. She'd started crying and begging her mother to go, but she just sat there until he came home. She closed her eyes and forced the memory back in the small box she kept the worst of them in. Like the one where he was burning her mother with lit cigarettes and her mother was making that noise—the night she called Breeze. She pushed that one back in the box, too. Sometimes it took a lot of energy, keeping everything down in that box. Thinking about the e-mail was a lot better.

She decided she couldn't say school was a drag—it would sound like she was whining. That was the quickest way to get her mother to go away. Her mother hated it when she whined. So she couldn't say everything was great, and she couldn't say everything was a drag. Where did that leave her?

Maybe things would be different on e-mail. A lot of kids said things on e-mail they couldn't say face to face. Maybe her mom would be like that. She started composing scenarios in her head. She and her mother would become close over e-mail, and one day her mother would show up to pick her up. She would have left that loser behind and . . . then what?

Well, they could live on the mainland where she could go to a bigger school, and they'd still be close enough to see Breeze and Betsy. She imagined the house, a cool house, really big with enough room for her friends to come and visit. And Betsy would come and take her for rides on the Harley, and she could go visit Breeze when she wanted to. She imagined what it would feel like to have well, like two aunts and a mother, but she couldn't. She'd be lucky if she ever even saw her mother again. She'd probably never get to live with her.

What if Betsy had been her mother? Or more like it, if her mother had been just a little bit like Betsy, enough not to take any guff from anybody. Betsy wouldn't let anyone hit her. She would have thrown that bastard out. Breeze, too. Still she didn't want Betsy for a mom or Breeze. She didn't think about them when she went to sleep at night, and she didn't cry like a stupid baby missing them.

She wondered what Breeze would think if she knew it was her, Lily's, fault that her mom was married to that asshole. That was definitely not something to think about. She pushed the thought back the way she'd learned to push the memories back—way, way back down in the box until they were so far away she couldn't even remember what they were.

Better to figure out what to say to Mom. She shouldn't wait forever to reply. She didn't want her mother to think she didn't want to hear from her. She'd have to say something that didn't upset her mother, that kept her writing. It was hard, getting the right tone. Something cheerful but not too cheerful. She had to make it clear she was glad her mom had written, and maybe she needed to act like staying here was just temporary, give her mom the idea.

She thought about Breeze wondering why she hadn't come out of her room. She stuck her head out, told Breeze she was tired, and said she was going to bed. But she didn't go to bed. She sat down at the small desk and wrote out responses. They all seemed dumb, and she kept crossing them out.

She went to bed but couldn't sleep. She kept thinking about the e-mail and finally, she got up after Breeze went to bed and snuck into the dining room where the computer was. She turned it on and then winced at the noise it made starting up. It didn't seem that noisy in the day. She read the e-mail again and then again. She didn't have the words for what she was feeling. It felt like she had something. A few hours ago, she had nothing. She was just a throwaway kid nobody wanted, a kid camping out in somebody's house who didn't particularly want her there. Now she had something. Maybe it wasn't much. Maybe it wouldn't turn out to be anything, but right now it was something.

Mac knocked on the door of Mandy's condo. He turned around while he waited and looked down at the pool in the center of the courtyard. He liked this condo complex, as much for the woods next door as anything. Beau, his dog, had certainly liked it when they had gone there for runs on the weekends when the two of them stayed over. The pool wasn't bad, either, and he remembered lying beside it with Mandy on Sunday mornings. What was it the man said, coffee and oranges and the green freedom of a cockatoo? He'd pass on the cockatoo, but the coffee and oranges sounded right.

The door opened behind him, and he swung around to see Mandy standing there in shorts and a halter top. She was short and compact and probably carried more weight than some men might like. What did they know? She'd been exuberant in bed, unselfconscious and full of mischief, and she liked to tease him until he couldn't decide if he wanted to fuck her or throttle her. She seemed to know just how far to go and then melted under him with the kind of sweet and joyous surrender that brought heat to his face just thinking about it now. How long had it been? Two years already?

"Hi," he said.

She looked at him steadily for a moment and then said, "Wanna come in?"

"No, I'd as soon stand around in the hall."

She turned and walked in the room. "Don't be like that," she said.

He saw the open suitcase through the door to the bedroom. "You going somewhere?"

"Uh-huh, a beach."

"By yourself?" As soon as he said it, he wished he hadn't. Mandy stopped walking and turned around. "No," she said. "I'm taking an entire troupe of Chippendale male strippers with me."

"I'm sorry," he said. She didn't reply.

He sat down. "No really, I didn't come to fight. I wanted to talk to you about the psychologist who came down from Washington State, what's-her-name." He paused, looking for a way to say what he wanted to say so it wouldn't anger her. He didn't find it. "You're not starting up with this again, are you?"

"You could have called me up to ask me that."

"I didn't want to telephone. Look, if you don't want me here. . . "

Now she sat down with a sigh and sprawled back in the chair, her eyes closed. "My turn to be sorry," she said. "It's good to see you. You look good. Now don't get all gooey on me but I miss you." He didn't know what to say to that, but he knew he'd think about it endlessly.

"Look, you might as well know, Pat's pulled another bonehead. She's got Trash thinking the psychologist who came down has got something on him. He actually tried to snatch her when she was here, if you can believe it. She's back home in North Carolina and rumor is he's going to take his act on the road."

"How do you get all this information?" he asked.

"Pat's secretary works out with me."

Then he put two and two together and said, "You're not . . ."

She grinned wryly. "Yeah, I am. Can't resist."

"For Christ's sake, Mandy," he exploded. "They'll fire you. It was that close last time." He held his finger to his thumb with no measurable distance between them.

"You going to tell them?"

"Right. Why are you doing this? This case is over. Nothing is going to happen. It's done."

"It's not over. It's never going to be over until we nail Sissy's killer. Besides, I'm just going up to keep an eye on the psychologist. I don't want him killing somebody else over this."

He wished then that he smoked or drank or something. He wished he was the kind of man who could backhand her and send her flying and then walk out muttering to himself that she deserved it, and feeling light and righteous with the world. Instead, his stomach started to hurt. Loving Mandy had given him an ulcer worrying about her.

Mandy didn't seem to notice how much it got to him. "You know," she said, "you make one mistake. One stupid, fucking mistake. And it seems it won't end, like some kind of fucking nuclear chain reaction. First there's Roosevelt and then Sissy and probably Crystal, too."

"Who?" he said.

She glanced at him in disbelief. The players were so familiar to her twelve years later that she could hardly believe anyone else didn't know who they were. "Roosevelt's girlfriend," she said, "the one who disappeared when he was killed. And now Leroy's going after somebody else. It's just one long endless chain."

If he said anything at all now, he knew it would be the wrong thing. He'd be back on the trail of lecturing and judging and browbeating that had ended it last time. He sat silently, wishing he hadn't come.

Mandy sighed and rubbed her eyes, then looked at him with something wistful on her face. "We haven't talked for a long time."

"I try to stay away."

"I'm sorry for the way it ended." He shrugged. No doubt she was talking about the night they got drunk together and ended up screaming, each one accusing the other of being the one to fuck things up. But it hadn't ended then. It had ended the night somebody had turned on the gas and left Sissy Harper curled up in an upstairs closet. He just hadn't known it then.

"I'd go another round," he said softly. "Any day."

She shook her head. "Can't do it. Can't even think about it till I finish this case."

But the case wasn't going to finish. If it hadn't finished in twelve years, it never would. He shrugged. There was nothing more to say. He couldn't stop her from going, and he couldn't stand the thought of what would happen to her if she did. They'd fire her for sure this time—that is if Leroy didn't put a bullet in her—and then what?

He could hear kids splashing in the pool down below, and suddenly he felt old and tired. His stomach hurt. His knee had stiffened up from the game the day before. Everything seemed futile and gridlocked, his relationship with Mandy, the case; even his body was falling apart. He'd come here to warn Mandy off the case, but she was way ahead of him. Suitcase packed. Back in it up to her neck. And once she was fired, who knew if she'd even stay in Dallas. Then what? Where would she go? What would she do? Mandy was a born cop. She'd be miserable doing anything except police work. He could see this thing playing out like it was locked in. Here he was right at the start of it and there was nothing he could do.

"Well, I guess I'd better go," he said. "Beau's locked up in the house." He got up and walked to the door but stopped right before he opened it. He'd said it before. Probably he'd say it again.

"Roosevelt was a born snitch, Mandy. If he hadn't been snitching for you, he'd have been snitching for somebody else."

chapter 17

A couple of days after Robert's call, I walked up my driveway one evening and found Mandy Johnson on my doorstep. At first I didn't recognize her. A baseball cap hid her short blond hair and she was sitting in the shadows of the lengthening dusk where I couldn't see her face clearly. She had given me a start, even though her posture was too open and casual to suggest a threat. She didn't get up as I approached, just waited for me. In the silence I could hear cicadas in the woods nearby.

"Mandy?" I said. "What are you doing here?" Looking at the cutoffs, the Nikes, and the T-shirt, I had a feeling it wasn't an official visit.

"I checked in with your daughter," she said, ignoring my question, "but I decided to wait out here. It's just too beautiful to be inside. I've never seen anything like this," she said, gesturing up at the night sky.

"She's not my daughter," I replied. "She's just visiting." I sat down beside her. "You can't really see stars like this in the city. There's too much ambient light."

"Are they always this bright?"

"Pretty much. I guess I've gotten used to it." It was true. In the city you only saw the brightest stars, single dots of light separated by endless space. Here, a thick cloud of glitter filled the sky from horizon to horizon, a shimmering carpet hooding the sky.

I didn't say anything more. I had already asked my question.

After a moment Mandy said, "I thought of not telling you I was here, just keeping an eye on things. Then I figured you'd spot me sooner or later, and if you saw a distant figure on a dune, you might think I was Leroy or somebody he sent. You'd probably shoot me or call the police. If it were me, I'd probably shoot, but you, you'd probably call the police. Then they'd roust me, and it would be a huge hassle."

"Because nobody knows you're here," I finished.

She nodded. "So I decided to come see you and check in," she said. "I have a cottage only a couple of doors down."

"You're here because of Leroy?"

"It sounded to me like you could use a bodyguard," but now her voice had changed. It had lost some of its wiry, thundercloud texture and it was brassier and more scratchy-looking.

"Maybe that's a piece of it," I said. "I'm thinking it's probably not the main reason. At least not the only reason. I'm sure a lot of people need bodyguards, but you don't take off work and fly across half the country to protect them."

She looked straight at me. "So maybe I'm just looking for an excuse to shoot Leroy Collins." She laughed. "Maybe this is part of an elaborate plan I've had for years to rid the earth of that scumbag." Her voice had lost its brassy edge and gone back to normal.

"People ever think you're lying when you're telling the truth and telling the truth when you're lying?" I asked softly.

"Sometimes," she said and then fell silent.

"I'm wondering if I'm better off with you here," I said. "I hate to be so blunt about it, Mandy, but I don't know if you'd be a help or not."

"Why not?" she replied. "Right now, you seem to think denial is a river in Egypt. Your security stinks. That kid—whoever she is—is in there alone where anybody could get to her. The door's unlocked. Nobody's outside keeping an eye on this place. I bet you're not even carrying. I don't think you have a clue who you're dealing with."

The comment about Lily hurt. I hadn't really thought of Lily being in danger. "She's the daughter of a friend, and she's staying with me temporarily. I can't see how she's at risk. She doesn't know anything."

"She could be here very temporarily," Mandy said. "if you don't get your act together. I think she'd better find another friend to stay with for a while."

"He doesn't have any reason to go after her."

"You need a crash course in security," she said, "or maybe psychology. Do you know any faster way to get to an adult than seize their kid? If I thought she was your kid, why wouldn't he?"

I thought about it. She was right. I'd have to send Lily to Betsy's. Probably tomorrow. But Mandy had sidetracked me, and I wanted to get back to the main point.

"You might not be a help because—put bluntly—you're more interested in killing Leroy than helping me. Tell me, Mandy, if you had a chance to prevent him going after me, or you could let it go to the point you had an excuse to kill him, which would you do?"

She didn't answer. "Well," I said. "I don't want any bullets going by my ears. Even snipers miss sometimes."

"I won't miss," she said.

"Why don't they want you on the case?"

"Why is that any of your business?"

"Because you're here. Because I have to figure out if it's a good thing or a bad thing. Because if you won't tell me, I'll have to call Pat Humphrey and ask her the same question. I think she'd tell me about it if I told her you were here."

Mandy rubbed her temples with her fingertips. After a moment she said, "All right. I don't want to get into a lot of detail about this, but I'll give you the highlights.

"I was a child protection worker before I became a police officer. Have you had much contact with child protection?"

"Unfortunately, yes," I said. "I used to treat victims."

"Then you know what a mess it is."

I nodded.

"The laws are made to protect parents, not kids," she said bitterly. "It's nearly impossible to get a kid out of an abusive home, and when you do get them out, it's about two weeks before the parents promise to do better and the judge sends them home. 'Family preservation,' they call it. 'Offender protection,' I call it, but it's the law. The first duty is preserve the family. I saw one baby sent home who had bite marks all over her, for Christ's sake. Hell, another judge sent a kid home whose family kept her in a cage. 'Let the healing begin,' the defense attorney said and the judge bought it. The only way the healing would have begun is if the parents were shot."

I didn't answer. What she was saying was true and one of the reasons I no longer worked with victims. What the offenders did to the victims was hard enough to take. What the system did to them was impossible.

"I knew Sissy," she said. "I worked on her case in child protection before I became a cop. She should never have been in that house. Her father had been dealing drugs since before she was born—dealing from the house half the time with her in it. Her worthless mother had taken off when she was still a baby. Roosevelt was usually too stoned to even feed her properly. She was always underweight. That's what they call it, underweight. Malnourished. The truth is she was half starved most of the time. She'd eat paint, trash, anything. Pica they call it when a kid eats anything. Nobody wants to say they're starving.

"We'd had numerous reports on her for neglect. The neglect laws are worse than the child abuse laws, and we couldn't get any judge to keep her out. Roosevelt could clean up nice when he wanted to and he'd get an attorney, get dressed up, and back Sissy would go.

"I quit child protection," she said, "because I couldn't cope with stuff like that anymore. I decided to become a police officer because at least they didn't try to preserve abusive families: they busted the scumbags. I went to the police academy and got on the force. I did pretty well," she said. "I did really well at the academy but once on the street . . ." her voice trailed off. "It seems I had forgotten something. I'd forgotten that the police don't get involved until after the damage is done. They don't prevent anything. They just punish people afterward.

"Anyway, I got on the force, and I tried to forget all about Sissy and the other kids I'd seen in child protection. To tell you the truth, Sissy was the hardest. Maybe because she was a survivor. She had learned to open cans when she was three years old so she could get something to eat. They had a dog, and once I went over to their house and she was eating dry dog food right out of a bag. Still, it kept her alive. She'd look after herself for days when she had to. She was definitely a fighter.

"Anyway, I got hooked up with Roosevelt. We nabbed him for extortion. I don't know why I'm telling you all this. Pat Humphrey doesn't even know all of it." She took a deep breath, and I thought she was going to stop, but she didn't.

"He was extorting money out of a minister who was using. The minister was very popular in the black community and was thinking seriously of a run for Congress. I don't know if his constituents would have cared about the drugs or not. The white bleeding-heart liberals who were providing the money would have. Roosevelt was as dumb as they come, but not dumb enough to miss that.

"We had him cold and we turned him. He was wearing a wire on Leroy. We already knew where the meth labs were. We were going to have a ton of evidence.

"Nobody knew. At least we thought nobody knew. We didn't tell Pat or anybody—not even the extortion victim knew we had him. Roosevelt wasn't tough like Leroy or Daryl. He was a fuckup. It wasn't that hard to turn him. I don't think he even really thought about what Leroy would do to him if he found out. All I could think about was I'd be the one to break the big, bad Leroy. Trash was going down.

"I knew he'd kill Roosevelt if he found out, but it never occurred to me he'd hurt Sissy. If I thought anything, it was that Leroy would be doing Sissy a favor if he took Roosevelt out. You know, the funny part is I might have been able to deal with it. Maybe. The last straw was that goddamn doll."

She had spoken this last so softly I wasn't sure I'd heard her. "I'm sorry," I said. "A doll?"

"A doll. A goddamn doll. When we found her, she was clutching this doll. I don't know if she had it the whole time, or she crawled to it after he raped her. She was curled up in a fetal position wrapped around that doll. She had it so tight the coroner had trouble getting it out of her hand. And the damn thing was a miserable excuse for a toy.

"It had one eye missing and the head was cracked and it was filthy dirty. It was just nothing, and the thing was, we searched the whole house and it was the only toy in that house. The only toy and it was something that you wouldn't even want your child to touch. You could tell what it meant to her in the way she was holding onto it. It was all she had. I don't know why it got to me, but it did. I just couldn't get the image of Sissy clutching that doll out of my head. And don't even think about telling me I'm being melodramatic. That's just the way it was."

I wasn't thinking about telling her anything. Working with victims you saw things that nobody could make up.

"We worked it for a while, but we didn't have any kind of physical evidence. Roosevelt dealt enough drugs that anybody could have done it—somebody looking to rip him off, somebody he'd ripped off, a rival, a business partner, a customer—who knew? There was just no evidence, no witnesses, no rumors, nothing. I didn't tell anybody he was my snitch. Nobody except Mac knew. It wouldn't have done any good to tell anybody. By itself, it didn't prove anything. Police were already looking at Leroy because of the drug connection. The case got cold, eventually, and everybody moved on."

"Except you."

"I couldn't seem to. I went through a phase of trying to prove somebody else killed her. I just didn't want to believe she got killed because of me. For a while I thought the extortion victim did it. He was a flimflam man himself and a shady character. He didn't know we'd found out about it, and he was a reasonable bet.

"I got kind of got obsessed with the whole thing. The big mistake I made was I took the files home. If I'd copied them, none of this would have happened, but I didn't. I took them home, and then someone was looking for them and they were missing and eventually they got to me. I should have lied and said I didn't have them, that they'd gotten lost somehow, but I'm not sure they would have believed me. The long and the short of it is I admitted I had the files, and they wanted to know why, and one thing led to another and they found out I'd been working the case on weekends on my own time.

"The whole thing was long and drawn out, and there's no point in getting into it. The bottom line is they told me to stop, and I didn't, and then the flimflam man, the charismatic, full-of-it asshole minister complained I was harassing him, and I got put on leave. I got put on leave and had to go to counseling. It was a mess and it took me six months to get reinstated. The price of reinstatement was that I'd never have anything to do with the case again. They just all took the view that I'd gone over the edge. Even the shrink. Especially the shrink."

"And had you?" It sounded to me like she had. I wondered if she saw it that way.

"Maybe. Probably. I don't know. Have you ever just wanted to go back and fix something that you fucked up? Have you ever gotten tired of things falling apart in your hands and said, 'That's it. That's one too many?' Do you know what I mean? Have you ever wanted to make something right—well as right as you could? I had gotten a child killed, and although I knew absolutely that nailing her killer wouldn't bring her back, I couldn't seem to live without nailing him."

"I can see it," I said.

"Well, it happened to me. I needed to solve Sissy's murder and somebody needed to pay or nothing meant anything."

"Mandy, I understand what you're saying, but the sad truth

is, you don't ever really solve the past by solving something different in the present."

"You're wrong about that," she said. "Something different in the present is all you can solve."

I thought about that. "Just remember one thing, Mandy," I said. "You're still guessing Leroy Collins was involved in Sissy's death and her father's. You said yourself nobody knew he was snitching, and that were a lot of other people who could have killed him." Of course, I thought he was, but that was based on seeing things, which was hardly evidence. And maybe realizing she didn't have anything would slow Mandy down a bit.

"Who are you kidding?" she said. "He wouldn't have bothered to come after you if he hadn't been involved. His interest in this whole thing—the fact he's looking for you—what do you think that means if he's not involved? He wants to know how much you know about it. If he wasn't involved, he'd have laughed you off.

"I'm not leaving," she said. "Maybe I can't get him for Sissy's death, but I can stop him from doing it again. Now you can call Pat or not. Either way I'm staying."

Later when I went in, Lily was waiting for me. She seemed happy to see me and hung around while I fixed dinner. I couldn't read Lily these days. She'd been so different lately. She spent tons of time in her room, but then, every book on teenagers I picked up predicted that. She was moody—sometimes high and silly, sometimes morose and irritable. Again, it was straight out of the books. Still something wasn't fitting. Lily had been with me long enough now that I knew her patterns, and this was different.

Drugs? Could it be drugs? A boyfriend? Sex at thirteen?

God, I hoped not. Surly was proving more than I could handle. The thought of a genuine problem with drugs or a pregnant thirteen-year-old made my stomach knot. But tonight I had something else on my mind.

"Wait, Lily," I said when she started to get up from the table. "Sit down for a minute. I need to talk to you about something." She sat down slowly, her eyes fixed on me. She looked almost panicky and as though she was holding her breath. "It's nothing," I said. "It's just that you may need to go to Betsy's for a while."

"What?" The reaction was instantaneous and hostile. It surprised me. Lily usually couldn't wait to get to Betsy's. Did she have a friend at school? Maybe she did have a boyfriend.

"Well, you usually like to go there. What's the problem?"

"I've got school." This was a new one. "I haven't done anything. Why are you trying to send me away?"

"I'm not," I said, perplexed. "Well, I am, but not for any bad reason. It's not you." I sighed. "You might as well know. I've got a small problem."

"What kind of problem?"

"A man, a criminal, thinks I know something I don't know. He may come after me to find it out."

"Here? He may come here?"

"That's the thought, although it may not happen, but why take a chance?"

"I don't think he'll come. Besides, what does that have to do with me?"

I gritted my teeth. The hubris of youth. As if Lily knew anything about whether Leroy would come or not. "It doesn't have anything to do with you, Lily, I hope," I said. "It's just not a good idea to hang around when someone that dangerous might show up. He is really a very scary dude. You might end up in the middle of it somehow."

Lily wasn't fazed. "It's got nothing to do with me. I'm not going, and you can't make me."

"Why, Lily? Spending time with Betsy isn't purgatory. Betsy's a hoot and you like hanging out with her."

"I don't want to go to Betsy's. Betsy doesn't even have a computer. I'm just getting used to school. I'm just making friends, and now you're trying to ruin it. I won't let you. You're not going to ruin this." The voice had risen, and it held an edge of hysteria that I did not understand. "I know you don't want me here, and you never have."

I started to speak, but she kept going. "Well, I'm here and I'm not leaving. If you make me go to Betsy's, I'll run away, I swear."

"Never mind," I said. "I'll think of something."

chapter **18**

S   till among the living, I see," Robert said. I had woken early, worrying about Lily and why she wouldn't leave, and was sitting on my beloved balcony with a cup of coffee mulling it over when he called. Robert, of course, was always up early due to his workaholic ways. He'd taken to calling me from his car on his way to work.

"Robert," I said, "calling me every day to see if I'm alive or dead is what, a way to reduce my anxiety?"

"No, it's a way to reduce mine," he said. "So, no problems?"

"Actually," I said, "I just found an armed bodyguard on my front steps." I told him about Mandy.

"Umm, I like everything except the possibility that you're being followed around by a woman Pat Humphrey—who is smart if not particularly kind—has said you should stay completely away from because something terrible will happen if she gets reinvolved in this case, and whose boyfriend is hinting that if he tells you anything at all about her, she'll get in a lot of trouble."

"On the other hand," I said, "she's carrying a .45 and a .9 millimeter."

"It's a point," he said. "How's her aim?"

"Fine, unless she's upset."

Robert laughed. "How come you're so far away, Red?" he said. "You're the most fun I have all day. Would you stay in mortal danger so I'll always have an excuse to call you?"

His voice sounded warm and easy and reminded me somehow of sunlight filtering through pines. Maybe it was the strain of waiting for something bad to happen, but suddenly I missed him. I missed the time I'd spent with him, and the house he took me to on the beach, and the sound of surf outside the window. I missed the long nights with his body close to mine while, eyes closed, he felt my face with his fingertips. The rhythm of his body on mine seemed to fuse with the sound of the surf until the roaring exploded somewhere in my head. All night I'd wake and the surf would still be there, and so would Robert, languid and slow in his lovemaking, slipping his hard body into mine in an increasingly sure and familiar way.

Just before daybreak, while he slept, I got up and walked on the beach outside. I had on a white cotton nightgown, and the sea breeze lifted it as I waded through the edge of the water. Even with the salt breeze I could still smell Robert on me. The waves lapped my ankles, and I felt somehow like the quintessential female, like I was Mother Earth herself. That was the problem, really. It felt like he was making love to the quintessential female, as though it could have been any woman in that bed.

Still, ever since then, the surf had had a sensual edge for me it had never had before, as though the memory swam up somewhere near consciousness every time I saw the sea. "Do you ever wonder," I said, "what happened to us?"

"No, I know what happened to us. You left me for your beloved island."

"It wasn't just that," I said.

"You didn't like my cat?"

"I like Hurricane fine," I said. "The scratches have all healed and you can hardly see the scars."

"What then?"

"I just didn't like that six-month expiration date stamped on my butt."

"You wound me. It wasn't that bad."

"I'll recant," I said, "if you can name a single woman in your life who's lasted longer than six months."

"My mother?" he said.

"She was drafted," I said.

"Ummm," he said, "I'll have to think about it. My memory's not what it used to be."

"That's the point," I said. "Most people could name their relationships on the fingers of one hand. Not too many people need a calculator."

"Maybe you jumped the gun too soon, Red. You didn't give it much of a chance. I was thinking," he went on, "maybe you'd be up for a visit sometime."

I laughed. "I admire your spunk," I said, "but you might want to pick some time when a crazed thug with a genuine track record for killing people isn't coming after me. Perhaps some time when I'm not being protected by a woman who carries loaded guns and whose stability is up for grabs.

"There'll be a time," he said. "You have a spare bedroom?"

"No," I said.

"Good," Robert replied, "We'll just have to share," and he wished me good day.

I was thinking about Robert and smiling when I saw Mandy's car stop in front of the house. I waved to her as she walked up the drive-way . She wore a T-shirt and cutoffs, this time with an oversized long-sleeved shirt over it. No doubt there was a small holster at her back that made tank tops impractical.

"Hi," she said, as she got closer. "I wanted to get your schedule for the day."

"Come on in," I said, getting up and heading in. I hoped in my soul she'd be easier to deal with about this than Lily had been.

"Look," I said when she had sat down, and I'd poured her some coffee, "you freaked me out about Lily."

"Good thing to be freaked out about," she said. "The sooner she's gone the better."

"That's not going to happen," I said. "She went bonkers when I suggested it. I don't know why. She's not that happy stranded here but she is not, capital letters, leaving."

"She gets to decide?"

"You haven't dealt with Lily. Yes, she gets to decide unless you have a gag and handcuffs ready. You can negotiate some things with Lily and other things you cannot. When she gets that panicky look in her eye—which I do not understand—then you are way past negotiation. I am not a mother," I said. "I am doing the best I can here." I took a sip of my coffee and steeled myself. "Which brings me to Plan B."

"Which is?" She raised her eyebrows.

"You. You've offered to help. I'm more worried about Lily than me. I would feel endless, debilitating, see-a-shrink guilt if she got hurt because of me. If you really want to do some good here, you can babysit Lily."

"Breeze," Mandy said, putting her coffee cup down and

sounding strangely official. She was using her cop voice, and for a second I felt like a criminal waiting for the full force of the law to come down on me. "I didn't offer to babysit Lily. She's at risk, sure, but you're more at risk. You're the only one I know for sure Leroy will come after. You're getting a freebie here. You don't get to dictate the terms."

"Such a deal I have for you," I said. "Lily's in school all day. You can follow me around to your heart's desire. Then, at night, we're both here most of the time. Again, a two-for-one deal. And we're together a good part of the weekend, so there you go. It's only those rare moments—OK, those not-that-frequent moments—when she's not in school and we're not actually in the same place that you need to stay with Lily."

"I'm sorry, Breeze. I can understand your wanting me to do it, but the answer is no. I've got to go with the primary target."

"Mandy, I am not a mean person. I don't think anyone in my whole life has ever accused me of being a mean person. But these are desperate times."

"Meaning?"

"It's a good deal. You should take it."

"What's the mean part?"

"The mean part has to do with calling Dallas if you don't."

She eyed me speculatively. "You wouldn't do it. With me here you've got Lily covered half the time. You said it yourself. Without me here, it's a cakewalk for Leroy."

"You wouldn't leave," I said. "No matter what they said. All it would mean is you'd get fired from your job and that would mean, if Leroy doesn't show up here, you'd never get another crack at him—or at solving Sissy's murder. The last I heard citizens don't get information from the police. They don't get to interview people and they don't make arrests. I can't see you putting yourself out of the loop."

She cocked her head and looked at me. I tried desperately not to blink. "It's not that bad a deal," she said.

I saw them both off—Lily to school and Mandy to pick up some equipment to strengthen our "wretched" security, and was settling down to work when the phone rang. Pat Humphrey's confident tones came over the line. For a moment, I thought she had figured out Mandy was here, but she was—unbelievably—calling to apologize. She was as close to contrite, I guess, as Pat ever got.

"I wanted to say I'm sorry," she said. "I fucked up. I should have thought it through."

"I know, Pat," I said. "It's just one of those things that blows up when you don't expect it to." Which was generous of me. Actually it was totally predictable and she did screw up.

"I should have known," she said. " I've been dealing with Leroy for a decade."

"I'm still here," I said.

"Early days," she said. "Listen, Robert says you won't leave the island, and that is just plain stupid. What I did is nowhere near as stupid as that." Always the diplomat, I thought.

"I've got my reasons," I said, not wanting to drag Lily and Jena into it.

"Do you have a gun?"

"No," I said. I heard her sigh.

"Look," she said. "Maybe I didn't get in enough detail about Leroy, or maybe you didn't read enough files. Do you remember a case where a woman looked out her window one night, just in time to see Leroy knife a man in an alley?

"No," I said, "I didn't get to all of them. I was mainly looking at the Sissy Harper case."

"Well, he found out about her, and he wanted to know if anybody else in her apartment saw it, too. So he cut off her fingers, one by one, until he was sure she'd told him everything."

My stomach turned. "Pat, I don't have any information that's worth losing a finger over," I said. "If you remember, I don't actually know anything."

"She didn't, either," Pat said. "At least tell me you've got a plan."

"I have a friend here looking after me," I said. "He's got a gun." I didn't think Mandy would mind being turned into a he to keep Pat from guessing who it was.

"And he knows how to use it?"

"Former police," I said. "Hey, Pat, one more thing. You didn't want me to speak to Mandy Johnson. Why was that?" Call me a skeptic, but even though Mandy's account had the ring of truth, I'd worked with too many offenders not to cross-check what I was told.

There was a long pause and then Pat said, "I'll tell you because I have a feeling she may try to insert herself in the case at some point, if she finds out what's going on. She worked the case before and got carried away. She started working it on her own. She got obsessed. When they went to retrieve the files, the entire living room had been turned into a sort of war room with pictures of Sissy, case files, hundreds of notes of interviews we didn't even know about. The whole thing was a mess. She had harassed a local minister so much we damn near got our asses sued off. The shrink thought she should quit the force altogether. We decided to give her one more chance.

"Not everybody agreed. They're just waiting for her to fuck up. Don't let her get involved, OK? It's her job this time. It's more than that. If you get her involved, you'll destabilize her and she's likely to get back into that whole obsession thing.

Listen, I know about obsession. I can't tell you how many stalkers I've prosecuted. It's an ugly business.

"Besides," she added, "despite what Mandy thinks, I like her. Women get a shitty deal in criminal justice. Mandy was a good cop—is a good cop if she stays away from this."

I thought about the picture of Mandy that was emerging: an unstable cop with an obsession. I wasn't so wrong the first time. Bullets by the ears. Worse, bullets by Lily's ears.

chapter 19

Lily had pretty much avoided the beach since she arrived. What was the point? Now she was stuck. Her teacher, Mrs. Carson, had asked the class of four students to bring in seashells for a science project. Lily had halfheartedly suggested to Breeze they buy them from one of the gift shops. Breeze just laughed, like she thought it was a joke.

Better to get it over with, Lily thought. It was a stupid assignment, but she'd lose the computer if she didn't keep her grades up, and that wasn't going to happen. How would she talk to her mother if she lost the computer? Her mother's e-mails were the only thing that mattered. Just thinking about them made her feel better. Go to Betsy's when she didn't even own a computer? Not on your life.

Mandy had offered to take her and armed with a picture of the shells she needed, she'd agreed. Probably all of the other kids, she thought, knew what the shells looked like. Mrs. Carson didn't say that, just handed out the pictures to everybody. She wasn't so bad.

She and Mandy walked together on the beach. The hard wet sand jiggled under Lily's feet like coffee-colored Jell-O. Mandy had been hanging around for a few days now, and that wasn't so bad, either. She was getting used to her. At least she talked more than Breeze, although she didn't mind Breeze so much anymore. Funny, since she'd been talking to her mother on the e-mail, she hadn't felt so angry with Breeze.

The sun was bright enough, even at this hour, to lay a yellow ribbon on the sand right up to Lily's feet. In front of her lay an array of shells that looked like the remains of porcelain dishes broken and thrown around carelessly. She peered among them, looking for the Scotch bonnets, razor clams, and knobbed whelks she had come to find.

On her left the breakers rolled steadily. It sounded like an endless heartbeat, she thought. Sort of like a giant animal breathing, and strangely, it made her feel better about everything. Maybe that's why Breeze spent so much time here. Maybe it made her feel better, too.

The light wind lifted the tips of her hair, and she felt the salt on her lips and thought this wasn't such a bad place, really—just not enough kids, but the place was pretty. That wasn't the right word. Maybe the town was pretty. The beach was bigger than pretty somehow. Pretty made it sound small and ordinary, and it wasn't. She looked out over the waves into the distance and thought, this thing goes all the way to France, which was really weird. If she could see far enough, she could see France. How weird was that?

Would her mom like it here? Would she want to live here someday—or at least come to visit? Her mom talked about mountains all the time. She used to anyway, before Jerry beat her into the zombie zone. This place was like the mountains in a way. It had that bigness thing she knew somehow was part of what her mother loved.

She looked over at Mandy and wondered how much she could say. Mandy was very cool. She had righteous hair and the guns seemed a sure sign she wouldn't take guff from anybody.

"Mandy?"

Mandy had turned around and was scanning the dunes as she did every few minutes. Now she turned back toward her. "Yes?"

She wasn't sure how to say it. "I saw a thing on television. About domestic violence."

"OK." Mandy didn't look at her, just started walking and watching the waves.

"I just thought you might know about it, because you're a cop. And cops get calls about it, right? So I was wondering. Why do they do it?"

"The perps? Why do they beat up on people?"

"Oh, no, not them. I don't care about them. They're just mean. I think they do it because they enjoy it."

Mandy looked at her in surprise and, it seemed to her, with a kind of approval.

"I mean the women. I bet you wouldn't do it. You wouldn't let anyone beat you. You'd leave. Or shoot him. Or if the cops came, you wouldn't tell them everything was OK."

Mandy just kept walking, then said, "I'm not going to lie to you, Lily. I don't have a good answer for you. I've never really understood it myself. I lived with it when I was a child, but I didn't understand it any better than you do. Now I'm grown and I still don't."

Lily's heart seemed to skip a beat. "What do you mean," she said casually, "about living with it."

"My mother had a series of boyfriends who beat her. I can't tell you why she let them. She'd no sooner get rid of one than another would move in. She drank, but that's no excuse. She felt worthless, I know, but I think now that a lot of that came after the beatings. To tell you the honest truth, I've never understood my mother. We were never close. I had a pretty lousy childhood because of her. I've spent a lot of years being angry about it.

"I'm better now, less angry. At least I think so. I don't seem to spend that much time thinking about it anymore. But I'm the wrong person to ask because I have never understood it."

Oh, no, you're not, Lily thought. You're exactly the right person.

They walked for a few more minutes and then Lily said, "Did you ever feel like it was your fault?"

"Sometimes," Mandy laughed. "Now I can't even remember why. Why would a child think something like that was her fault? It makes no sense. I did feel it though."

"Somebody might think that," Lily said slowly, "if it was because of her that her mother got involved with the guy in the first place."

"Kids don't choose who their parents get involved with," Mandy countered. Lily didn't answer.

"Is that the reason you're here?" Mandy said gently. "Does your mom have a problem like that?"

Again Lily didn't answer.

"You don't have to tell me, Lily, but I've been pretty straight with you. And I won't tell anyone what you say to me."

Lily felt like she was pushing on a door that was really heavy, one she'd never been able to move before. Finally it just seemed to give way. "My mom has had some problems like that," she said, keeping her voice flat. "It's not like she's a bad person. Really, she's not."

"No," Mandy said sadly. "I'm sure she's not."

"The thing is," Lily said, "my mother wasn't always like that.

I remember when I was little, and Jerry didn't live with us. She was really pretty, and we did things together, all kinds of things. She told me stories about the mountains."

"Mountains?"

Lily sighed. "My mother has a thing about mountains, really big ones in South America and the Himalayas. She's a climber, a mountain climber, was anyway. She has pictures. It's true. She didn't make it up." She looked up at Mandy then, as though Mandy was sure to think her mother was lying. Mandy didn't reply. "You can ask Breeze. They used to talk about the mountains when they were little. She knows."

"I don't doubt it, honey," Mandy said. "I was just wondering which was worse, having a mother like mine, who was never anything but a doormat, or one like yours, who used to be different. Beats me. Sorry, that's not a pun."

"The thing is," Lily said. "That's why it's my fault. My father died. He was a climber and he fell and died, and then there was only my mother to look after me, and it meant she couldn't climb anymore. Then she met Jerry, and he was a climber and he reminded her of the mountains. So she got hooked up with him because he was her connection to the mountains. That's what I think anyway, but it's true. If she'd had the mountains, she wouldn't have needed him." She was talking quickly, and the words seemed to fly out of her mouth before she decided to say them.

"This is your idea?" Mandy said. "This is what you think?"

"It's true," Lily said, stubbornly, wishing she hadn't told her.

"It could be," Mandy agreed. "I promised I wouldn't lie to you. It could be true."

Something massive eased in Lily, like she'd lost that ten pounds of baby fat she still had. She didn't think any grown-up would admit that. Lily knew it was true. It had that feeling of something real, something you don't make up. But she never thought any adult would talk to her about it.

Mandy scanned the dunes again, then flopped down on the beach. "Let's sit," she said. Lily obediently sat down beside her and Mandy leaned back on her elbows and stared out at the water. After a moment she said, "So, let's say it's true. So what? It was going to happen anyway, you know. Sooner or later she was going to get too old to climb, or she'd have gotten an injury that kept her from climbing. Or she wouldn't have had the money. The point is, your mother's problem was that she loved one thing and she couldn't live without it. It just happened to be a child that stopped her. It could have been anything."

"I wish it had been something else," Lily said.

"She could have done other things," Mandy went on. "She could have taught rock climbing, or she could have opened a climbing store. Why this guy? And why not leave when it went bad? He's not reminding her of the mountains now. It doesn't explain why she didn't leave."

Lily didn't answer.

"It's only a piece of it," Mandy said. "She had a lot of choices, and he's the one she chose."

But Lily wasn't listening now. She was thinking about what Mandy had said: that her mother could have done other things. That sounded true, too. So why hadn't she?

"Can people like that ever change?" Lily said finally. "Get back to who they used to be?"

"Your mother might be able to," Mandy said. "She has something to get back to. I don't think my mother can. She's never been any different."

"My mom sounds different lately," Lily said hesitantly. "She's talking about leaving him, but I never know whether to believe her. She's said that before. She used to say it a lot. Then for a while she quit even pretending she'd leave. She just seemed to give up, and she was spaced out all the time. I could hardly even talk to her.

"I don't know, now she sounds different again. More like before, only better. How am I supposed to know? She didn't leave him before, even when she sounded like she would. I don't know."

"They say people give up cigarettes ten times before it sticks," Mandy said. "Who knows? Maybe this is the time it sticks?"

Maybe, Lily thought. And maybe it's one of the ten.

"Mandy," Lily said. "You said you used to be angry. What did you do about it?"

"Nothing good," Mandy replied. "I just sort of let it fuck up my life, over and over. Sorry for the language. Sometimes you don't sound thirteen and I forget. It isn't gone entirely. I still get angry at some things, but it's not all the time any-more and it's not at everything. There's one thing I'm still angry about," she said. "I can't seem to get over it. I don't think you can grow up like I did and not be angry," she added.

"I don't even notice when I'm angry," Lily said. "Some-times. Sometimes people tell me I'm angry, and it's like I don't know what they're talking about. Then I notice I have this knot in my chest. I think that's anger. It gets really tight and— I don't know how to describe it. If it isn't anger, I don't know what it is."

"It's anger," Mandy said, "if it feels like an animal chewing on you."

"Yeah," Lily said, "that sounds about right."

◄○►

Robert Giles was working on a brief when the phone rang. He didn't look up, just waited to see who it was before he answered: if he took every call, he'd never get anything done. He didn't recognize the woman's voice and started to turn the volume down when it dawned on him the voice was Southern. He didn't know many Southerners in Seattle, and he thought of the Texas connection and wondered if this had anything to do with Daryl Collins. He hesitated, then turned the volume up.

"Mr. Giles, I need to talk to you. I jus' got a question. I called the prison, but they didn't know the answer, and they told me to call you. I'll call back . . ."

Robert picked up the phone. "This is Robert Giles."

"Mr. Giles, you don't know me, but I got a question 'bout Daryl Collins, and the prison said I should ask you."

"Whom am I speaking to?"

There was a pause. " That don't matter none. I jus' got a question."

Robert put his pen down and sat up straighter. "OK, then, what can I do for you?"

"Is it true you're fixing to let that man go?"

He thought for a moment. It was public information. Why not? "Maybe," Robert said. "We're not sure. There's a chance he'll stay in, but his time is up in a few months and he'll probably be released."

"What do you want to do a thing like that for, let a man like Daryl Collins go?" she said. "Seems like once you got him, you'd hold on to him. It done took you long enough to get him. Now you're gonna turn around and let him right back out? He'll go right back to doing what he always done. You let that man out, some people gonna get hurt."

"I know people who feel the same way you do," Robert said, "but he's served his time."

"He ain't served his time for all the things that man has done."

"So I hear," he said, "but witnesses are hard to come by."

"You can't do no witnessing against that man," the voice said. "What you talk nonsense for? You might as well take a bullet and put it in your own brain yourself. You really gonna let him go?"

"I don't think we'll have a choice," Robert said. "If you'll give me your name and number, I can make sure you're called. Daryl Collins doesn't need to know anything about it."

'Won't do no good," the voice said, "giving you my number. I got to move. Again. I got to tear everything up and go. I got to be long gone 'fore that man show his face outside those prison walls."

"Why do you . . . " but she had hung up.

He sat for a moment and thought about it. Probably it was just someone Daryl had met up here who had reason to fear him. Robert had read the file and Daryl hadn't been in Seattle long before the robbery, but there could still be people here afraid of him. Daryl probably had people afraid of him everywhere he went.

But the woman had a Southern accent and that seemed like too much of a coincidence. And how did he know she was even calling from Seattle? She could be calling from Texas. He remembered the voice mailbox always gave the number the person was calling from and it had picked up before he did. He dialed it and found the area code was 206—the call was from Seattle. He wrote the rest of the number down, turned to his computer and looked up a reverse phone directory. The number belonged to a woman named Gladys Parks.

He picked up the phone and dialed Pat Humphrey, then hung up quickly when it started to ring. Maybe Pat wasn't the right person to ask about this. Pat had jumped the gun before and endangered Breeze. She was irrational about Leroy Collins, and he wasn't sure she wouldn't do something impulsive again. He stared at the phone while he thought and then called Breeze instead.

"How well do you know the file on Daryl Collins?" Robert asked when Breeze answered.

"As well as you can know three thousand pages of records," Breeze replied. "Which is to say, not that well."

"Ever see reference to a woman named Gladys Parks?"

"No, who is she?"

"I don't know," he said, "but she just called me," and he told her about the phone call.

"If she's from Texas," Breeze said slowly, "maybe somebody on the case would know her."

"If she is," Robert said. "I started to call Pat and then changed my mind. I don't want to get anybody else in trouble with Leroy or Daryl. This woman's already afraid of him. I suspect she's got good reason."

"How about Mandy Johnson, my new bodyguard? She took Lily to the beach and they'll be back soon. You know she's not going tell anybody down in Texas about Parks. If they find out she's here, they'll fire her. And she probably knows this file better than anybody. Besides . . . she added, and then paused for a moment thinking.

"What?"

"It never made sense to me why Daryl left Texas. Why'd he come to Seattle? Maybe this woman knows something about that."

"Talk to Johnson," Robert said. "I'll be here."

chapter 20

Who's Gladys Parks?" I asked Mandy when she and Lily arrived a little while later. Lily had immediately headed for her room and her headphones.

"Gladys Parks?" Mandy frowned. "Where did you hear that name?"

"You first," I said.

"Crystal Parks was Roosevelt Harper's girlfriend. She was just a kid—I can't remember her age exactly, but she was young—and she was wasted pretty much all the time. She lived with her mother. I think her mother's name was Gladys. It started with a G anyway.

"I tried to find Crystal after the shooting, but she had disappeared. I thought they probably had killed her, too, but her body never showed up. That kind of thing happened. I don't know where they were dumping bodies, but several people went missing and never turned up. We never found her or her mother. I've gone back to the neighborhood lots of times, but nobody has ever admitted knowing what happened to them. Your turn. Why do you ask?"

"Gladys Parks is in Seattle. She just called Robert Giles and wanted to know when Daryl Collins was getting out of prison."

Mandy froze for a moment, the coffee cup in midair. "Are you serious?" she said. "For real?"

"I shouldn't say that," I said. "Somebody called from a phone listed in Gladys Parks's name. There's no way to know who it was for sure. All we know is the accent was Southern."

"Did she mention Crystal?" she asked.

"Not that I know of," I said.

"How do you know it wasn't Crystal?" she said. "How do you know it was Gladys?"

"Whoa," I said. "I don't know anything, and I don't think Robert does, either. All we know is what I told you. A woman with a Southern accent called Robert inquiring about Daryl Collins and said if he got out of prison, she'd have to move. Then she hung up before he could ask her any questions. She wouldn't tell him her name. He got the name from the reverse directory. That's all I know."

"She said that, that she'd have to move?"

I looked at Mandy curiously. The words seemed reasonable enough, but her tone held a sharp sense of urgency. The voice was still thundercloud gray, but it had become small and compacted. It matched the stillness in her body which now had the quality of a rubber band that was pulled too tight. I had the feeling it was taking all she could do not to throttle me to get the information out of me faster, but I had told her everything I knew. I thought about Pat Humphrey's comments about Mandy's obsession with the case. She's still got it, I thought, just like before.

"Does he know where she is?"

I shrugged. "I don't know. The reverse directory would have the address."

"I want to talk to him. Vouch for me, will you?" She looked at me and waited.

I thought for a minute. "OK," I said, but I had my reservations. I went back to drinking my coffee.

"Does Pat know about it?"

"No," I said. "He thought about calling her, but she's a bit of a loose canon about Leroy."

Mandy smiled at that and I couldn't blame her. No doubt she'd been called a loose cannon over this case many times, and some of them probably by the woman I was referring to. But it was Pat and not her that Robert and I didn't trust enough to tell.

"OK," she said.

I just sat for a moment sipping my coffee and she said impatiently, "So . . . "

"So what?" I asked, not sure what she wanted.

"So call him," she said.

"Right now?" She just looked at me like I was an idiot. "Right," I said.

Mandy paced back and forth while I was on the phone with Robert. When I handed her the phone, she grabbed it like she was dialing 911. I listened for a few minutes, and then, feeling oddly disturbed by the intensity radiating from her, I went outside and hung with Grandma. Grandma's leaves were almost all out now and she looked dressed for the first time since she'd stripped last fall. Compared to other trees, Grandma was a good-looking nude—trees got better looking as they got older—but I liked her better dressed. I stood under her branches and watched her olive leaves flash silver in the sunlight.

In a few minutes Mandy joined me outside.

"How'd it go?" I asked.

"It's all set," she said. "I fly to Seattle tomorrow, and Robert and I will go out and interview Mrs. Parks. He doesn't know the case so it wouldn't do much good for him to go alone. He could call Dallas, but he seemed OK with me coming instead, which I am grateful for. This case is old enough that most people barely remember it. I know it a whole lot better than anybody else does."

"You're leaving?" Suddenly I felt a little forlorn, a little left behind and abandoned.

"Just for a few days," she said. "Got to. Mrs. Parks knows something or she wouldn't have disappeared when Sissy was killed. And maybe she's got Crystal with her. It could be the whole ball game if Crystal's there. Who knows? We might have ourselves a witness to Sissy's murder." Her eyes had a tight brightness that looked like a fever.

She read the look on my face. "Look, you're set up pretty well. You've got the new dead bolts, the peephole in the door, lights with motion sensors. We've got everything set up except the camera for the outside, and since we can't find that here anyway, I'll pick one up in Seattle."

But I wasn't thinking about security gadgets. What about Lily? Lily had taken to Mandy and she was not going to understand being deserted like this at all.

"What about Lily?" I said.

"What about her?" Mandy said, but she seemed to be studying Grandma now and not looking at me.

"You're going to have to tell Lily yourself. You can't just walk out like this without telling her."

She paused, then said, "I can do that. She'll just have to understand."

"Understand what, Mandy?" I said. "You've told her Leroy's

dangerous, and you're here to protect her, and now you're telling her that protecting her isn't all that important because you have something else you'd rather do." I was surprised at how protective I felt of Lily, and how pissed I was at Mandy for leaving her.

"Look, we don't even know for sure he's coming."

I stared at her. "Mandy, you're the one who's said he's definitely coming."

"All right," she said. "The truth is I can't help it. I have to go. If Crystal's alive, she's the key to the whole thing. She disappeared instantly when Sissy was killed. She and her mother both. She had to know something. If I don't go, the two of them may disappear again, and then we'll never find them."

"Mandy," I said. "Don't do this. Sissy's dead. You'd be endangering a live child to help a dead one."

"I have to. You don't understand."

"But it doesn't have to be you."

"Yes it does," she said, turning away. "I don't know why," she said softly, "but it does."

We went round and round about it but it didn't do any good. Finally, we sat in silence while Mandy screwed up her courage to tell Lily. She was leaving right away, tomorrow at the latest so it couldn't wait. She waited until Lily emerged from her room for a snack. Mandy hadn't seemed all that anxious to call her out. "It's all yours," I said.

"Thanks a lot," she said. We followed Lily into the kitchen.

"Lily," Mandy said, "I need to talk to you about something."

Lily smiled and held up the potato chips.

Mandy shook her head and went on quickly, "A possible witness has turned up to a murder that Leroy committed a long time ago. She ran away last time, and if we don't stop her, she'll probably run away this time. I've got to go tomorrow to interview her." She spoke almost formally, and I guessed she had been sitting there rehearsing it.

"OK," Lily said, turning back to her potato chips. "Where are you going?"

"Seattle."

Lily looked up quickly. "You're leaving, like really leaving?"

"Just for a few days."

"Who's going to be here?"

"Breeze will be here." Lily glanced at me with the look of someone who's been told the pilot's gone and the passenger in seat 2C will be taking over.

"Breeze? What's she supposed to do?"

"Lily. . ."

"Are they making you go?"

"No," Mandy said. "Nobody's making me go. I just need to."

"Can't someone else do it?"

"Nobody else knows the case like I do."

"But somebody else could do it," Lily said slowly. Her face seemed to stiffen as she said this. I wanted to turn away and not see it. "And nobody else will be here with Breeze and me. So even though somebody else could do that, and nobody else will be here to do this, you're still going. And that's the deal, isn't it?"

Mandy looked like she didn't want to answer. "Lily, I . . . "

"Don't start," Lily said. "I know all about excuses. For a kid, I'm pretty much an expert on excuses. I could write a term paper about them. You've leaving us to that man Leroy. That's what you're doing, isn't it? All right. You want to leave us? Go ahead. You say you're going. So go."

Mandy looked at me, and I shrugged helplessly. Lily was no dummy. There was no way to sugarcoat it. Mandy tried a couple of more times to talk to her, but Lily kept eating potato chips and ignored her. Mandy gave up and left. I stayed in the kitchen with Lily and leaned on the counter next to her. I had an urge to put my arms around her, but I could feel bumpers radiating from her. She could not have said "don't touch me" any more clearly if she had yelled it. She was putting peanut butter on the bread, spreading it very carefully and taking a long time to get it right. The house was so quiet I could hear the clock ticking in the living room.

"I don't want to make excuses for her," I said softly. "What she's doing isn't right. It's lousy and you've got a right to be mad. The problem is she's driven. She's out of control about this thing. I don't really get it, either. It's some kind of obsession with her."

"You said you don't want to make excuses for her," Lily said sharply. "So don't." And with that she picked up her peanut butter sandwich and headed to her room.

chapter 21

T he Seattle sky was clear and cloudless, and the air held a sweet crispness like a promise when it's first made.

Mandy sat silently, staring out the window, watching Seattle go by and seemingly unwilling or uninterested in talking. Robert noticed how rigidly she sat, how flushed her face was, and wished he'd asked Breeze more about her. He also noticed how heavy her purse seemed to be when she put it in the car, nor did he miss the bulge in the small of her back.

"How did you get the guns through security?" he asked.

"You just check them in your luggage," she said absent-mindedly, "and show your badge so they don't get upset when they find them." She didn't say anything more and started staring out the window again. Robert decided just to shut up and drive. It was clear she didn't want to talk. He wondered how she'd take it if no one was home to interview.

They had driven through a series of middle-class neighborhoods, but now the area was getting poorer. The street where Gladys Parks lived wasn't as bad, though, as Robert had feared from the address. The neighborhood was poor, but there were no bars at the windows, no abandoned houses with syringes lying on the floors. Maybe there wasn't enough money to keep things up, but the social fabric hadn't shattered. They saw people waiting for the bus to go to work, and only a few young men was hanging on the street corners.

The house was small and rundown, but a few early flowers were budding in the front yard. The door was opened by a short, heavy black woman who appeared to be in her early fifties. Mandy tried to hide her disappointment that it wasn't Crystal.

"Mrs. Parks?" Robert said.

"Who's asking?" she said.

"I'm Robert Giles. I believe we spoke the other day. You called me about Daryl Collins. This is Mandy Johnson, a police officer from Dallas. May we come in? We'd like to talk to you if we may."

Mrs. Parks sighed and opened the door. "I knowed you'd be coming someday," she said, leading them into a small living room and gesturing toward a sofa. The furnishings did not remember being new, but the place was spotless. "I was just looking for a little more time," she said. She sat down heavily across from them. "But what I want more time for? My baby's been dead a long time now. I had me too much time; I don't need no more. Ain't right, a child dying before her momma." She fanned herself a little and waited, her heavy chest going up and down like a bellows.

"Crystal's dead?" Mandy asked, Robert could hear the disappointment edge ridges in her voice.

"Oh, my baby died a long time ago," Mrs. Parks said. "But you're not here to hear about an old woman's grief. You want to hear about Leroy Collins, 'bout Daryl Collins. I know you want to get 'em something bad. I know'd it. But you want people like me to do it for you. I don't know how black folks get along in this world. We got you on one side, and we got men like Leroy Collins on the other. Neither one of you give a damn what happens to us. Ain't that much difference between you, to tell the truth."

"Oh, there's a difference," Robert said quietly. "You're not running because of us." Beside him, Mandy had seemed to wilt at the news of Crystal's death and was silent. "Anything you might know about them might help us. You said you'd have to move if Daryl got out of prison. May I ask why that is?"

Mrs. Parks sat back on the chair and straightened out her legs. She wore long socks folded over and her ankles looked swollen. She probably works on her feet all day, Robert thought.

"Long time ago now. Back in Dallas. My girl Crystal, she got messed up with the dope. My only child—Lawd, she was pretty as a movie star. All the men were hanging around by the time she was fourteen. I loved that child—God knows—but she didn't have no sense. She liked pretty things and she liked the drugs. I thought she'd get herself straightened out one day, but that day never come.

"She got to running around with Roosevelt Harper, that cousin of Daryl and Leroy's. He weren't nothing, just a no-'count drug dealer. He weren't never going to make nothing of himself and he weren't never gonna let her make nothing of herself. I tried to tell her that, but a sixteen-year-old girl don't think she got to listen to her momma."

Neither Robert nor Mandy interrupted. It was clear that Gladys Parks had a story to tell and she was ready to tell it.

"One night she call me. I ain't seen hide nor hair of her for two days and she only sixteen years old. But I couldn't keep her in. Weren't no way to do it short of tying her up. She call me, and she was one scared little girl. She said I had to come get her, that she'd lost her pocketbook and the Collins brothers was after her. She didn't have no money for a cab and no way to get away from them. I took it serious. I came right away. She was crying and carrying on like I never seen the beat of.

"I picked her up right on Bay Street where she told me to, and I started to take her home. She started crying real hard and said we couldn't go home, they'd come get her. So I drove around for a while and then I parked in the back of a gas station and I got the story out of her.

"She'd been up at Roosevelt's house. She said she'd taken some drugs and stayed up all night then slept through the day. She was upstairs and just waking up that night when she heard somebody yelling real loud downstairs. She said Daryl and Leroy was there—she could hear their voices, and Daryl was yelling at Roosevelt. She said she tiptoed to the stairs and looked down and saw Daryl and Leroy and Roosevelt standing in the kitchen. She said Leroy weren't yelling none. He was talking real calm like but it was cold and the look on his face scared her something bad.

"She said they didn't see her and didn't know nothing 'bout her being there. She could see Roosevelt from the stairs and he scared her worse than Leroy. His voice was all high and shaky and she said he looked so pale he looked like he was white. Anything scare Roosevelt that bad got to be bad, so she started thinking maybe she ought to get out of there before something real worse happens.

"She turned to go back in the room—she was gonna try and get out the window—when she heard a shot. She looked back around and saw Roosevelt lying on the floor with blood everywhere, and then she saw Leroy step up and shoot him again, right in the face. She saw Sissy run over to her daddy. She didn't know Sissy was there 'cause she couldn't see her from the top of the stair. When Sissy got close up to her daddy, she started screaming and tried to run away. Crystal didn't wait no more. She ran over to the window and got it open. She could hear Sissy's footsteps coming up the stairs and Daryl yelling, 'Come back here, you little bitch,' and she heard his footsteps coming after Sissy.

"She got that window open and the screen was tore off, thank God, or my baby would of died right then and there. She climbed out of that window and jumped. She busted up her ankle when she hit the ground. It was all swole up, but she said she didn't even feel it. She started running, and it wasn't till she got away she remembered her pocketbook was still upstairs.

"She knew they'd be after her. She knew it. Her pocketbook was in the room and the bed was all messed up and the window was wide open in the winter time. She didn't have good sense about men and drugs, but she weren't no fool. She knew they'd go looking for her, and what they'd do to her when they found her. Everybody knew that. You didn't have nothing on the Collins brothers and live.

"I knew she was right. We couldn't ever go back home. I had cashed my paycheck that day, thank the Lord, so I had enough money for gas and food. I put that car on the highway and I kept going. I didn't go home to get nothing. I had a cousin up in Seattle and I decided that was as close to Texas as I wanted my baby to be."

"You've been up here ever since?" Robert asked.

"We have, but it didn't do no good. The Collins brothers may of scared her, but she weren't ready to change nothing. She still into the dope. And she didn't have the sense to keep her mouth shut. We'd been here for a while and then I heard her on the phone, telling some friend of hers in Dallas she up in Seattle. I told her she was a fool, but she said her friend wouldn't tell nobody. Then one day I see Daryl Collins on the street. I knowed he up here looking for her, and I knowed we got to move again.

"But she wouldn't go. We'd been up here almost a year, and she had a new boyfriend and she figured Daryl and Leroy ought to know if she hadn't said anything by now, she weren't never going to. I tole her it don't work like that, but she wouldn't listen. I don't think she was right in the head by then. She was always high on something.

"It weren't too long after that I got a call from the police. She was dead in some crack house. Lord, I don't know how a body can hear news like that and not have your heart just plain give out. I done the best I could with what I got left, but it would of been a whole lot better if my old heart had wore out when they first tole me."

Mandy asked softly, "What happened to her? Did Daryl kill her?"

"I don't rightly know. Maybe Daryl did get to her. I guess I'll never know. But she had done so much bad stuff to herself, it was just a question of time. It was coming sooner or later. If she kept messing with the drugs, it was just a question of time."

She stopped and rocked for a few minutes. Nobody spoke. Then she started up again. "After Crystal died, I didn't much care what happened. He could come and get me if he wanted to. I got a little bit more straightened out after a time, but by then I'd seen in the newspaper he got arrested. I didn't think he could do much from prison. so I just stayed."

"How did you know he was getting out of prison?" Robert said.

"My cousin call from down home and tell me he's heard a rumor Daryl's getting out. I was gonna move, but I'd just as soon talk to you. It don't matter anymore and I'm too old to keep running."

"Did Crystal know what they were fighting about?" Mandy said, "Why they killed him?" She could feel her whole body get tense when she asked.

"If she did, she never tole me," Mrs. Parks said, "but I don't think she knew."

The room seemed to swim around Mandy for a moment. If Crystal didn't know, nobody would ever know. Mandy would never know for sure if making Roosevelt a snitch got Sissy killed or not. Which meant, she thought, she'd never get the monkey off her back. But she felt relief, too, at the answer. The only thing worse that not knowing would have been to know for sure she caused her death.

Robert was looking at Mandy curiously now, waiting to see if she had more questions. When she didn't, he turned back to Mrs. Parks. "We'd like you to come down to the police station and give us a statement about this."

"Is it gonna keep Daryl Collins in prison?"

"It might well be enough to put him in prison on a new murder charge."

"And Leroy?"

"Same with Leroy."

"But it's hearsay," Mandy said to Robert. "Crystal was the witness and she's dead."

"Ah, but it's a special kind of hearsay—'excited utterance.' Crystal was upset when she said it. It followed immediately after the killings."

"It's admissible?"

"Oh, yes, it's admissible. She was fleeing from them. She was still in the throes of emotion from the killing. I don't see it as an issue. I doubt there's a judge anywhere who wouldn't admit it."

"You're saying I can testify against Daryl and Leroy even though I didn't see nothing myself?"

"That's what I'm saying," Robert said. "If you're willing to."

"But I got to live long enough."

"I don't think Leroy has the reach here in Seattle that he has in Dallas," Robert said. "I think we can hide you well enough for now. But I won't tell you there's no risk."

"Oh, I knowed that. I knowed it. Anytime you dealing with the Collins brothers, you got risk. You got the risk you won't wake up the next day.

"But I guess I'll do it. Like I said, I already had me too much time. And I don't really want to run no more. Worse thing that can happen is I die and quit studying on Crystal."

It was late and Mac was just getting ready to go to bed when the phone rang.

"It's me," Mandy said.

Mac reached over for the remote and turned off the TV.

"You all right?" he asked.

"Mac, I'm in Seattle. We've got a witness."

"Seattle? What are you doing in Seattle?"

"Mac, are you listening? We've got a witness."

"To what? What are you talking about?"

She told him. "It counts, Mac. It's called 'excited utterance.' She can testify."

Mac was stunned. Who would have thought after all this time that there was a witness? He had been sure this was just another in a long series of wild-goose chases. "Fucking unbelievable," he said. "Does she know why Roosevelt was killed?"

"No." Mac let out a disappointed breath. In the best of all worlds, Leroy would have killed him for anything else other than snitching, and maybe that would have brought some peace to Mandy. "She doesn't know," Mandy added. "If Crystal knew any more about the argument, she didn't tell her mother."

Mandy sounded strange. She was excited all right, but something else was in her voice, too. Always before, even she had even a tiny lead, she had sounded like she'd won the lottery. But not this time. "How do you feel?" he said carefully.

"I don't know," she said. He waited. "I think I did it again."

"Did what?"

"Same thing I did last time. Breeze said I was helping a dead girl," she added, "and endangering a live one."

"What's she talking about?" Mac said.

She told him about Lily and about leaving her and Breeze despite knowing Leroy was coming. Mac hoped Mandy wasn't going to ask him if he thought Breeze's comment was true.

"I don't feel good about this. I was really pissed at Breeze when she said it, and all the way here I'm arguing with her in my mind. But then, I started running the videotape back in my head, you know? Replaying the conversation with her, sort of watching myself like I was looking at myself from the outside? I feel like an idiot."

Now she really had his attention. "What do you mean?" he said carefully.

"I still think," she said slowly, "that Roosevelt was killed because he was snitching for me, that I got so carried away with nailing Leroy that I didn't even think about the fact that he had a four-year-old in the house and what they might do to her."

He opened his mouth to object then shut it. He'd made the old objections hundreds and hundreds of times. All snitches had family of some kind. Who would have expected anybody—even the Collins brothers—to kill a four-year-old?

"But then I got so, I don't know, so carried away with it, I couldn't even see anything else. I mean now, after this thing started up again, when it turned out that Leroy really was involved, it was just like the old days."

"But," Mac said, "we still don't know if Leroy killed her because her father was snitching."

"That's not the point, Mac," she said.

He was lost. "The point is there's another kid in this thing and I just did the same thing to her. I forgot all about her. Because I was carried away with Sissy. What am I doing? I'm chasing my tail. I'm going from one thing to another and not paying any attention to who gets hurt along the way. I'm doing it again. I don't know what's wrong with me. I can't seem to find my balance on this thing."

"Are you coming home?" he asked, wanting badly for her to say yes.

"No, I've got to do one more thing tomorrow. I've got to make sure Ms. Parks is set up with protection, then I'm going back to Blackbeard's Isle, probably tomorrow night. Leroy doesn't know about this. He's still coming. But Mac, pray to God that he doesn't get there before I do. I can't go through this again."

"You want me to come?" Mac said. "Between the two of us, we could cover both of them."

"It could be your badge, too," she said. "If anybody finds out."

"Fuck 'em," Mac said. "if they can't take a joke."

Mandy laughed. "Let me go check it out," she said. "If Leroy hasn't shown up yet, I'll call you. I could probably use the help."

Well, that's a first, he thought. Mandy taking help from him on anything.

"We were always better as a team," he said and then wondered if he had gone too far.

But Mandy only said, "Yeah, I know."

Lily waited until Breeze went to bed and then came out and turned on the computer. Sure enough, there was an e-mail from her mom. The e-mails had grown longer lately, and more frequent. Her mom sounded less spacey all the time, like she was waking up or something. It hadn't seemed like anything you could trust at first—I mean how dumb would it be to get excited about a few e-mails? But now . . . it was hard to know. The old feelings she had about her mom seemed to be easing—that hard, knotlike thing that used to be inside her all the time. Lately there was something different, a sort of fluttering feeling, like some kind of hopeful thing, but she didn't dare trust it.

She opened the e-mail.

Hi Lily,

I wanted you to know I got a kitten today. I was going to name him, and then I thought perhaps you might want to. I know you always wanted one, sweetheart, and I'm sorry I didn't get you one before. I just couldn't seem to stand up to Jerry about it— about anything. But it's getting easier. He told me I couldn't get one this time, and I told him I was going to anyway and nothing bad had better happen to him. He's orange and black and very sweet. Do you have any ideas for names?

By the way, he hasn't hit me in a long time now. I guess your leaving really woke him up. I hope you get to see the kitten soon. Love, Mom

Right, Lily thought, as if Jerry gave a shit about her leaving. She read the last line again. Jeez, what was her mother saying about seeing the kitten soon? Was she going home? But not if

ANNA SALTER

Jerry was there. Even if he wasn't hitting her mom, she never wanted to live under the same roof with that termite again.

Lily didn't want to think about going home. She definitely did not want to get her hopes up about that. That wasn't even worth thinking about. So what to say? She hesitated. What she really wanted to tell her mom about tonight was Mandy. About Mandy leaving them and all.

But could she do that? Her mom didn't know anything about Mandy. If she'd told her mom that, she would have to tell her why. She was pretty sure her mom wouldn't want her in any kind of danger. The whole time Jerry lived with them, the one thing he had never done was lay a finger on her, and she was pretty sure that was some deal her mom had made.

But if she told her, would her mom call up Breeze and say she had to go to Betsy's? Betsy didn't even have a computer. Without a computer she couldn't talk to her mom. Somewhere inside there was fear, smooth and hard as a marble, that if she lost her mother this time, she'd never get her back. Maybe she'd never even see her again.

She didn't want to think about that either. But maybe she could talk about Mandy a little if she down played the whole thing. She really wanted to talk about it.

She started slowly:

> Hi Mom,
> I have an idea for a name, but it's kind of a stupid name so you don't have to use it. I was thinking about naming him Blackbeard. That's where I am right now, on Blackbeard's Isle, so I wondered if you thought it would make a good name for a kitten. I'll think of some other names if you don't like it.
> Something happened today I wanted to tell you

about. It's not a big deal or anything but there was a friend of Breeze's named Mandy who was here on the island for a while. Some guy threatened Breeze and Mandy is a police officer and she was kind of keeping an eye on Breeze to make sure this guy didn't bother her. But then Mandy got something else she wanted to do and she just left. It's not a big deal or anything but I think it hurt Breeze's feelings. It was weird to have her just leave like that.

She read it again, but it seemed OK. It didn't sound like she was in any danger, so hopefully her mother wouldn't make any dumb suggestions that she should leave the island. If anything, it sounded like people leaving would hurt Breeze's feelings. She hit the send button, and then sat back and waited. Sometimes her mom wrote back right away. If she didn't get something soon, she'd give up and check in the morning.

While she waited, she thought about the fluttering feeling. She always got it when she was waiting for e-mails from her mom. She liked it. It made her want to giggle sometimes. It was weird, though, not worrying about her mom and not being angry all the time. "I hope you get to see him soon," her mother had said. You never know. Ten times before they quit. The e-mail gong sounded and she reached for the mouse.

chapter 22

I let Lily sleep for a few more minutes. No need to get her up yet. No need for me to get up. The window beside the bed showed a seamless expanse of blue powder that seemed deeper and richer than any ordinary blue. Sunlight flittered silently across the sheets. I watched the bright full-ness for a while, then got up and made some coffee. Cup in hand, I headed out on the balcony.

I sat down in the white rocker and put my feet up on the rail. The chirping of the birds made a sweet weaving of tones that seemed to shift and complement each other. Who knows? Maybe they sing harmony? Rehearsals under the pines. OK, now the chickadees will come in on the second robin chirp . . . hey, sparrows, you listen up . . . A light breeze tickled my bare toes. There was nothing like a Southern spring. Leaves and flowers burst forth like firecrackers exploding out of the ground. Up north, spring came grudgingly, slowly, as though mother nature had to pull the flowers up one by one, all the while harassing and nagging.

Mandy's late night phone call had blown me away. By God, they had a witness to Sissy's murder, and by God, it was just what I saw. I had seen Sissy hanging around Daryl at the prison. I never saw her when I watched Leroy or even when I spoke with him. It was Daryl who raped her, as I had thought, and I'll bet it was Daryl who turned on the gas. I knew about "excited utterance." Robert was right. Sissy would indeed get her day in court through Crystal's mom.

Mandy had sounded strangely subdued and said she'd be back as soon as she could. I could hear in her voice the unease and guilt about dumping us and her anxiety to get back and make it up to Lily.

So probably we only had a couple of days to get through until Mandy got back. Maybe Leroy wasn't even coming. It would be fine with me if he decided to skip his visit, but it was too soon to call off the watch. It had only been a week since he called Daryl.

It was true that we were in pretty good shape for gadgets. I had even had to pull an iron bar out of the track of the sliding glass door before I could open it to get out on the balcony this morning. Maybe Lily and I had been too hard on Mandy. She had set us up pretty well. It was frightening now to think of how accessible we had been before she came.

I heard the sound of a car and looked down in time to see a police cruiser go by. The officer waved and I waved back. Mandy had met with Carl, the local police chief, before she left and asked him to keep an eye on us while she was gone. Carl was a thin, wiry man in his forties who had retired to Blackbeard's Isle from Chapel Hill when he had gotten tired of drunk college kids tearing up the world. Tired, too, of the endless alcohol on a college campus and the endless parade of athletes arrested for vandalism or sexual assault or fighting whose cases quietly fell apart when victims sporting new cars decided to withdraw the charges.

Mandy had pronounced herself happy with him: Carl was a good cop. He had pulled up Leroy Collins's track record on his computer and then looked at me thoughtfully. He had said he didn't have the manpower to keep a guy at the house—but I knew that before I went. He could have his officers ride by frequently, and he'd run off a mug shot and show it to the ferry workers.

That might or might not help, I knew. More and more tourists were coming on the island as we got closer to summer, and if someone drove on the ferry and stayed inside their car, nobody would even get a look at them. That was especially true on the Hatteras end of the island, where the ferry was free and no one even had to get out to buy a ticket. Carl didn't like my odds, he told me: Leroy was a pro. He, too, thought a trip wasn't a bad idea, but he didn't argue when I told him I wasn't going.

The best plan I could think of for the next few days was to drive Lily to and from school and then just stay home, cell phone at hand. Lily would be all right in school, and I should be all right if I skipped the beach for a few days and stayed put. Mandy had seemed to think it was the transitions—getting from the car to the house, going out on the beach alone—that were the biggest risks. Leroy was unlikely to do anything in the grocery store or any other public spot. I was probably worrying for nothing anyway. We'd have to be extraordinarily unlucky for Leroy to show up the few days Mandy was gone. It didn't sound to me like my odds were all that bad.

I went downstairs to wake up Lily for school but she wasn't in her room. Puzzled, I checked the bathroom, then the rest of the house, all the time calling her name, then went outside to see if she had finally developed an affection for Grandma.

I called her from the yard, but didn't get an answer, and by now my stomach was getting tight, and fear was running like electricity up and down my arms. I told myself not to panic. Lily was upset with Mandy. Maybe she went for a walk. I went back and checked the house again, then ran out to the jeep.

What was she thinking, going for a walk right now? I'd kill her when I found her. I backed my jeep out the driveway and started down the road toward the beach. One good thing about Blackbeard's Isle—there weren't that many roads. I drove everywhere I could think of, even out on the beach, but no Lily. Where the hell was she? I drove home hoping she'd come back while I was gone but the house was silent.

Where else could she be? Had I looked under the bed? On the roof? Jena and I climbed out on the roof at night as kids. Why hadn't I thought of it? You could see the sea from there. I walked all around the outside of the house, looking at the roof and calling her name, then went back inside. I checked the house again, this time every closet, under every bed—even ridiculous places like under the couch where she wouldn't fit anyway.

I stopped in the middle of the living room and just stood while I tried to think. There was no place else to check. My heart rate felt like the buzzing of a bee, and I could hear the sound of my own breathing. I started to go out to the car again, then turned back, walked over and reached for the phone to call Carl when suddenly it rang. I grabbed it and said, "Lily?" without even thinking. There was a pause, and I heard Leroy Collins's voice on the line.

"No," he said slowly. "I'm calling about Daryl Collins. I got some information you might want."

I sank onto the couch. "Don't play games with me, Leroy," I said. "I know your voice." I was holding the phone with both hands now and mashing it against my ear as though I could get through the line at him. "You better not have hurt a hair on that child's head. If you ever, ever expect to get any information out of me, you had better leave Lily alone."

This time the pause was longer. "I ain't gonna hurt her, if I get what I want," he said finally.

I had my hand on my forehead now and my eyes shut, the better to see his voice. The voice didn't change at all when he said he wouldn't hurt Lily. He was telling the truth. I'd bet on it.

"Where is she?"

"What you got for me?"

"What do you want?"

"If you know so much, I'm thinking you know what I want. I want to know what's going on. Why're the cops all fired up about Sissy Harper?"

"This is not a problem, Leroy. I don't care about the information. I want Lily back. As long as she is unharmed, I'll tell you whatever you want to know. "

His voice sounded almost amused at my quick capitulation. "I ain't done nothing to her," he said smoothly. Again, the texture of his voice did not change. I opened my eyes.

"So what now?" I asked. "What do you want to know?"

"I want to talk about this up close and personal," he said. "Momma didn't raise nobody stupid enough to talk business on the phone."

"So where?" I asked. "Bring Lily with you," I added.

"I'm thinking I ain't spent no time on the beach," he said. "I expect you know a nice quiet spot where nobody be bothering us."

I thought for a moment about a spot. Why not? "I do," I said. I told him how to get there. "If you can't find it, ask anybody. It's right where Blackbeard's hideaway used to be. It's well known."

"All right," he said. "I'll be seeing you round midnight."

"What? Midnight? Come on, Leroy. What's the point in waiting? You want the information. I want Lily back. I can meet you now."

"Tonight'll be soon enough," Leroy said smoothly. "Too many tourists out in the daytime. I don't like nobody around when I'm talking business. Now here's what you're gonna do. You're going to take the phone off the hook today and you're going to turn off the cell phone. You ain't gonna to talk to nobody, you hear me? You ain't gonna see nobody or talk to nobody. I be checking on you. I can see your house from where I am, and I'll know if you go out. I'll be calling that number to make sure it's busy. You don't want to get nobody killed with your foolishness."

"No problem," I said.

"You just stay put and have yourself a fine day at home. I'll be seeing you round midnight. And," he added, "you remember what I said. Don't you even think about calling the police. I ain't done nothing to Lily, and I won't so long as you come alone."

I put down the receiver and just sat back with my head on the couch and my eyes closed. How the hell had he gotten her out of the house? But he couldn't have. Upset about Mandy or some such thing, she must have gone for a walk, and he grabbed her. I didn't even notice the tears until I needed a Kleenex for my nose. I got up slowly. Why did Leroy want me in such an isolated place in the middle of the night? There was no good answer to that, but the important thing was that he wasn't going to hurt Lily. The look of a voice couldn't be faked, and Leroy's hadn't turned brassy or changed texture in the slightest.

I walked over to the window and wondered where Leroy was that he could see the house. The sky was still an all enveloping blue and the bright yellow disk just over the horizon seemed to signal that God was in his heaven and all was right with the world. But nothing was right. The day had lied to me.

chapter **23**

While Lily had waited that night, the e-mail she was hoping for was being written. It was read and reread and fiddled with until there were no more changes to be made. The plan was risky, but it couldn't be helped.

Dear Lily,

I've thought a long time about this, and I think the time has come to leave Jerry. I know I've said this before and I haven't done it, but I feel different now. Maybe it took your leaving to wake me up.

Anyway, I want you to go with me but it won't be easy to get away. I know Jerry will try to find us, but I won't let that happen.

I want to protect Breeze so I don't want you to tell her anything about this. If she doesn't know anything, there's nothing she can tell Jerry, no matter how much he tries to trick her. I'll call her from the road as soon as we're safe. Please don't tell her anything, or leave a note or somehow Jerry might find us. I know this sounds crazy, but I feel our best chance is if nobody knows about it but you and me.

I've worked it all out and here's what I want you to do. I want you to get up early in the morning—tomorrow morning, if that's ok. I know that's not a lot of notice but I just found out Jerry's leaving tonight and won't be back until tomorrow night so that would give us a head start.

Don't pack much. Just bring a backpack with what you need for the day. I'll get you new clothes. If your clothes are gone, Breeze will know you've left for good and she'll worry.

I've checked the ferry schedule. There's one at 5 AM. Can you make it? I'll arrange to have a ticket at the counter for you, all paid for. You'll just have to pick it up. If you take the ferry, I'll have a limousine to meet you on the other side. Don't worry about finding it, the driver will have a picture of you and he'll recognize you when you get off the ferry. I'd pick you up myself but I can't leave until Jerry leaves tonight, and that means I can't get there in time.

The driver will take you all the way to Raleigh and drop you at a motel. He has the address. The motel will have a room for you in my name. I've talked to the hotel, and they know you'll arrive before I do. They'll give you a key to the room. Don't worry. The room is all paid for. If I drive straight through I can be in Raleigh by tomorrow night.

Order room service for food. Just tell them to charge it to the room. Oh, and you can watch movies too. Just charge them to the room also.

I think the plan is a pretty good one. I'll tell you
more when I arrive. My boss Dave has been helping
me work it all out. I didn't want to tell you until I
was ready, but I've been working on this for a while.

My sweet girl, I can't wait to see you. We're leaving
and we'll be free of Jerry forever. Love you, Mom

He read it through one last time and then hit the send button.

Lily stood on the ferry and watched Blackbeard's Isle shrink
to nothing behind her. She'd been there almost an hour early.
It crossed her mind that she was a little like Mandy, leaving
Breeze alone when that man Leroy was after her. But even if
she stayed, what could she do? And this was it. She might not
have another chance to get her mom away from Jerry. Breeze
would understand that. Besides, she was a whole lot better
able to take care of herself than her mom was. She wished she
had a copy of the e-mail, but she'd been too afraid of waking
Breeze to print it. It didn't matter. She knew it by heart.

Turning back to watch the bay ahead of her, she strained her
eyes to see the mainland, but it would be another hour or so
before land came into view. Somewhere over there a limousine was waiting, or maybe it was still on its way—that is, if
her mother hadn't changed her mind. Which she could do.
But somehow she didn't think her mother would this time.
She had never made plans like this before, really detailed
plans. And she'd been sounding different for a while.

The time dragged. All she wanted was to see her mom walk
in that motel room. She waited and waited for land to appear,
but when it did, she had a sudden moment of regret and
turned back to look behind her. What if she never saw Breeze

again, or Betsy? Leaving had happened so quickly, like a giant wind had just swept her off the island. She'd kind of been blown on the island and now she'd been blown off, like some sort of seed being thrown around by the wind. After a while, would the whole thing seem like a dream, that she'd never been there at all? But she didn't really believe that. Black-beard's Isle now seemed more like home than the house with Jerry in it did, and she promised herself she'd go back soon. With her mom.

She walked off the boat and, as her mother promised, she saw a man scanning the crowd. He spotted her and then started walking toward her. She had a moment of fear, remembering what she had always been told about not getting into cars with strangers. "I'm an idiot," she thought. "Nothing but a big baby." She walked toward him, smiling nervously.

chapter 24

I walked down the beach toward the place I told Leroy to meet me. I had thought immediately of the section of beach near Blackbeard's hideaway where I had run into Charlie, though I couldn't say why. But now I wished I hadn't. Nobody hung out there much in the day, nobody except Charlie, and for sure nobody would be here at night. I didn't see anyone when I arrived, but Leroy must have been hiding in the marsh beyond the dunes because only a few minutes after I got there, he seemed to materialize in the nighttime fog on top of a dune.

He walked down toward me and stopped only a few feet away. He had a gun in his hand, hanging down by his side, and the fog gave him an ethereal look, like he was one of the specters I saw. A sharp fear wrapped around my heart like a large bird's talons, and it was for a thirteen-year-old girl I hadn't even known I liked. Somehow, worrying about her had taken all the fear away. The talons felt like they were puncturing my lungs.

"Where's Lily?" I said. "You better not have hurt that child."

"I got no reason to hurt her," he said, "not if you tell me what I want to know."

"What do you want to know?"

"What do the police have on Daryl and Sissy Harper?" Leroy said.

"Nothing, basically nothing."

"Now don't be playing games with me," he said.

"I'm not playing games," I said. "A woman named . . . Lucy Sparks . . . called the prison," I lied. "She wanted to know if Daryl was getting out. She said she had a friend named Crystal a long time ago, when Daryl first went to prison, and Crystal told her Daryl had killed a four-year-old girl back in Texas. The prison officials called the police. The police interviewed her, and she said Crystal saw the killing. She said she was afraid Daryl knew Crystal told her, and that he'd come after her if he got out of prison." I stopped and shrugged. "That's it."

"Tell me the rest," he said. "What they gonna do about it?"

"Nothing," I said. "There's nothing they can do about it. Crystal's dead. She's been dead for a decade. Without her, it's just hearsay evidence. Lucy wouldn't be allowed to testify, and there was never any forensic evidence to begin with. It's a dead end, but I saw a note in the records about the interview so I asked Daryl about the girl. That's all. All this is for nothing. It's a done deal." Behind him, down the beach in the fog, I saw a man sitting on the rocks by the jetty. Probably Charlie. Sweet Jesus, what was he doing out here at this hour?

"How do I know Crystal is really dead?" Leroy said.

"I don't know," I said. "All I know is the story I was told. Crystal was a drug addict, and supposedly she died of an overdose.

"Crystal went up to Seattle with her mother," Leroy said. "Where's she?"

"Her mother?" I said. "How would I know? I didn't see anything in the records about Crystal's mother. Maybe she's dead by now, or maybe she went back to Texas. It was all a long time ago."

Leroy digested this, then switched the topic. "Daryl says you're trying to keep him in prison."

"I don't care one way or the other," I said. "I'm an outside evaluator. Sometimes I think offenders meet the criteria of the law to stay, and sometimes I don't. It doesn't affect me either way. As a matter of fact, Daryl doesn't meet the criteria. He's going to be released on time. Now I've told you everything I know. Where's Lily?"

"Who the hell is Lily?" Leroy said, grinning. He raised the gun and pointed it at my face.

"What are you doing? You've got no reason to kill me," I said.

"I got no reason not to," he said. "Besides,"—he grinned again—"sometimes I got to kill somebody, just to remind people who I am."

Over his shoulder I saw Charlie walk up behind him. Oh dear God, on top of everything, don't let that poor old man get killed.

"There's somebody behind you, Leroy," I said. "It's an old man and he's harmless. Just let him go."

Leroy swung around, his gun pointing at Charlie.

Charlie saw the gun and stopped, staring at Leroy. "Ain't no sense in it, Cap'n," he said. "I ain't done nothing wrong. You just leave me be now. We be coming up on Beaufort Inlet soon. You ain't got no better pilot. You have Abe take you in, you'll be lucky if you don't break the old ship in pieces. Leave me be now."

Charlie was dressed as he always was, in old pants and a dirty shirt, and tonight he had a red bandana around his head. In the daytime he just looked poor and unkempt, but in the darkness and half-light of the clouded moon with fog creeping across the beach, he looked like some kind of unearthly creature that had sprung from the marsh and the dunes. When he spoke, he sent a chill up my spine, even though I knew who he was.

He must have affected Leroy the same way because I saw him take a step backward and stumble as he did so. He seemed struck speechless, and the gun dropped to his side.

I started backing into the water. Maybe Charlie had caught Leroy by surprise, but it wouldn't be long before he realized Charlie was just a crazy old man, and he'd kill him, too. I couldn't stop Leroy by rushing him. He was bigger and faster and he had a gun. But maybe I could draw him off. I kept backing into the water, all the time watching Leroy, who was still staring at Charlie. When I was thigh-deep, I turned to dive, but just as I did so, I was dragged backward by a giant hand so powerful it knocked the breath out of me. A riptide had caught me. I could see nothing but black water, and I could feel myself getting dragged rapidly out to sea. When I surfaced, the beach was already some distance away, and I saw Leroy running toward me. Charlie was still standing, so Leroy hadn't shot him yet.

I saw Leroy briefly in snapshots after that, each time I fought my way to the surface. I saw him once up to his knees in the water looking for me, and the next time I surfaced he was gone. The riptide, like a huge animal reaching out, must have grabbed him too.

I got my wits about me and started swimming sideways, parallel to the beach. That was the one and only way to beat a riptide. They were too powerful to swim against, and anyone trying to get straight back to shore would exhaust themselves and drown, all the time getting taken further and further out to sea. But riptides were narrow, and if you swam sideways, you could get out of them and then head for shore.

It seemed to take forever. By the time I was out of the riptide, the shore was so far away, I could hardly see it. If there hadn't been something of a moon left, maybe I wouldn't have. I started the long swim back in.

When I finally dragged myself up on the beach, I was too tired to even think. Charlie was nowhere in sight, so I figured he was alive or there would have been a body. For sure Leroy hadn't moved it. I hiked back down the beach to my car and drove straight to the police station. I had the officer on duty call Carl. He came on the phone, instantly awake, and I told him that Lily was missing, and what had happened with Leroy. Carl was at the station no more than ten minutes later, and I went through the whole story again, this time in detail. I was still dripping wet but wrapped in a blanket an officer had given me. Carl spoke calmly, but I could see the anger behind his eyes.

"I don't meant to fault you, Breeze. I know when a child's life is on the line, people do crazy things. But people like Leroy don't play fair. You had to know he was planning on killing you if he insisted on meeting you on the beach in the middle of the night. If he was going to kill you, he would surely have killed her, too, if he hadn't already. Otherwise, she could testify against him. I wish you'd called us." I opened my mouth and then shut it. In the light of reason, without the heart-stopping fear for Lily, and without knowing Leroy had passed my synesthesia truth test, what I had done looked stupid.

He picked up the phone to get all his deputies in. They'd start searching the island now. They'd call all the motels and inns to find Leroy. I told him I was 99 percent sure Leroy was dead because what could he possibly know about riptides? He said until the body turned up, he'd keep on looking for him. I could see something in his eyes that said he thought he might find Leroy alive, but there was no chance he'd find Lily. I was pretty sure he was wrong about Leroy. I hoped to God he was wrong about Lily.

"Just one thing, Carl," I said hesitantly. "What if he doesn't have her? He did say, 'Who the hell is Lily?' What if she's somewhere else? She was upset. Maybe she ran away."

"It's a possibility," Carl said calmly, with the same degree of conviction as if I had suggested she'd swum to the mainland.

I went home and not knowing what else to do, I called Mandy. Her cell phone was off, which was not a surprise in the middle of the night. I just said it was an emergency, to call me back.

She returned the call at 4:00 a.m. I had been dozing on the couch and I told her briefly that Leroy was on the island and that Lily was missing. I was too tired to get into much of the rest of it.

"Shit," she said. "Shit, shit, shit. I knew I shouldn't have left. Jesus Christ."

"I brought in the police, Mandy," I said.

"Good thing," she said sharply. "You should have done that before. He would have killed you." I couldn't defend myself if I wanted to. The point was getting Lily out alive. How could I tell anybody that I believed Leroy wouldn't hurt Lily if I did what he said because the texture of his voice didn't turn scratchy?

"Mandy," I said. "are you coming or not?"

"What?" she said, surprised. "Of course, I'm coming. I told you I was coming back as soon as I could. I took a red-eye. I'm in Raleigh and on my way down. I'll be there in a few hours."

"Not a trace," Mandy said. "Not a fucking trace." She was pacing back and forth in my living room and looked completely wired. Betsy was watching her and thinking. The skin around Betsy's eyes was stretched and dark with worry and lack of sleep.

"What did he say?" Betsy said thoughtfully, "'Who the hell is Lily?'"

"That's the thing," I said. "He should have been bragging about having her, but he wasn't."

"I don't get it," Mandy said. "He told you he had her, right, on the phone?"

"Sort of," I said. "But maybe not exactly. When I run it back in my head, I think I told him he had her. He called right after she disappeared, and I just assumed he did."

"What if he didn't have her? Maybe she went to see her mother," Mandy said.

"I don't think so," I replied. "She couldn't possibly think she could hitchhike all the way to Chicago, and she wouldn't have just run away somewhere else, because then her mother wouldn't be able to find her. Besides, she didn't take any clothes and she doesn't have any money."

"Still, maybe she went with her mother," Mandy persisted. "She said her mother was changing, that she was better, that she was thinking of leaving Jerry."

"What?" I said. "Her mother isn't better. Why would she think that?"

Mandy thought for a minute. "She said she was *sounding* better," she said finally, "when we went to get the shells on the beach. It sounded like they were talking. I just assumed you knew."

"You're kidding," I said. "She must have made it up. She hasn't been talking to her mother. I have the phone bills. I went into my bedroom and opened the drawer in my desk that kept my bills. I came back out with the phone bill in my hand. "Here it is. No calls to Jena."

"What about the cell phone?" Mandy asked. "They only record minutes."

"It doesn't work here," I said. "No towers. I only keep it for when I'm on the mainland."

"She was in contact with her," Mandy said. "I'm sure of it." We looked at each other for a moment, and then we both turned toward the computer.

"Oh jeez," I said, moving toward it. "I thought she was talking to her friends. Why didn't she tell me?"

It wasn't hard to find the e-mails. We pulled the latest one up first.

"She's gone with her mother," Mandy said, relief in her voice.

"No, she hasn't," I said. "That isn't Jena."

"How do you know?"

"I know what kind of shape Jena's in. I call her boss every week. Jena is having trouble ordering paper clips right now. No way in hell could she make a plan like this. But we can find out for sure. The e-mail says Dave's helping her." I picked up the phone and called him.

"Jena's gone with Jerry," I said when I hung up. "They've gone on a trip. She asked for a couple of days off. And no, Dave hasn't been helping her make any plans."

Betsy stood up. "Call Carl," she said. "Get the Raleigh police involved. The son of a bitch has kidnapped her. If there's a God in heaven, he'll will go to jail till the sun don't shine."

"Betsy," I said. "You can't accuse Jena of kidnapping her own child. She's in the car with him and she has legal custody. She can rescind my guardianship anytime she wants to."

"But ten to one she wasn't in on this. She probably doesn't even know they're going to pick Lily up."

"Almost certainly she doesn't know," I agreed.

"So she can tell them she didn't agree."

Mandy and I just looked at each other. Betsy knew nothing about battered women. "She won't stand up to him, Betsy," I said gently. "She's completely and totally under his control. She's been beaten so much she's lost all sense of herself. She'll say whatever he tells her to say."

"God damn it, Breeze," Betsy exploded. "We're not just going to just sit here and let this happen."

"I don't know what we can do about it," I said.

"We can steal her back," she said.

"Oh, right," I replied. "And how do you feel about a kidnapping charge?"

"Breeze, don't give me that bullshit. We're not going to let the son of a bitch get away with it, and that's all there is to it."

"What exactly do you think we can do? Once he's got her, he'll find a way to make her say she wants to stay."

"Breeze, I cannot believe you. You sound so namby-pamby. This has got to be coming from that hippie momma of yours. You got some of that Arizona peace-and-love stuff stuck in your soul. It ain't Southern, that's for sure. We never forgive and we never forget and we never give up. There are rattlesnakes that deserve to live more than that son of a bitch. Personally, I doubt the police would care a whole lot if we shot him and fed him to the crabs, once they find out what he's done to Jena."

At the mention of my mother I bristled. I was exhausted and worried sick, and my emotions were stretched to the point where the rubber band snaps back. But Betsy didn't even notice me bristling. She was looking for a fight, and I was handy.

"Let's not get into nostalgia for the South, Betsy. It's bull-shit."

Mandy started to interrupt, but Betsy waved her off.

"Don't start in on the South," Betsy said. "I know we've made our mistakes. At times we've been about as wrong as a people can be. Just about. But you got to make a distinction between the content and the process. We just got the content wrong, but being loyal to your family and your kin and your part of the world was never wrong. We understand loyalty. It runs like layers of granite through this whole part of the country. You can't treat folks the way he's treated those two and not have some of their people get in your face. And we're all the people those two have got.

"If I wasn't a lady," she added, "I'd say the son of a bitch needed killing."

"We aren't ladies," I said.

"Well, then, he needs killing." We all fell silent.

"Mandy?" I said.

"She's going with or without us," she said, getting up. "So I say we go. Thank God," she added, "I'm the only one with a gun."

chapter 25

J erry looked over at Jena sitting quietly and staring out the window beside him. It had gotten to the point that she was damn near worthless. She couldn't even drive the freeways anymore. He hadn't counted on that. She drove to work every day. How the hell was he supposed to know she'd get confused driving somewhere she hadn't been before? He remembered with a shudder waking up to the sound of the tractor trailer horn. The bitch had drifted over right in front of him. You never know, it could have been deliberate. She'd cut her arms a few times, but none of that seemed serious. A tractor trailer was pretty goddamn serious.

It meant he'd had to drive the whole lousy seventeen hours. And that meant a new problem. He'd planned on going back the same night he picked up Lily, but now that was impossible. He couldn't drive a day and a half without sleep. They'd have to stay over at the hotel, which was risky. It was hard to know how Lily would react.

This whole thing was on its last legs anyway. It was time to start thinking about cutting his losses. Jena wouldn't be able to work much longer, and if she couldn't work, she had to go.

But he had unfinished business at home yet. How did the little bitch think she'd get away with it? As if it were up to her if she walked away. Time for her to learn she couldn't pee without asking him first. He had to admit, though, at first he'd enjoyed Lily being gone. No prying pair of eyes. No potential witness. No competition for Jena's attention. Total isolation.

But it hadn't worked. Without Lily, he had no real hold on Jena. She'd retreated to someplace where he couldn't reach her. Nothing made a difference. She was oblivious to pain, and she didn't seem to even register humiliation. She'd gotten to the point where he suspected she hoped he'd kill her, so threatening her did no good. The only thing she still feared was that something would happen to Lily.

You never could tell with Jena, though. Every time he decided she was completely out of it, he'd catch her looking at him, and for a moment the old intelligence would be back— further down in the eyes, maybe, but still present. There was still something he didn't own.

Not that it mattered. She was going downhill so fast, it was just a question of time. But he thought she had one last hurrah in her. One more round. He smiled as he remembered how it used to be: the frightened eyes so wide the whites showed all around, the pale, tremulous skin quivering around the mouth, the shock and fear printed out starkly in the tight skin and the rigid lines. It was better than crack, better than cocaine; a high that didn't come with anything else. He might have a year, he thought, more or less, of the old days. But only if he got Lily back.

He saw the sign for the motel and pulled off the highway. He stopped the car under the canopy and glanced over at Jena, but she hadn't changed expression or made any move to open the door. She hadn't asked where they were going or why.

He said, "We're going in to pick up a room key. I want you with me."

She looked over at him. She knew better than to question him.

He opened the door and started to get out, then sat back down. The clerk might mention it, and he didn't want her reacting in front of him, so he'd better tell her now.

"Lily's here. We're taking her home. If the clerk mentions it, keep your mouth shut."

A shock wave seemed to rise from the depths behind Jena's eyes and explode in her face. She looked at him and the old Jena was back in the eyes, as though she had just woken up. He wasn't imagining it. She still had something left.

"What did you think," he said quietly, "that I'd let her go? You know me better than that. You say one word to that clerk, and I will take her home and hold her hand down the garbage disposal until it's shredded. I'll make you watch." Jena said nothing. "Now, let's go get the key." He got out of the car and headed for the door, sure that Jena would follow.

The clerk was a tall, skinny kid with hunched-over shoulders and anxious eyes. He glanced at Jena once, and she braced herself for his scrutiny, but it was only a cursory glance. He turned his attention immediately back to the smiling Jerry.

Jerry turned on the charm and Jena watched the hapless clerk fall under it. Had that been her, she wondered, a long time ago, shuffling from one foot to the other, nervous in the presence of what seemed like grace?

She followed Jerry silently to the room. As they approached, she started getting dizzy, and the image grew in her mind that the top of her head was coming off. The insides were floating away on the air like Jell-O floating in water. She wondered if she should hold her hands on her head to hold her head on, but she didn't have the energy to lift her hands. It was probably too late anyway. She couldn't feel the top of her head, and she had a distinct feeling of cool air running over her brain, so it was probably gone already.

She concentrated on counting the doors as she passed. She wanted to stop and finger the numbers of the doors. Every door had numbers, every single one. If she could just stop and run her fingers over the numbers. Why would anybody ever leave if they could just stand there and do that? She hoped to God there would be an odd number of doors before they got to Lily's. What would she do if they ended on an even number?.

Lily wouldn't be in that room. She couldn't be. It was all wrong. Breeze would never send Lily back. Breeze would take care of her. He was fooling her, but even as she said it, she knew it wasn't true. He never made empty threats. But maybe he'd made a mistake. He wouldn't outfox Breeze. Lily wouldn't be in that room, and the cords would stand out in his neck when she wasn't. She didn't care what happened after that—as long as Lily wasn't there.

They were getting closer to 116 now, Lily's room, and her body started feeling heavier, as though she were on Jupiter. She felt herself getting bigger, but mostly from her hips downward. Her stomach felt so heavy she wondered if she looked pregnant. She didn't dare look down. Her legs and ankles must be enormous.

She saw Jerry stop in front of the door, slide his plastic key in the lock, then step quickly into the room. She heard Lily cry out at seeing him and then the sound of a blow through the open door. Then mercifully it happened. She was floating somewhere high up, looking down on herself and the scene.

Everything below seemed remote, like she was watching a movie.

From her high vantage point, she saw Jerry grab her arm and yank her into the room, saw herself stare at Lily, who was lying on the floor. Lily was sobbing hysterically and covering her face with her arms. She saw Jerry kick her twice, then pick her up and throw her in a chair. He grabbed the arms of the chair and got his face very close to Lily's. He pulled a gun out of his pocket and pointed it straight in Lily's face. He wasn't yelling, just talking quietly. Lily's face drained of color. Then Jena saw him backhand her and send her flying out of the chair. Lily's head hit the wall as she fell.

—◦—

Jena sat up in the darkness in the motel room and listened to Jerry's ragged breathing beside her. She wondered if Lily was sleeping or awake next door. Maybe she was gone, but Jena didn't think so. She could almost feel her presence. That's the way it had been since she was born. Some part of her was always listening for Lily.

She looked down at Jerry and wondered what it was like to love him. It had been so long she couldn't remember. When did it stop? Sometimes things end, and it takes a while to notice. It had been like that. She never saw it go. But the rest of it—the feeling she didn't exist without him and the taste of fear always in her mouth—that had seemed to last forever.

Until now. Now it just seemed to have run its course, like a fever that finally breaks and disappears. But that didn't seem right, either. It was almost like taking one step too far and you've gone through a door and everything's all different. Just one step.

If Lily hadn't come back, maybe it wouldn't have happened. The image of Lily's head hitting the wall played and replayed in her mind, as if it were running an endless loop. It had been so much easier with Lily gone. He'd lost some giant hold on her when Lily left. They both knew it. And now Lily was back, and he was beating her, too.

Lily had been the last step through the door. Certainly it wasn't the beatings. They were the same as always. Not like the night Lily left. Nothing had happened like that for a while, no cigarette burns or plastic bags over her head. She had thought when they left on this trip that they'd go back home, and things would go on like they always had. She'd get up in the morning and go to work, like she always did. Jerry would be waiting when she got back, like he always was.

Sometime in the night she had woken up and it had all broken down. She had lost the thread of things, the script. Then she realized she hadn't actually woken up. She just noticed that she wasn't sleeping.

Jena got up. Nothing seemed connected to anything. She had no idea why she was standing there. She had no plans or ideas or any place to go, and she wondered what she would do next. She stood for a moment looking around. Everything seemed different, clearer and sharper somehow. The edges of a bureau stood out clearly in the moonlight coming through a gap in the curtain. Everything was still. He was lying on his side, sprawled and careless, and a line from a poem came to her: "You were so close, I could have touched the dead childhood in your face." But that wasn't what was different. She felt like that a lot when he was sleeping.

What was different was that she wasn't afraid anymore. That scrunched-up thing in her was gone. Her chest felt like some tight wrapping had loosened that had kept it all closed up.

She took a deep breath for the first time in . . . what? She couldn't remember, some kind of forever. She just didn't care anymore. More than that, she couldn't remember what caring had been like. She felt like a ghost, like she didn't exist. She had no sense of herself, no real belief she was real or her body was real. Her legs didn't feel heavy anymore. She felt light and insubstantial. She was made of air or something lighter even.

She closed her eyes and saw herself hovering over the earth, just floating above the earth like a Macy's Thanksgiving Day parade balloon, with one faint tether still connecting her, a line that led straight to a small figure holding it and looking up. Lily was the only thing that could take her back, back to that scrunched-up place where she was afraid all the time.

The moonlight slipping through the curtain drew her, and she walked over to the door and opened it. She didn't even glance to see if the noise woke him. As if it mattered. Outside, the parking lot lights seemed like giant fireflies hovering in the air over a black pond. She wiggled her toes up and down on the wet payment and marveled at how distinctly she could see everything. Cars and lights and, beyond the parking lot, a row of trees—all seemed imbued with an unreal clarity. She saw water dripping from the leaves, a small dent in the light pole, and she wondered how she could see them so far away. She didn't remember taking any drugs.

It was very quiet. She could hear a car going by a long way away, its motor a distant buzz like a solitary bee making night rounds. She sat down on the curb and felt wetness from the rain soak through her nightgown. It must have been cold because she had goose bumps on her arms, but she couldn't feel anything.

She could hear her heart beating loudly in the quiet. She thought she might dance. She just needed a scarf, like Isadora

ANNA SALTER

Duncan. If she danced, she would need someone to dance with. If she danced, would her mother come? Her mother had gone so long ago, just seemed to drift off day by day until she was hardly getting out of bed anymore. Then one day she didn't get up at all. Maybe she would come if Jena danced. She'd never thought of that.

She got up and walked back into the motel, and surprised herself by opening the drawer to the bedside table next to Jerry. She'd seen him put the gun in there, just like he did at home. The blue steel danced when the moonlight caught it, and she picked it up and ran her hand over it. She never realized what a beautiful thing a gun was, but the deep shine on this one mesmerized her.

She sat down in the easy chair next to the bed. The gun lay on her lap. Her hand felt right holding it, as though the gun was part of her or maybe she was part of the gun. The gun had its own ideas about things, she knew. Maybe the gun knew what was going to happen. She marveled at how right the gun looked lying in her lap. Should she keep a gun in her hand forever, like Michael Jackson wearing his glove? She sat there waiting, but for what? She wasn't sure. She just sat and waited to see what would happen. While she waited, she watched Jerry sleep.

It must have been a while. Probably it was, because daylight was streaming through the curtain when he woke. Lily's room next door was silent. His eyes just came open and then he sat bolt upright. "What are you doing?" he said.

She didn't know, so she didn't say anything. It wasn't a fair question, really. She wasn't doing anything.

"What the hell are you doing?" he said again, this time louder and she heard fear in his voice. Strange to hear fear from him. That was new and sort of embarrassing. "Give me that," he said, and reached out for the gun.

"Oh, I can't do that," she said, the gun rising automatically up in her hand and pointing right at him. Why was he talking to her? It wasn't up to her. "I'm just waiting," she said, trying to explain it to him.

"Put that thing down," he said, but not strong like he usually said things.

She looked at the gun. "It's not up to me," she said. Couldn't he see that? He just sat back, staring at her. "I don't think it matters a lot," she said. "I wouldn't worry about it."

"What the hell is wrong with you?" he whispered.

Was that true? Was there anything wrong with her? She felt fine: calm and light. She had almost been dancing. She watched the gun to see what it would do next.

"You don't want to do this," he said. "You'll go to jail. You'll never see Lily again."

That was a surprising thing to say. She felt a faint tug when he said Lily, but jail produced no feeling at all. He might as well have said she'd eat asparagus.

"It's like eating asparagus," she said.

He looked really alarmed then, and she tried to calm him. "Don't be afraid." She wanted him to understand but he didn't seem to.

"What are you going to do?" he said. Was he really whimpering? Was that possible? She felt puzzled. She didn't know this man. Who was he? Jerry never asked her what she was going to do.

I'm waiting to see what will happen," she said. "You can wait with me if you want."

"Why don't we call someone?" he said. "You need help. You need a rest. Why don't we call the police?"

"The police?" she said, even more puzzled. "You told me not to call the police. I'd have to show them my neck. And my back. But it doesn't matter, does it? Why would we call the police?" Cocking her head to the side, she watched him and the gun and wondered what would happen next.

They sat and she waited and he kept looking at her. Honestly, she thought he should have been looking at the gun, not her. He had a funny nose, really. She wondered why she had never noticed it. It was red like he'd been crying, but she didn't see any tears.

"Do you have a cold?" she said.

He looked at her like she was crazy. She wondered if she was.

"Why is your nose so red?" That was all she could see. It dominated everything. And it seemed important to know why.

"This has gone far enough," he said. "Give me that gun." He leaned forward with his hand stretched out. She knew immediately he shouldn't have done that. Even she knew enough to leave the gun alone.

The sound deafened her. It was a lot louder than on TV. The recoil knocked her hand back and the gun flew out of it. It was just as well. It was heavy and she was tired of holding it.

Her ears were ringing and she couldn't hear anything. He was saying something or trying to, because his mouth was moving. Red was spreading over the pillow and it was messy. It would be hell to clean those sheets.

She saw Lily in the doorway between the two rooms and she looked like she was screaming. In any case, her mouth was moving, but she heard no sound at all. She sat waiting, not even wondering what would happen next.

chapter **26**

gotta find some country," Betsy said, turning on the radio. "I can't stand just sitting here doing nothing but worrying about Lily. How much longer, do you think?"

"Stop, Betsy," I said. "You know this road as well as I do. We're barely past Goldsboro. We've got at least two hours to go." Betsy had spent the trip thus far ranting about Jerry, and she wasn't the only one who needed a break from it. Mandy had her eyes closed, and was leaning against the window in the backseat, and I thought even Josie, my beloved car, was tired of it.

My cell phone rang and I answered it.

"Breeze, It's Carl. We found Leroy Collins."

"Dead?" I said.

"Very," Carl said. "A fisherman hauled him in early this morning. Crabs got to him but not too bad. We'll get DNA to confirm it, but he still looks enough like his mug shot that it's just a formality. It's him. But I'm sorry. We haven't found any trace of Lily."

"Oh, Carl," I said. "I should have called you. I don't know what I was thinking. Early this morning we found some e-mails from Lily to her mother, or someone she thought was her mother. We think it's her stepfather. He was beating on her mother and that's why she was here. He tricked her into going to . . ."

I heard Betsy yell. I looked over and saw her face registering shock. "She's in Raleigh," I said to Carl. "We think so, anyway. Got to go. Betsy's yelling about something. I'll call you back." I hung up and turned to Betsy.

"What?" I said. "What is . . . "

"Shhhhh," she said. She reached over and turned up the radio.

> . . . Mrs. Jensen was found sitting in the room next to her dead husband after another guest heard the shot and phoned the police. Sources near the police say she has not spoken, and they believe she may be mentally ill. The couple's thirteen-year-old daughter was with them, in an adjoining room at the motel.

I stared at the radio, too, and then looked up quickly. I had drifted halfway off the road. "Oh, my God," Betsy said. "She shot him. She shot the son of a bitch."

"I can't believe it," I said, and I couldn't. "Oh, Jesus, where's Lily?"

Mandy was learning forward now. "That's him? You're sure?"

"Oh, that's him," I replied. "It's got to be. How many Jena Jensen's were in a Raleigh motel last night with their thirteen-year-old daughters?" We all stared at the radio, but the announcer had moved on to another story.

"Find another station," Mandy said from the back seat. "See if you can catch it again."

I started to reach for the radio, but Mandy said, "You drive. Let Betsy find it." Betsy hit the scanner repeatedly, but the news was ending everywhere, and music was coming back on.

"I'll call the Raleigh police," Mandy said. "See if we can verify it and then find out where Lily is and what jail Jena's in. I'll tell them Lily's been living with you and you have guardianship. Did you bring the papers?"

"No," I said, "but I can get somebody to go to the house and fax them if I need to."

Mandy called and got a better reception than we expected. Lily had been asking for us, and they had already called my house. We had left early and missed the call.

After Mandy hung up, Betsy held out her hand. "Give me the phone," she said. Mandy handed it over.

"Who're you calling?" I asked.

"I've got a cousin in Raleigh," she said. "Member of the school board. Country club type. Knows everybody. I'm going to find that girl a lawyer."

Mandy turned to me, "You think it was because of Lily?"

"Don't you?" I answered.

"God bless that child," Betsy said.

We drove straight to the police station that held Lily. They had taken her statement and were now waiting to locate someone who would take her home. Lily was in a small interview room wrapped in a blanket. In the corner a woman from social services sat reading a magazine.

All three of us walked into the room, and Lily dropped the blanket and flew across the room toward us. I wrapped my arms around her, and Betsy stroked the top of her head. Her face was swollen on both sides and starting to turn purple. She cried hard against my shoulder for a few minutes, and Betsy murmured low in my ear, "Drive a stake through the son of a bitch's heart."

"She shot him," Lily said finally. "My mother shot him. There was blood everywhere, and she wouldn't even talk. She looked really spacey. It was like she was crazy or something. Will she be OK?"

"Probably," I said. "She's probably just in shock from all that happened."

"It was self-defense," she said. "I heard him beating on her through the walls. And then I heard him say he was going to kill her, and then there was like a struggle and the gun went off." But her voice, always smooth as orange sherbet, had changed its texture and now looked rough and scratchy.

I kissed the top of her head and whispered in her ear. "I think it was Lily-defense," I said, "not self-defense."

She turned her head and whispered back, "But you can go to jail for Lily-defense, can't you?"

"You could," I said.

"You don't go to jail for self-defense," she said.

Carter Bennington III turned out to be a well-dressed, portly man in his sixties. He moved and talked slowly, but the bland look in his eyes hid something further back: a pool of intelligence as clear and deep as a well. From the references Betsy got, it was clear to me he was the kind of attorney I feared the most when I was on the stand, the kind who would lull you with folksy stories, all the time weighing and assessing your weaknesses with computer-like efficiency. The jury never saw the strategic maneuvering. They just saw a folksy, likeable man talking casually with a witness and wondered why they hadn't realized earlier the witness was a fool.

He ambled slowly up to our small group. We were sitting in the hall at the psychiatric hospital where the police had brought Jena, but as her attorney, only Carter had actually gotten in to see her.

He introduced himself to the four of us, then turned to Lily. "You must be Lily," he said, and mentally I gave him kudos for speaking to her first. Lily was sitting in a chair, and Carter squatted down to talk to her eye to eye. "You've been through quite an ordeal," he said. "Did they check you out at the hospital?"

Lily nodded. "I'm OK. What's going to happen to my mother?"

"Nothing, if I have anything to say about it. Don't you worry your pretty little head about that. I understand it was self-defense?"

"It was," Lily said, too quickly. "He would have killed her. He was trying to. I heard him." She was looking down now and avoiding his gaze.

I saw Carter cock his head at her appraisingly, but he said nothing. "Can I speak to Ms. Breeze here for a moment?" Lily nodded hesitantly. "It's just some legal formalities," he said reassuringly. "Bore the hell out of you."

I walked aside with him. "I'm not sure the woman in that room is competent to assist with her defense," he said. "Hell, let me rephrase that. I'm sure she isn't competent to assist with her defense. She doesn't seem to know what day it is, maybe what year. What the hell is wrong with her?"

"She's probably dissociating," I said. She's surely got post-traumatic stress disorder and sometimes people with severe PTSD space out. I don't know how much you know about the case, but he's been beating on her for years. Really bad. She's got cigarette burns, ligature marks, God knows what else. Basically he's been torturing her. You should talk to her boss. He's gotten depressed just from watching it happen."

Carter shook his head. "Sum'bitch," he said. "You mind calling her boss, giving him my number?"

"Sure," I said.

"What about the kid's story?" he asked.

I didn't say anything for a minute and then I said, "I think she'll stick to it. That's all I can say."

"So what really happened in that room?" he asked.

"My guess is she just lost it. Jena sent Lily to live with me, to get her away from Jerry, the maniac husband. Jerry lured Lily out of my house by e-mailing her and pretending to be her mother. I'm sure his plan was to take Lily back to Chicago with him. I doubt Jena knew anything about it until she got here. She had the shock of seeing that he had gotten Lily back, plus he beat Lily up. You saw her face. He'd never done that before."

"Interesting," he said. He stared down the corridor for a moment. "Folks around here don't have that much sympathy for battered women," he said. "Think they ought to just leave the bastards. Don't see why they have to shoot them. Ordinarily, she'd be facing a long prison term."

I started to speak and he held up his hands. "Now don't you worry about it. I talked to the docs already. She's got enough scars to maybe change their minds. Plus I'll get a psychiatrist in here this afternoon to evaluate her mental state. I'll invite the police to do the same. I don't think the prosecution can even find a court whore who'll say she's mentally competent right now."

"And Lily's story?" I said.

"I'll say this," he said. "I like that lady's chances anyway, but it never hurts to have a little insurance. There's nobody here to tell the tale but Ms. Jensen and her daughter. The deceased isn't going to contradict Miss Lily, and I doubt Ms. Jensen even remembers what happened. If the girl sticks to her story, she'll be OK. Depending on which prosecutor gets the case, we may not even have to go to court."

It was a somber group that gathered in a hotel room for take-out Chinese that night. Plans to go out had been cancelled when Lily had gotten a headache that grew steadily worse. I had finally called the hospital and learned that Lily's injuries were worse than I knew. She had a fracture of the occipital bone around the eye and a bad concussion. By the time she went to bed, she couldn't brush her teeth because the jarring shook her head too much. She was sleeping now in the adjoining room.

"I don't know about you," Betsy said, "but I am worn out. Worrying is a miserable business."

No one disagreed. The relief that Lily was out of Jerry's clutches had been replaced by mind-numbing exhaustion.

"I'm going home tomorrow," I said. "I'll take Lily with me. If we can't see Jena, there's nothing more we can do here for now. Anyway, that's what I'm thinking. Mandy, what about you?"

"Me?" Mandy said. "I'm leaving too. I've got unfinished business to take care of."

"Seattle?" I asked. "Are you babysitting Mrs. Parks?"

"Nah," she said. "They don't need me. I shouldn't have gone in the first place."

"It wouldn't have made any difference if you were here," I said. "Nobody anticipated Jerry tricking Lily."

"It could have made a huge difference," she said. "With Leroy. How many times is a crazy person going to bail you out? Except for some kind of weird fluke, Leroy would have killed you, and I would have been in Seattle, sitting politely on a couch and listening to Robert interview a witness."

"Don't be too hard on yourself, Mandy." I said softly. "Sissy had a real hold on you."

Mandy looked at me quickly, then looked away. I thought about asking her what would replace the search for Sissy's killer in her life but didn't feel I had the right.

"So what's the unfinished business?" Betsy asked.

"A guy. You met him," Mandy said turning to me. "Mac."

I looked at Betsy. "Total hunk," I said. "Abs like a washboard."

"Well, la-tee-da," Betsy said, "what have we here?"

"Probably nothing," Mandy said. "We used to have something, but I fucked that up, too. Anyway, I'm going home. I might come back and visit—if nobody minds. I feel like I owe Lily. I let her down."

"You just come on down here anytime, honey child," Betsy said. "We got ever'thin' here. We got criminals and orphans and people who see colors when you talk to them. Hell, we got crazy people wandering around thinking they're Blackbeard's first mate. Could be, for all I know. Don't mind me," she said, getting up and stretching. "I'm going to bed."

Epilogue

I t was three weeks before the docs let anyone see Jena. By then Carter Bennington III had her legal case well in hand. Dave and his wife had flown down to talk to the police about Jerry's treatment of Jena. Apparently they couldn't shut Dave up. He also put them in touch with the detective whom he'd brought in a year or so earlier to try to talk Jena into leaving Jerry. Between Dave, his wife, the detective, and Jena's scars, they established beyond a doubt that Jena had a long and horrible history of abuse at Jerry's hands. Dave said if anybody questioned it, just let him know and he'd start sending his employees down to testify, one by one.

Carter had gotten a forensic psychiatrist in to see Jena the day I met him. Since Jena was mute and completely out of touch, he had no trouble finding her temporarily insane, although no one was sure about the temporary part. Carter had tried to get the police to have their own psychiatrist examine her right away, but they declined to send one over, on the grounds that it was a job for the prosecution. The case wasn't referred to the DA for a few days, and after that it took the prosecution a while to get organized and hire an expert.

It was a mistake if you wanted to prosecute her—and maybe the police didn't. By not examining her early on, whomever the prosecution called as an expert witness later wouldn't be able to say much about her mental state at the time she shot Jerry— not compared to the docs who saw her the same day. The docs who were treating her turned out to be the best witnesses of all. They'd seen Jena as soon as the police brought her in. They were adamant she wasn't faking it.

The prosecutor was a decent man named Martin Steinberg whom Carter knew well and respected. Carter called him up and told him he'd make his client available to talk to him at any point. Martin Steinberg took him up on the offer and emerged from the session shaken. Who knows? Maybe the eight-by-ten glossy photos Carter had made of the damage done to Jena's body helped. All we found out later was that after he saw her, he added up the facts. Jena had a horrendous history of abuse. She had also been pretty clearly psychotic at the time, not to mention there was at least an auditory witness to the incident who was certain Jerry was trying to kill her when the gun went off.

Carter called Lily and me a few weeks later to tell us it was all over but the shouting. Nothing official had been announced yet, but over drinks Martin had told him it was self-defense, pure and simple. There would be no prosecution.

As for Daryl Collins, he was toast. Pat Humphrey flew up to talk to Mrs. Parks and found to her delight that she was an impressive witness. Pat had an indictment within days. She transferred all her other cases and went after Daryl with a zeal that was almost frightening.

As for me, I had only one more thing to do regarding Daryl

Collins—a call to Sarah Reasons, the therapist he had raped in prison.

"It's over," I said, and explained that Daryl had been indicted for the murder of a four-year-old girl more than a decade earlier. "I can't see him wiggling out of it," I added. "He's got the prosecutor from hell, and she's got a witness who doesn't care if she lives or dies, so she can't be intimidated. Without Leroy around, she isn't in much danger, anyway."

"Are you serious?" she said, sounding as though she didn't believe me. "Are you really serious?"

"Oh, yes," I said. "I am. Indeed I am. I know," I added, "that it won't solve everything, maybe not most of it, but at least you won't be getting any more anniversary cards and he is most certainly not going to be coming after you. All that's left," I said, "is the Daryl Collins in your head."

There was silence for a moment and then she said, "I'm working on it."

I didn't know what else to say, so I wished her well and started to hang up when she said, "Wait a minute. One more thing. Did you do this? How did you get him for this after all this time? That murder was years and years ago."

"It wasn't me," I said, "not me at all. It was the four-year-old. Her name was Sissy Harper."

"But she's d . . ."

"Yeah, she is," I said, "but some people are like that, I guess. She just wasn't anybody he should have messed with."

Lily and I drove up as soon as the docs said it was OK. Lily almost hummed with nervous energy on the seat beside me, unable to concentrate on a magazine or even a conversation.

I tried to make small talk but gave up. She had a backpack with some presents for her mom. She kept going through it and worrying about whether her mother would like them. She had spent days deciding what to buy.

Later, when she came back out of Jena's room, she was smiling and I felt myself relax.

"How'd it go?" I asked.

"Good," she said. "She's a lot better. She's talking and everything. She sounds like herself. It was good. Your turn. Now don't say anything to upset her." I smiled at Lily's protectiveness and went in to see Jena.

She was sitting in a chair by the bed, wearing jeans and a T-shirt, and she was still very thin. All in all though she looked a lot better than the last time I saw her. Her hair was washed and combed. It didn't look quite like a lion's mane yet, but it didn't look quite so dispirited, either. Her clothes were neat, and she looked right at me when I came in. She still had dark circles under her eyes, and the memory of pain was written bone deep in the face and eyes—the eyes especially: they had the kind of darkness that seems to absorb all light. Nonetheless, I could see the old Jena in there somewhere, and she didn't have that zombie look anymore. She looked more like someone recovering from a train wreck.

"Hi," I said, hopping up on the bed. "You look good."

"I'm better," she said. "A lot better. I still don't remember a lot of it, especially the last few months. I don't remember shooting him at all.

"The last few years—I know I lived it, but it all seems so incredible to me, like it happened to someone else and I was watching. Who would have thought when we were kids, that my life would end up like this?"

"It ain't over," I said. "It ain't ended up anything yet."

She shook her head, as though trying to shake the years off, and then said, "Lily seems really good. I have you to thank you for that. She seems like a different kid."

"She's doing good," I said. "You should be proud of her. I am."

"I don't know when I'll be able to take her back," she said. "I have these flashbacks where I see Jerry. He seems so real, sometimes I find myself wondering if he's really dead. I'm still not right all the time."

"Oh, he's dead all right," I said. "I'm pretty sure Betsy drove a stake through his heart just to make sure. But don't worry about Lily. She's always got a home. You can take her tomorrow, or you can leave her until she's eighteen. But if you take her tomorrow, you're going to have to put up with me coming to visit—a lot."

"The memories of Lily are the worst of it," she said. "Especially in the motel room. He started in on her just like he did on me."

"Cut yourself some slack," I said. "I think what you did was amazing. It isn't easy when you're falling out of a twenty-second-story window to catch someone else and throw them back in. Isn't that enough for one day's work?"

She held up her hand. "Oh, Breeze, don't patronize me. I don't have anything to be proud of," she said. "I let a monster take over my life. After a while I didn't feel anything for anybody, even Lily. I was totally numb, high on drugs and gone somewhere in my head I can't even describe."

"But it isn't true," I said. "If you didn't feel something for Lily, he would never have come after her."

She was silent for a moment. "Maybe," she said finally. She paused and looked away. "I was taken in so completely when I first met him. I never saw any of it coming. The truth is, I don't think I'm that good with people anyway. I'm just not that social, and I've never felt at home around people, not really."

She looked away again, and I was almost sure she was thinking of what she was good at, the climbing. "Patagonia?" I said gently.

"Yes," she said, and rubbed her fingers on her palms. "I wish I could take you there someday. You wouldn't believe how the rock feels under your hands, what it's like to be in the middle of all those white peaks in a kind of silence that's so powerful it feels like it has weight and mass. And the wind. Oh my God. The wind is like some kind of dangerous animal you have to constantly watch out for. You drop a rope in that wind and it stands straight up."

"It's a great place to rehab," I said.

"I can't go," she said. "I need to get set up so I can take Lily back."

"Lily's not doing badly where she is. I think she wants to see who you really are, at your best."

She looked at me thoughtfully.

We talked for a while longer, then Jena just seemed to wilt.

"Listen, you look beat," I said, getting up. "I'm leaving before they throw me out. We'll be back next week."

I headed for the door, then stopped and turned around. "I still think you did all right," I said. "You did better than I would have. I can't even cope with commercials."

◄○►

So that's what mothering is, I thought as I walked down the beach on Portsmouth. Mothering is picking up a gun when you don't have anything left in you—when you're so bad off you hardly know your name—and firing it into a man's chest, not because he's taken everything away from you, but because he's starting in on your daughter. And maybe, too, mothering is that sharp bird's talons cutting into my chest when I was standing on the beach with Leroy that night. Maybe it's Betsy hollering into the phone at the Raleigh police, "If the son of a bitch isn't dead, shoot him again." Maybe some people get more than one mother.

And maybe other people get a mother when it's too late. Mandy had searched for a four-year-old's killer for twelve years because she felt responsible for her death, and because the kid had no one looking out for her except a broken doll—for all the good her quest did Sissy.

And maybe some people get no mother at all. My mother had never felt those sharp talons in her chest. Those talons wouldn't let you leave a two-year-old wandering around the house hungry and dragging a feces-filled diaper—not for all the oceans of color in the universe. There was no point in going to Arizona after all. I might find a very nice woman there, but I wouldn't find a mother.

It was a new thing, thinking I had a little mothering in me. I glanced over at Lily and Betsy walking toward me on the beach.

"This," Lily said proudly, "is a buttercup lucine." She held out a round, smooth bivalve.

"And a fine specimen it is," I said. She and Betsy fell in step beside me, and we walked in companionable silence.

"This is a neat place," Lily said.

"Consider yourself honored," I replied. "I've only taken a few people to Portsmouth Island. It's you and Betsy and one old boyfriend."

"It's quiet," she said, "There's something big about a beach and this one is the best one yet. Will you take my mother here someday?"

"As soon as possible," I said.

"Breeze," she said hesitantly, "I want to live with Betsy and go to school on the mainland."

"OK," I said contentedly, "if it's OK with Betsy."

"Sure," Betsy said.

"It isn't you," she said. "It's just that this school is too small. Way too small. I don't have any friends and I can't even get the courses I need for college. I want to live here on the weekends."

"That's OK with me too," I said.

"Is it really true, Breeze?" she said. "They're not going to charge my mom?"

"Nope," I said. "They probably wouldn't have anyway, but I have to admit your testimony cemented it."

Lily grinned sheepishly. "I don't feel one bit bad about it," she said. "He was a scumbag. My mother shouldn't go to jail for shooting him. Betsy says he needed killing."

I glanced at Betsy. "He did," she replied.

"Ordinarily I'm not a big fan of killing people," I said. "But truthfully, I think the planet is better off without him."

"I should have thought about doing it myself," Lily said. "I knew where the gun was."

"Are you sure you're not Southern?" I asked. And truly I wondered. Maybe Southern didn't have to do with geography. Maybe it had to do with that combination of passionate loyalty and deep stubbornness that were admired by all when you were right and a complete disaster when you were wrong. And in Lily's case, I didn't have it in me to say she was wrong. Not just because she had helped Jena, but because lying to protect her mom had also done something for Lily, something to ease the helplessness and guilt she felt while watching her mother being beat to death in front of her.

"What's going to happen to her," Lily asked, "when she gets out of the hospital?"

"I hope that she'll come live with me for a bit. I think it will take her a while to get back on her feet."

"She'd like it here," Lily said. "I know she would.

"Breeze," she added, "she needs to get back to climbing, doesn't she?"

"Probably," I said.

"I think so, too. My mother was happy climbing. I bought her a climbing magazine, and I've ordered her a subscription. They have trips in them you can sign up for. I thought maybe she could start with just a trek somewhere." Maybe, I thought, sometimes mothering is upside down.

We kept walking, and nobody seemed to feel the need to talk. Lily wandered off looking for more shells.

"What about you?" I asked Betsy.

"Me?" she said, smiling. "I'm going to be busy. I'm going to have a teenager in the house again."

She glanced over at me. "I know," she added. "You think sooner or later I'm going to need something else in my life. That I need to go to work or something. But I tell you what, girl. I am a mother. I know there are plenty of women who are mothers and airplane pilots and what all, but I'm a mother, pure and simple. I'm an OK wife but I'm a great mother. So you can shove thinking I should move on, get a job, whatever. I don't want to. When Lily leaves, I think I'm going to take in foster kids."

"Oh, Betsy," I said. "That would be great for the kids, but I have to warn you: there is so much heartbreak in dealing with child protection. These families get the kids back, and sometimes the kids are dragged kicking and screaming from the house."

"What'd Joplin say?" Betsy asked. "'Freedom's just another word for nothing left to lose.' Well, maybe heartbreak is what happens when you got something to lose, but having nothing ain't better. I'll take the something. Maybe some of these kids will sneak back, after school, on the weekends, maybe just for Doritos and a Coke. Maybe they'll stay in touch when they get out of school. Don't get me wrong. I'm not doing this to save the world. I'm doing this because it's what I do best. But I doubt it will be wasted."

"You got no problem with me, Betsy. Sounds like a plan."

Betsy stopped and sat down. She said that was as far as she felt like going. I kept walking down the beach, watching Lily flit back and forth, zigzagging her way from shell to shell. It wasn't Lily who was on my mind; it was Sissy. She had fingered Daryl Collins from the grave—not a mean feat. It was ironic, really. The one witness who truly couldn't be intimidated was one who was already dead. Nothing left to lose. Who would that child have been had she grown up? I had always thought it was something special about me that made me see her, but I had it all wrong. It had been something special about Sissy.

Robert was coming in tomorrow. He had to prepare for a trial, he said, and needed a quiet place to work for a week or so. We'd see how it went. I'd be lying to myself if I said I wasn't glad. After the fear and the worry, I wanted warmth and loving and his fine wit and good company. But the longevity of it was another matter. I couldn't see him spending much time with his feet up on the balcony rail, and there was no part of my soul that could ever live in a city. But no matter what, I'd find solace in it while he was here.

I watched Lily turn and walk back toward me. All around her—the dune grass, the shells, the sand, even Lily herself—all seemed to be enfolded in layers and layers of southern light, light that seemed to bathe everything around it in a kind of glory. Much of the comfort in the world, I thought, came from its glory. I glanced up at the sun shimmering in the distance, closed my eyes and felt the breeze slide salty fingers across my face. I still didn't understand so much of it: why Jena didn't leave early on; how Sissy could have shown up as she did, how Charlie knew someone was coming.

But why even try to figure it out? Sometimes it was better just to watch the sun surf the waves and to lick the salt-covered fingers of the wind. Sometimes it was better just to watch southern light confer grace on everything it touched, and not think of anything at all. Jena and I were not so different. That was the thing. That had always been the thing.

Lily held out her shell as she walked up. She'll figure out a way to make it work, I thought. She'll get her mothering from all of us, a little here, a little there. She'll even do a little mothering of her own. I slung my arm over the shoulders of the dark-headed daughter beside me and we turned and headed home.

ML   2/07